MW00959817

COLOR
OF
FIRE

JMW

Color of Fire

Copyright © 2017 J.M.W.

All rights reserved. No part of this book may be used or reproduced by any means, graphic, electronic, or mechanical, including photocopying, recording, taping or by any information storage retrieval system without the written permission of the author except in the case of brief quotations embodied in critical articles and reviews.

This is a work of fiction. All of the characters, names, incidents, organizations, and dialogue in this novel are either the products of the author's imagination or are used fictitiously.

Scripture quotations taken from the New American Standard Bible®, Copyright © 1960, 1962, 1963, 1968, 1971, 1972, 1973, 1975, 1977, 1995 by The Lockman Foundation. Used by permission. (www.Lockman.org)

Scripture taken from the Holy Bible, NEW INTERNATIONAL VERSION®. Copyright © 1973, 1978, 1984, 2011 by Biblica, Inc. All rights reserved worldwide. Used by permission. NEW INTERNATIONAL VERSION® and NIV® are registered trademarks of Biblica, Inc. Use of either trademark for the offering of goods or services requires the prior written consent of Biblica US, Inc.

Scripture taken from the Holy Bible: International Standard Version® Release 2.0. Copyright
© 1996-2012 by the ISV Foundation. ALL RIGHTS RESERVED INTERNATIONALLY.

Because of the dynamic nature of the Internet, any web addresses or links contained in this book may have changed since publication and may no longer be valid. The views expressed in this work are solely those of the author and do not necessarily reflect the views of the publisher, and the publisher hereby disclaims any responsibility for them.

Any people depicted in stock imagery provided by Thinkstock are models, and such images are being used for illustrative purposes only. Certain stock imagery © Thinkstock.

ISBN-13: 978-1981656592
ISBN-10: 1981656596

Published by:
Elite Online Publishing
63 East 11400 South
Suite #230
Sandy, UT 84070
EliteOnlinePublishing.com

TABLE OF CONTENTS

"More than a half century ago, while I was still a child, I recall hearing a number of older people offer the following explanation for the great disasters that had befallen Russia:

'Men have forgotten God; that is why all this has happened.'"

Alexander Scholzhenitsyn

"For God so loved the world, that He gave His only begotten Son, that whoever believes in Him shall not perish, but have eternal life."

To my grandsons . . . I see the hero in each of you.

Prologue

He stood in a recessed doorway soaked to the bone watching his subjects herd a group of young girls into a building. The girls were no more than eighteen and ranged from, his best guess, thirteen, although the one he was after was only eleven. Cole felt that old devil (or maybe it was an angel, as his sister kept telling him) inside him raising its head; happened every time he witnessed evil perpetrated on the innocent . . . especially the young. He waited patiently. Not even the devil could push Cole before he was ready. His team was en route, and he knew the time had come to retrieve what he had traveled the two thousand miles for.

It was raining and raining hard! Cole had not seen rain like this in years. Good, he thought, they might just sit this storm out long enough for us to do our thing.

He waited in a corner restaurant called Abarrotes Universidad. He guessed they'd named it that because there was a university off of Paseo Niños Heroes and Nicola's Braveo, a block or so away. He thought, how apropos, these bad guys brought kidnapped victims to an area of Culiacan that had a preparatory school and a university. No one would pay any attention to a bunch of kids being transported from one place to another and shuffled in and out of buildings; especially off a street named the Passage of Child Heroes. His blood began to boil.

The Same Day

Eighteen hundred miles to the north, a different kind of gathering was taking place, another young and promising girl looking haggard and beleaguered; her tears overflowed on a face that carried the fear of innocents trapped by destructive heresies. Joan wondered what on earth was happening. It seemed girl after girl was confessing to sexual sins. Joan kept thinking, *I'm just a Bible teacher. I see these kids on Sunday mornings and that's it. What's going on?*

The truth was that Joan was so compelling in the classes she taught at the Pimsler Community Bible Church that the Word shone like a beacon from a lighthouse and these kids were responding to her teachings. The Holy Spirit was working overtime on them. But something dark, almost sinister, was happening that Joan could not put her finger on. The pain was too great, too deep, and too emotional. Her heart was breaking over these girls.

But as with all things made by man, Pimsler had a dark side, a profound sadness that could not be comforted. As God spoke of Egypt, "There shall be a great cry in all the land of Egypt, such as there has not been before and such as never will be again. For what will come to light will terrify the mighty and horrify the weak." Only God could vanquish some evil, and Pimsler's cup had been full for too long.

1

Beauty does not always guarantee peace.

Joan had moved to the mountains of Colorado eighteen months ago and settled into a pristine community surrounded by purple mountains, clean air, deep-green pastures looking almost manicured, and skies so blue one could lose themselves in the depths of the expanse. She had not ever witnessed such beauty. This town of Pimsler, Colorado, was voted the prettiest town in the state and best place to raise a family. Joan had relocated to Pimsler due to a corporate head hunter looking for a human resource manager for that area. Joan Cusiak, being an avid outdoors person and loving the beauty of God's high mountain creation, had jumped at the chance to work in Pimsler. She had left everything and started a new life that brought her much needed peace, along with a new lease on life she was sharing with about twenty-five girls on Sunday mornings and a night or sometimes two during the week. Her last position in the great state of Georgia almost killed her. The heat and humidity were at times unbearable, not to mention the grueling work hours. But the true pain came from the divorce that had devastated her. The loss of love and hope. The pain of constant reminders of places and things was debilitating her. A thirty-something, attractive, professional woman starting over. She was ill from depression, the heat and humidity most of the time; and when the opportunity of cool Colorado came up, she had no hesitation whatsoever. She sold her furniture, and some of her clothes and other furnishings just to expedite the move. She was so completely ready that she accepted the job after the first visit to Pimsler and a tentative offer from G. B. Booker Manufacturing Company.

After eighteen months, Joan was nested down completely. She built her life around her and all those she loved. She drew people to her like bugs to a blue-light bug zapper on a moonless night, but, of course, the attraction was mutual. Joan made soup for the sick, cookies for the kids at church, and cakes for all the bake sales. She had her garden of herbs and veggies in the backyard. Always had an excellent recipe, with a good cup of coffee for her girlfriends and fresh herbs for those who were ailing. Once Joan settled into the new career and her newfound church; she gave herself completely to the body of believers. Not because they needed her so much but because she needed them. After all, there were none immune to what chases humanity (and Joan was running like the rest of us, even if she did not know she was running). As soon as the brothers and sisters saw her talents and that she used them everywhere for the cause of Christ, they began the "We need Joan" campaign. Before long, the preacher couldn't do without her and added to her list of "Hey, Joan, can you help me with this?" In the same period it took to settle in, Ms. Joan had become the patron saint of Pimsler, Colorado. Loving life in the body of Christ, just where she wanted to be!

And one fateful day she was asked to teach the high school girls Bible class on Sunday morning. No one knew it, but life was about to change for the whole church. The rumblings would be felt all the way to the state capitol.

2

Your adversary, the devil, prowls about like a roaring lion seeking someone to devour.

I just wish it was that easy to see him.

In every community, the clean coexists with the dirty; the good with the bad and the righteous with the evil. Pimsler was no different. This was not an across-the-tracks sort of thing. This was a wicked sort of thing. You do not see it in daylight so much, and if you do, you often don't recognize it. But if it is at night or dark and shadowy, then you feel it more than see it. But don't kid yourself—you can see evil . . . and evil can see you.

Pimsler was beautiful, like a queen dressed in her robes of glory imitating the Egyptian royalty that had gold threads woven into their clothes so that they would sparkle and dupe the people into believing that they were gods.

Streets were swept every night and often washed with river water drawn from the nearby Colorado. The buildings were always freshly painted, with only the city's paint standard in mind. Downtown had flowerpots and convenient trash receptacles placed at appropriate distances throughout the entire city. Clean was important if Pimsler was to live up to the coveted standard of the most beautiful town in the west. Signage was a key also . . . not too tall, not too gaudy; it had to match the city's code, all had to look alike or close enough to lend to the "beauty." Even the residential areas were strictly coded and regulated, from the style of houses built to the plants, landscaping, grass, trees, and the type and style of fencing. The whole city seemed to be under a home owners' association of sorts. If you did not comply, procedures were in place that would . . . well . . . assist you in compliance. Perhaps the town's ideals were not as militaristic as it seemed to Joan at the time, but it was clear that there were even restrictions on outside materials or suppliers. The citizenry was forbidden to bring in outside labor to assist in any construction. All in all, the regulations were for the good of the town, of course, so as to keep all working for the betterment of the community. "We share and share alike. We take care of our own," said the mayor in an afternoon speech on one of Pimsler's 'High' days. Keeping things orderly and at peace created the atmosphere of, well, Pimsler.

And so, life went on in Pimsler, and Joan's excitement for life grew in her glorious chosen city. What a place Pimsler, Colorado, was!

3

Culiacan, Mexico, 2113 hrs

The rain was falling harder now. It had not let up since he arrived almost four hours ago. He knew there could be any number of doors these guys could remove the one he came after through but he was betting that the weather just might keep them a little longer.

His earpiece crackled. "BC, you copy?"

"Read you 5 by 5, what's your ETA?" His entire team had dubbed him BC. Newbies thought it meant that he had been doing this so long that the team nicked named him BC, which meant "before Christ." Nothing so cryptic, though. Just his initials, which stood for Brady Cole. Brady Cole Williams often felt he had been doing this type of work "before Christ," and with his luck was probably going to be doing it after Christ's return as well.

"Three clicks out." Came the response from the encrypted radio answered by his best and most respected friend, Wayne Gilford. Wayne and BC went back to the Marine Corps days where Wayne had picked up the name Hatch. During one of their deployments, Wayne's pack snagged during an exit from an armored personal vehicle hatch. As he forced himself out of the hatch, he fell to the ground, with the pack coming over his head knocking his helmet off and losing his hold on his weapon. Totally discombobulated, by the time he regained his control, the fight was over. He never lived it down. Wayne was not overweight, he was just huge. Thick, massive, and at that time had about 4 to 5 percent body fat. Just a big boy, and with his pack on he could not easily squeeze through the hatch. He survived to tell the story and became the brunt of jokes for fifteen years . . . so far.

"Copy that. You northbound on Teofilo, Noris?"

"Affirmative." The voice was flat and emotionless.

"Ten-four. Need you to turn off of Teofilo West onto Miguel Hidalgo y Costilla. Go to the first intersection, turn north onto Rodolfo G. Robles. Next intersection is Gral Angel Flores. On the southwest corner is a blue rock façade restaurant. I'm in the doorway."

"Copy that. Hey, they serve hamburgers there?" Hatch loved hamburgers.

Cole stepped out and looked up at the sign above the building. Rain pelted him in the face. "No, they serve *hamburguesas* and *desayunos ricos*, just for you, my boy."

Wayne laughed. "Well, I got the *hamburguesas,* but the other I'm at a loss for."

"Rich breakfast, my son. We might have to have a take-out order depending on how our package looks."

"How far from your location is the parcel?"

"One minute." A wave of tension came over the two, knowing what lay in store.

4

But the Spirit explicitly says that in later times some will fall away from the faith, paying attention to deceitful spirits and doctrines of demons.

1 Timothy 4:1

It was another Pimsler day! Ever since Joan's arrival in town, she began to call these bright, cool, sunny days Pimsler days. Days so full of sun and crispness it was almost too good to be true, all this beauty and a great career to boot. And now the preacher's wife was coming over for some tea and cookies! Joan was so excited and curious about this meeting. Joan was at work when she had received the call from Mary Donny.

"Joan, dear, how are you?" Mary asked as Joan was winding up an HR meeting with a group of Booker employees.

"Hi, Mary, I am so glad you called. I am fine. How are you?" Joan responded, a bit distracted by the paperwork in her hands left over from the meeting she just concluded. It always disturbed Joan when she notified twenty for a meeting and generated twenty booklets and only nine showed up. Mr. Booker was going to hear about this. She heard Mary say something. "I am sorry, Mary. I didn't catch that. Could you repeat that, please?"

"I said, 'Do you have plans for this afternoon after work? I would really love to drop by and chat with you for a minute.'"

Joan, being the efficient HR manager that she was, immediately ran her afternoon schedule through her head as she juggled the booklets, the phone, and hurried down the hall to her office. She turned the corner and collided with Charles, and dropped some of the paperwork. "Oh, I'm sorry, Charles." Joan quickly stated in frustration.

To which Mary replied, "Excuse me?"

Charles had worked for the G. B. Booker Company for eleven years. Single, desperate, and hawk-eyed on Joan, he bent down and began picking up the papers, grunting out, "Joan, Joan, Joanie! You need to slow your roll, girl," never taking his eyes off of her. Joan was not exceptionally beautiful but was for Colorado standards, where women generally, wore pants, didn't style their hair, and wore no makeup. She was very eye pleasing, especially her figure. Joan always dressed with flare and had the cutest clothes, which accentuated the accent, if you know what I mean. Charles was always there looking and wanting to help. No matter what it was! She would go to the copy room, and there was Charles; she would go to the break room, and there was Charles. Leave the building to go pick up supplies, and there was Charles! He showed up like a ghost out of the mist except there was never any mist, just Charles! After eighteen months of *just Charles*, Joan was getting a bit concerned about Charles. If it weren't for the other women in the office assuring her that he was quite innocent, Joan might have talked to Mr. Booker about him.

Of course, Charles couldn't leave well enough alone. "Hey, I'm headed to the Or House after work. Wanna come?"

"I'm on the phone, Charles." Holding up one finger, hearing Mary say again, "Excuse me, Joan? Are you there? I must have a bad connection—these crazy cell phones," Mary said to no one.

"I'm sorry, Mary, yes. I'm here. What was it you were saying?" Joan's frustration was growing as she realized that Charles was following her down the hall.

Mary laughed. "These crazy cell phones, I thought I heard someone ask me to go to the Or House with them." Joan laughed just thinking of the preacher's wife sitting in the Or House with a desperately clingy Charlie. "Well, anyway," Mary continued, "I was asking before all the static, if you're not too awfully busy this afternoon, I would love to stop by for a minute or so. Would that be all right?"

As Joan entered her office, she realized Charles was in his stalking mode. Still on the phone, she stepped through the door and quickly shut it without turning, hoping Charles thought she did not see him or try to come through the door with her. "Of course, Mary, I would love for you to come over anytime. You know that."

"Wonderful. Joan, you are the sweetest thing."

To which Joan wanted to say, "Well, bless your little heart," but held her tongue.

Mary continued. "I will see you about five thirty? Okay?"

To that, Joan replied, "Five thirty it is. See you then. Bye, bye."

As soon as she clicked off, there was a sharp knock at her office door. In her mind's eye she saw Charles standing on the other side drooling like Pavlov's dog after hearing the bell. Normally Joan was a very patient person and kind, but enough was enough! She marched around her desk to the door and flung it open, prepared to give Charles a bit of womanly advice.

As she prepared herself and the door swung quick and wide, she was taken aback.

"You could have just said, 'Come in,'" Mr. Booker said with a broad, cheery smile.

"Mr. Booker! I thought it was . . . someone else." Joan said, peering out the door with a start in her voice.

"Charles?" Booker said with a chuckle.

"Well, I, uh, well, yes, actually," Joan replied, feeling a bit embarrassed.

Mr. Booker walked across the room to an office chair. As he sat down, he said, "I will speak to Charlie if you like. I would guess he's probably not your type. Please leave the door open, Joan."

"Well, Mr. Booker." Joan felt flushed and didn't want to say too much. Booker knew it too, so he cut in, holding his hands up in a defensive, palms-out posture. "I know you're a big girl, and I am sure you have handled his type before. But, Joan, there are some things a computer programmer doesn't understand, and as far as I can tell, Charlie has a tough time understanding the word *no*. So if it gets too heavy for you to carry, just tell me and I can help him understand, okay?" Joan's look caused Booker to add, "Don't worry, he'll be fine and you two will still be friends. I've handled a hundred Charlies."

Joan, visibly relieved, said, "Thank you, Mr. Booker, you have always been so kind to us all. And while I've got you here, there is something I would like to speak to you about, if you have a minute."

"Let me guess—your meeting didn't go as planned."

"How did you know?"

"Well, they don't call me Booger Booker for nothing." They both laughed. She was amazed at how well he knew everything about his company and employees. How could he read people's expressions and answer their questions before they even asked? And he was almost always right! He amazed her, and she loved working for his company.

"Well," she started, "I was a bit concerned with the turnout as you had said this was a mandatory training session."

"What does your schedule look like for tomorrow, Joan?" Still holding the smile on his face, he said, "This is important, and they all know it!"

"I have a few things to accomplish in the morning, but the afternoon looks good." She had her eyes in her day planner.

"Great. I will have all the ones who missed today attend, if you can handle a class of thirty-one instead of the usual twenty?" Booker said with a bit of determination in his voice.

"No problem with the class size. I just know this material will assist in the development of a more positive attitude when we are ready to change to the new computer system. People seem so afraid of change at times."

Mr. Booker stood, signaling that his part of the conversation was over. "Joan, I want to say that you are doing an excellent job. I have been reviewing the employee evaluations, and they are outstanding. I am proud of myself for having the foresight to hire you!" He headed for the door, laughing.

"Really, Joan, you're doing a great job, and we are all happy you're with us."

Joan was beaming. Mr. Booker was the father figure she had not had and a boss that she thought didn't exist anywhere in the world. "Thank you, sir."

"Don't call me sir. Booger will do." His back was turned as he departed through the door, still laughing. Mr. Booker was truly an amazing man. Never rattled, always seemed to be on a Sunday stroll everywhere he went. Joan thought, if someone screamed fire, Mr. Booker would be the last out and he'd come strolling and laughing. What an amazing man.

It was close to five. Joan gathered her things to leave. Backing out of her office door, she closed it, and down the hall she heard a voice call, "Hey, Joan! You didn't answer me about the Or House. Ya wanna go?"

Oh, brother. *No!* She screamed in her mind. She glanced over her shoulder, and as she did she saw Booger stroll up behind Charles and say, "Charlie—just the man I need to speak to," in his gentle, firm, fatherly way.

That said, you have no choice in the matter, Charlie, and if you say anything but 'Yes, sir,' I will pull your pants down and spank you like a three-year-old right here in the hall. And I will do it too! Joan was kind of stuck in limbo watching this little scene play out. Charlie, with a look of uh-oh on his face, along with total surprise that Mr. Booker came up behind him without a sound; Mr. Booker putting his arm around Charles and turning him the opposite direction in the hall, all the while looking at Joan with a twinkle in his eye and crooked little grin on his face.

"Charlie, have you ever heard of the term sexual harassment? Let me help you understand the legal ramifications of that detestable term," she heard him say as she saw Charlie take on the stroll effect of the Booger.

Joan was running late to her 5:30 with "The Preacher's Wife." Joan always thought the term "The Preachers Wife," sounded like it needed to be in caps. So in her mind it was capitalized. As she turned the corner onto her lovely, clean, tree-lined street, feeling relief to be going to her little dream cottage that she absolutely loved, there was the preacher's wife's car, parked in front of her house.

Joan pulled up in the drive and jumped out almost before it came to a stop. Mary was already standing on the stone sidewalk leading up to her house. "I am so sorry for being late, Mary!" Joan said, looking over the top of her car.

"Late?" Mary said, lifting her arm up and straining to see the watch on her wrist while she held an arm full of study guides against her bosom. "You're not late, honey. I just got here. Don't worry yourself."

Joan thought, *Everyone seems so sweet, even after I've been here for more than a year*. Joan cleared the front of the car and said, "Thanks, Mary. Come on in."

Joan unlocked the front door, and as it swished open her senses opened up to the sweet aromas of home. She then stood back, letting Mary enter first. "Just put the books on the coffee table and have a seat. Would you like some tea? Or coffee? I have some delicious low-cal brownies I have been dying to tear into. How about you, Mary, would you like one?" Joan said as she headed to her kitchen.

Mary had not put the booklets down yet and had not taken a seat but was standing in the entryway with her mouth open, looking at Joan's beautiful home. "Joan, your home is so . . . so . . . I don't know what, so . . ." Joan helped her speechless friend, "Messy? I'm sorry. I have been working so hard lately. I just have not had the time to pick the place up."

"No, I was going to say beautifully homey. I just love it. I was admiring the outside, but the inside is . . . I just don't have the words to express how impressed I am with your design abilities and taste. I love it. You're going to have to come over and tell me what I need to do around my old place!" She inhaled deeply, letting the wonderful aromas of the house settle into her lungs.

Joan came back into the living room having put the teapot on to boil and pulling the brownies out of the fridge and putting them in the microwave.

"Okay," Joan said, kicking her shoes off and plopping down on her favorite love seat as she loudly exhaled, looking expectantly at Mary . . . living up to her reputation of "How can I help?"

Mary Donny, for all intents and purposes, started out in life with one goal in mind, and that was to marry a preacher, which she had. Peter Lahey Donny and the pretty Miss Mary Ann Shelley met at their denomination's seminary over twenty-five years ago. They'd fallen in love and were married in the seminary's chapel. Life was good early on for the young couple, but as time went on, things changed and blurred . . . what was that old cowboy saying? "Life's good as long as you don't weaken?" Poor Peter had heard a different gospel. Neither were even sure when it sounded, but nonetheless it had hollowed both Pete and Mary. Oh, Mary jostled about with the ladies club and church functions, as did Pete, with all the "normal" ministry duties, and occasionally the Spirit would grab him and he would even preach a semi-coherent and meaningful sermon. But most of the time he and others in the "Church" walked a different path than the one originally set by Jesus Christ the author and perfecter of the faith.

5

Culiacan, Mexico 2145 hrs

A white eighteen-passenger Ford van pulled to the curb, the door swung open, and the passenger moved between the front seats to the rear of the van. BC jumped in, wiping rainwater from his face, all eyes on him, the men waiting silently.

BC turned a quarter turn in the front passenger seat in order to see the three others.

"First," he said," I saw her clearly in the group of girls that were delivered to the safe house. It's a green stucco building with some blue graffiti on the lower part of the wall and large red letters over the windows that read "Victoria." The building has a brown door. We can go in blind, or we can wait until we have some movement, which means a bunch of gringos sitting outside in a white van looking like foreigners, and *that* will draw attention. But the alternative could be bloody . . . Your reactions?" Cole was not going to risk the lives of any one of them without their input and agreement.

Scottie, the second most senior man behind Hatch, asked, "You said 'group.' How many is a group, and are they all girls? Are they all American, or are we going to have to speak Thai, Spanish, and Swedish? Are we going to try to take them all, or what's your thinking?"

"More than likely they are all abducted, and yes, we will take them all. There are about eight to ten in the group I saw, but I do not know how many are inside. With them were two perps. I could not see weapons, but the girls' body language suggested they don't need any weapons to control them. I will bet that there are weapons in the house. I will also bet that there are more than the two I saw. If I am right, I am going to say we split up and bide our time until we have movement. Someone has to come out. Once they exit, we grab them and get them to take us back in. Once in, we take the house."

Blake was the youngest and most aggressive of the team, hence the name "Blake the Snake." "Waiting might bring a crowd. Don't you think it's better to pop the door and see if we can surprise the bunch?"

BC responded. "Well, that is an option, and waiting could compromise the mission. The door is a steel door with a two-by-three-foot wire smoke-glass inset. Remember, we have no idea what is on the other side nor who and what 'who' has in their hands. The door also opens outward, which will create a bottle neck and slow the entry. Shotgun will have to go first. Kids may be everywhere, and the bad guys will use them for cover. You can bet on that. What say you, Shotgun?"

Shotgun was the last man in the group and the most reserved. He preferred to let the shotgun do the talking. Shotgun was the oldest of them all and had been breaching doors and collecting bad guys for almost twenty-five years. Shotgun preferred the shotgun but not just any shotgun. Since the design and development of the AA-12 shotgun, Clint Bercelli, aka Shotgun, had been the man and had his weapon of choice for any entry situation the team might encounter. Here was another tough entry challenge, and as usual, Bercelli was up for the dare.

"Do you think we can pop the door and drop a concussion grenade in the room and then enter? It would give me the time to enter, assess, and defend. Then we could clear the house."

"Guys, this is partly a residential neighborhood. We go loud, we are blown, and then we will have to fight the policia. Not my idea of a quiet E and E (escape and evasion). Snake, if I give you the breaching tool, do you think you can pop the lock and open the door without much noise? I'm betting the front room is not where they keep the girls, and I'm betting some of the local cops are in on this little business venture as well."

"Whatcha got on your mind, BC?" Hatch asked.

"I'm thinking we wait until around 3:00 a.m. or so. Breach the door and take control of the house. Take each perp down and then quiet the children, call the priest to take the others, and get out of town before daylight. Any questions?" No response. "Snake, you have to be quick and silent. We prep for slam bam, thank you ma'am. We travel light, the night vision equipment is in the bag behind the backseat, our sidearms will be the H&K 23's. Clint on shotgun; Hatch, you and Snake carry duel canister Carbon 15 Model 4s short barrels. We may need the firepower. Scottie and I will carry the MP-5SD3s suppressed. Snake, breach the door. Shotgun first in. I will be second, followed by Scottie and then Snake. Wayne, you'll be on our six. Everyone okay with the order?" All agreed. "Once we have control and have secured every room, we round up the kids and explain the situation and what we will do next. Then we exit, hook up with the priest, take our catch, and head to the boat. Then to La Paz. We good with the plan?"

Hatch spoke for the team, "We're good." There was a long pause. "Now the tough part . . . we wait."

6

For everything created by God is good.

Pimsler Community Bible Church was the largest congregation in the city. It was by far the most opulent and gaudy in the whole area. People on vacation would drive by, stop, ooh and ahh, and stare and take pictures. Pete even became a little commercial with them and would charge a small fee to have one of the older parishioners take interested tourists on short tours of the structure. Pete called it a donation, and the tour was focused around missions, if anyone was to ask. But nothing was saved, and the only blessing was the donation that Pete picked up every day during the tourist season. Yes, things were good in Pimsler—on the surface, anyway.

Mary began, "Joan, I am going to get right down to the brass tacks." Joan could tell Mary was excited about whatever it was she was preparing to talk about.

Mary sat on the edge of her seat with her hands folded on her lap, her ankles crossed, and leaning slightly forward. "All, us girls at the Church have been hashing over who we need to help us with certain responsibilities. We have been short a few teachers, you know." Mary took a sharp breath drawing out the word know. "And as we discussed the girl's high school class" a slight pause indicated this was very important, "everyone all at once said your name!" Mary kind of spit the last part out as if Joan would stop her before she had time to finish the sentence.

Joan sat with a blank look on her face with no response. Then she slowly said, "My . . . name?"

"Yes, your name! It's got to be a sign. All of us at once thought of you to teach the girls Sunday Morning Bible class. You know how desperate we are to have that position filled buy a competent instructor." That sounded better than *teacher.*

"You want me to teach the high school girls?" Joan replied flatly.

"Yes! Not just teach but mentor them . . . well, sort of, I guess. What do you think?" Mary was trying to read Joan's face and was getting a little anxious, thinking she might have come on too strong.

The microwave bell dinged in the kitchen. Without a sound, Joan stood and walked straight to the kitchen. Mary could hear her with cups and saucers, and a minute later Joan reappeared with the snacks.

"Joan, what are you thinking, sweetie?" Mary was becoming concerned. Joan was perfect, and everyone had thought of her and agreed that she was perfect. Poor Mary didn't see any problems at all. You did what you were asked in Pimsler, you know.

Joan handed Mary the plate with the low-cal brownie and the cup of tea and said, "I think I would love to." Mary instantly clasped her hands in delight, bringing them to just below her wide grin, obviously delighted in her astute negotiation abilities, then grabbed and ate that rather large brownie in one massive bite. Joan was a bit taken aback with the enormity of Mary's mouth.

All Joan let slip was, "Wow, good brownie, huh?" as she watched Mary devour her prey.

Mary finished the tea and brownies (several), left the study guides, and Joan walked her to her car saying their goodbyes. Mary drove away, not feeling the least bit guilty about the brownies she slaughtered.

Joan picked up one of the study guides and remembered that the gift of teaching given by the Holy Spirit seemed to be the one gift most desired. She picked up her Bible and turned to 1 Corinthians 12:28 and read, "And God has appointed in the church, first apostles, second prophets, third teachers, then miracles, then gifts of healing, helps, administration, various kinds of tongues." As she looked through the study guide, she was struck by another verse that gave her pause. "Let not many of you become teachers, my brethren, knowing that as such we will incur a stricter judgment." Joan was resolute in that she would study herself approved at whatever cost, not just for the girls but for herself and her loving God.

7

A very wise man once said, "Whole people, people who are internally connected to conscience, to common sense, to God and who therefore possess a certain natural reverence for other souls and their autonomy— are not attracted to obtaining power over others."
Kupelian

Peter and Mary Donny lived life as normal as anyone else in Pimsler. With one exception. It was a total lie. Life in their home was not centered, as one would expect, around the things of Christ and the church but on an idea which had taken seed only a few short years ago. Interestingly enough, as with people who believe a lie to be true, they did not even know their faith had shifted into dark waters.

Brother Pete loved all the parishioners and the church building. Loved the town and went teaching his weak and twisted gospel everywhere in Pimsler. Mary followed right behind and was the respectable and dutiful wife all preachers wanted and needed. The couple had one adopted child, a teenager, who was a bit of a rebel. Not in any way that would bring reproach publicly but a child that had a, well, wild streak that brought Peter certain benefits.

Simone Donny was tall for sixteen years and attractive, with threatening dark eyes; sleek, shapely legs; and long, thick, and luscious jet-black hair. She had come into her teen years with a bursting figure, porcelain skin, and full, voluptuous lips. Most men and women found her almost captivating and had a hard time not staring for two different reasons. She loved their eyes on her and dressed accordingly, whether at school or church. She flaunted the attention and loved to see the women talk, point, and jab their husbands in the ribs as she floated by, but not one spoke of the impropriety. (For all depravities that are allowed to live in any body of believers have tails that wrap and sting others with nefarious delight).

All the men of the church gave Simone singular, concentrated interest, and she knew she could ask anything of almost anyone of them and have her wish granted. She knew this instinctively, almost as if she had been instructed. But there was one she had always been given special attention from, even when she was a younger girl. Deacon David Thomas Clark was a powerful and wealthy man in the church and community, a fine-looking man and younger than the other deacons. Simone often thought if he were not married they would make a wonderful couple with gorgeous children and, as young foolish girls conceive in their fantasies, they would live happily ever after. But not so for the couple, for the web of lies and secret sins would soon capture their hearts and lives in a silent hell created by themselves and fashioned by unseen hands intended for all!

David Clark married his second wife two years ago. Together, they had one three-year-old child. David's ex-wife and he had had three children after an eight-year marriage that ended in a vicious divorce, with David permanently denied access to his children. During the divorce, it became known, not only of David's proliferating promiscuity but his strong addiction to pornography of all kinds. This opened the door to discovering his participation in the film industry, implying his involvement in possible financing of porn films. Of course, this would return huge dollars to David's bottom line, if true. David did not seem to hold a day job, nor did he have an office outside his home. He traveled alone, assumed alone. Had meetings around town with different, alien, unusual looking people. Most said they were Hollywood types, not knowing what else to think. One thing was true. David lived life large and fast . . . and was best friends with Pastor Peter Lahey Donny. Such a curious friendship.

David too was relatively new to Pimsler, as new comers go. His arrival was normal until he purchased a twenty-eight-thousand square-foot mansion perched on top of a large hill just outside the city, overlooking Pimsler. It was a king's palace, to say the least; a twelve-car garage with a quarter mile heated driveway, house-servant quarters, a gardener's house, heated horse barns, and a four-thousand square-foot guest home (with its own pool, of course). The main house had several living areas, including a private media room, two kitchens (one on the third floor and one on the main floor), a large office complex, a full tennis court in the basement, and nine bedrooms with eleven bathrooms. Yes, one could say "Fit for a king." Let's not forget about the Olympic size swimming pool in the back with the three Jacuzzis perfectly stationed around the pool. Waterfalls inside the house and in the gardens, David entertained often, and the Donny's were always invited, and David never allowed them not to bring that strikingly beautiful girl of theirs. The Donnys were more than obliged to do so. It was said that the interior doors were made from Australian tiger wood costing $11,000 each. There were more than fifty doors in the house.

So "King David" lived well, entertained often, and held a certain power over all those who graced his opulent home. Some graced it more often than others.

Peter's office phone rang. "Hey, Pete!" the voice said before the pastor had a chance to say hello. Pete responded with, "We partying down this weekend?" to the voice on the other end of the line.

David replied with a certainty that only those who think they are ten foot tall and bulletproof have. "You betcha! I thought we would just hang. Let the staff cook some steaks, and if you guys want to stay out here, feel free. Julie took the boy to visit her mom and dad, so I'm bachin' it this weekend." David failed to explain that Julie and his son had not been home in several weeks and were not expected to return. But who would know since David and Julie came and went . . . most of the time without anyone knowing anything about their activities.

David also had a plane on full standby at the small executive airport for any trips . . . to anywhere. Not very many could afford a G5 with three crew members just waiting in the wings. There seemed to be much more to David than appeared at first glance, or even at deep levels of friendship.

Pete informed David, "Dave, Simone is having some girlfriends over Saturday night, so I'm not sure we can stay the full weekend or not." He hoped David would allow all the girls to come with Pete and Mary.

"I tell you what. If you and Mary don't mind, how about we give the girls the guesthouse? We can stay in the main house, do our thing, and they can stay out there doin' theirs. The guesthouse kitchen is fully stocked. They can prepare their own food, or I can get our kitchen staff to prep some meals and wala, we all be happy! Talk it over with Mary, and let me know. Meantime, tell Mary to pack her swim suit and get ready to get some sun!"

"We'll do, brother-man!" Pete said as he thought how lucky he and his family were to have such a great friend in David. "What else do I need to bring to this bash?" Pete always offered, but knew the answer he would receive.

"Nada, mi amigo, just whatever you need to get ready for our lesson on Sunday at church. I got the rest of it handled."

"Sounds good, my friend, see you in a while. I'll call Simone and see if she and her buddies are up to a night in the penthouse and let you know." Pete hung up the phone thinking of all the blessings that came to him through David.

David smiled to himself and turned on his in-house CCTV system and checked the guesthouse's full-color cameras to see if his pan, tilt, and zoom capabilities were all functioning. Naturally they were. After all, he used them last night when he had other guests stay at his mansion.

Simone's voice was husky and deep for a girl, something Pete and Mary noticed even when she was little. It used to be cute, but now it was downright seductive, and Simone knew it.

Her cell phone rang in her purse, "Hi, Daddy," she said in that alluring tone of hers. She could not help herself. She had seen how

Peter looked at her, and she liked it.

"Say, I know you're planning a sleepover Saturday. But David called and invited us up for the weekend. He is even willing to let you and your girlfriends stay out in the guesthouse by yourselves. What do you think? You want to have a night in the penthouse suite?" He knew how much his friend enjoyed her company. After all, it was innocent, was it not? He assured himself it was.

Without hesitation, Simone said, "Sure, Dad. I would love to stay. I know the girls have not seen his place and to have the guesthouse to ourselves, wow! That would be great!" Simone was suddenly sounding like an excited sixteen-year-old high schooler. She knew what was in store for her anyway; she had been to David's many times before and was always looking for an opportunity to return that would not raise questions, for lust of the flesh had caught her, and she loved the taste and feel of it.

Pete called Dave back and told him he was going to be hosting four crazy teenage girls.

"Wonderful. I will make sure they are well taken care of, my good friend," David switched on the top-of-the-line motion-sensitive camera system, smiling and anxious to the point of restless anticipation. At times, anxiety build up so deeply in his spirit that he could not control his lust. Patient expectation was not in his vocabulary. He paced nervously as his eagerness built to the point of bursting. He was frustrated with just looking, he wanted to touch and satisfy. Could he? He wondered? Would she? He breathed out. Closing his eyes and seeing her stand before him, he trembled with malevolent desperation claiming its will over every part of his being.

The deal had been struck long ago. The die cast. The lamb slaughtered for lust, pride, and vanity. He suddenly felt powerful with the hold he had over the entire Donny family. His lustful craving for their daughter consumed him.

8

Cole had made the call to the Priest earlier and had requested asylum for the children he was going to bring to him. Cole had also requested medical supplies standing by for any injuries that any of his team might receive or for the children. This could become a hot extraction. Always prepare for the worst expecting the best. Victory loves preparation, and Cole always prepared. Even down to the clothes his men wore, to weapons, fighting knives, and backup weapons; one vehicle for the extraction; then a mile or so away another for the transportation to the Priest, a change of clothes for all, even if it was just a poncho to give a different look. Ball caps, sunglasses, anything to confuse identity. The second vehicle had extra ammo and an emergency combat first-aid kit along with water, a liquid concoction that replaced the body's electrolytes, and high-calorie, meal-replacement bars. This was Mexico, so the second vehicle could not be left unattended. This is where the fifth man came into play; known as Goose, Cole's pilot had been flying for Cole for twelve years and was seasoned and unafraid of weather or bullets. At least that's what he said. Goose was a combat vet and could fly fixed wing or rotary blade and had a 150-ton-boat captain's license. Float, fly, or fight, Goose was your man. He was, at the present time, sleeping in the back of another passenger van a mile or so away, waiting with bated breath . . . well, he was waiting.

The rain had let up, and Cole had placed his men in strategic areas around the compound in order to watch any comings and goings.

0215 hours

His earpiece came alive, Snake asked, "What does In-sti-tuto del De-Porto mean?"

"Where do you see that?" Wayne chuckled.

"I'm at the corner of Noris and Flores. There's a big white building that has that over the doors."

"It means we will not have to travel far to get kicked out of Mexico if we get caught taking these kids back." Wayne laughed as he said it.

Snake again. "I've got movement here; standby one." Dead silence. "Clear. It's an old woman. Wonder what she's doing out here at this hour?"

"What is she doing?" Cole asked.

"She's just walking down the street."

"What's your 20, Snake?"

"I'm one block west of your location, across the street in the plaza under some trees. She would need night vision to see me, and I don't think she is wearing any."

Everything fell to a silence that only comes late at night. Darkness was always so different from day. The sounds were different, the atmosphere felt heavier, smells were even different . . . it was all different. Cole loved the night; it was his time to shine. Night seemed to heighten one's senses and to magnify sound, any sound. The slightest sound could be heard for a hundred feet away, giving away location, putting one in mortal danger. All the men sat still, absolutely quiet. It was still muggy and not any cooler, even though it had rained and was dark. Beads of sweat streamed down their faces and soaked their shirts. Everything seemed to hold moisture tonight. Cole was glad the sun was not beating down on them, topped with a 110-per cent humidity.

It was time . . . 0300 hours. Cole saw Snake walk around the corner, his head on a swivel, checking the area. He had his CAR 15 slung over his back, the breaching tool in one hand, and a can of WD-40 in the other. He eased up to the door and soaked the hinges. The wind kicked up a little, and Cole could smell the sweet cake-icing chemical aroma of WD -40 from sixty feet away. He guessed Snake used the whole can. Snake stepped to the knob side of the door with his back against the wall and waited. Shotgun moved like a shadow from around the opposite corner from the one Blake came from and stepped in behind Blake. As Cole began moving, he saw Wayne appear from the dark gloom of an alleyway across the narrow street. Scottie was suddenly there, appearing from nowhere. They moved soundlessly. These guys were spooky, all trained well and all loving their job. No one spoke, all knew their place and what each other was thinking and would instinctively do in any given situation.

Snake turned, faced the door, placed the breaching tool into the crack between the jamb and the lock, and began to ease into the bar. Snake was young and one of those types that didn't know how strong he really was. He pushed on the bar a little harder. The metal creaked. He stopped. He waited. He eased into it again, and, as pretty as you please, the door made no sound at all as it opened. Snaked looked up at Shotgun and grinned a big, toothy grin. Snake gently, slowly swung the door open. Not a sound. Shotgun entered the totally dark room. There was a refrigerated air conditioning unit loudly rattling in the house. Perfect, Cole thought. Shotgun pulled his night-vision goggles down over his eyes, as did the rest of them as they singly entered and took strategic positions around the room. Last one in gently closed the door.

9

Therefore putting aside all malice and all deceit and hypocrisy and envy and slander, like newborn babes, long for the pure milk of the word, so that by it you may grow in respect to salvation, if you have tasted the kindness of the Lord.

Peter

The first Sunday class was upon Joan, and she was a bit nervous. She had studied all week and was determined to teach out of her abundance of knowledge rather than teaching off the written script Mary had provided with her study guides. She had made a short outline based off her study. Joan had reviewed the guide and concluded that those responsible for the education of these children had not taken into consideration their age. These were teens capable of understanding rather deep concepts. Smart kids. The study guides were weak and watered down. Consequently, being the student that she was, Joan used the study guides as a suggestion and developed her own approach to the class. Needless to say, it was much deeper and convicting. Joan knew that victory loved preparation. Her brother used to say that all the time.

Therefore, class began with Joan more nervous than she thought she would be. Joan came in after all the girls were seated. Approaching the podium, she looked out and was shocked at what she saw. She had been here for over a year and a half and she was really looking at the girls for the first time. Why had she not perceived this before? She didn't know. The essence in the class room was that of languor. The girls slumped and looked disheveled. This was not at all what she expected. Joan had been so energized by Mary that she was expecting the girls to be as pumped up as she was. Not so. Not so at all. And where were the rest of them? For a church the size of Pimsler Community Bible Church, there should have been at least thirty girls or more.

Well, there was not anything to do except begin . . .

So Joan's first class began with only one female who wanted to be there.

"Hi, girls, for those of you that don't know me, my name is Joan

Cusiak and I am going to be your Bible teacher for a while." Joan had a big smile on her face and realized that not one girl was looking at her. First question Joan started with after her "Good morning, everyone," was, "I wonder if anyone can answer this question: 'Who is this Jesus we call the Christ, Savior and King above all kings?'" No one, not one, even looked at her. She tried again. "Do you believe the Bible is the inspired Word of God?" A girl changed position in her seat, and Joan exhaled a sigh of relief, thinking, *Well, at least they aren't dead.*

Joan attempted to engage once again, "Say, girls, please grab your Bibles and turn to John 1, and we will begin reading in verse one." No movement. Joan thought, *This is horrible!* A moment of panic set in. Joan gathered herself and began reading John 1:1.

As Joan read the passage, she began to regain strength in the knowledge that her God was the most powerful force in the universe and He was going to help her through this nightmare.
So she read:

In the beginning was the Word, and the Word was with God, and the Word was God. He was in the beginning with God. All things came into being through Him and apart from Him nothing came into being that has come into being. In him was life and the life was the light of men. The light shines in the darkness and the darkness did not comprehend it.

"I would like to take the first four verses of John, verse by verse, or maybe word by word." She distinctly heard someone snoring. *My word, a girl snoring!* Now she was afraid to look at the class, embarrassed and angry. *These girls—what is wrong here?* Joan said a silent prayer and continued.

"The term in the beginning is referring to before the Creation, before time. John is explaining that the Word was in the beginning with God, depicting a continuous relationship, and relates to quality or same nature as God. The Word was face-to-face with God. You see?" One of the girls stirred. "Yeah, we see." She sounded as if she was half asleep or worse—hung over.

"So verse 1 puts the Word into the eternal, or coexistence concept with the Eternal God of heaven. Giving the Word eternal essence! Verse 2 gives the Word personality, 'He.'" Joan looked out and saw the most disinterested group of kids she had ever seen in her life. It almost made her sick. A couple of the girls were talking, and one was painting her nails. The rest looked like they were in a flophouse.
She stopped speaking; she stood and starred out at them, not moving, not speaking, just looking. Silently looking; unable to believe these girls were so detached from God's Son. She wondered if the boys were like this as well. Was the whole church like this? Had she been here for

this long and hadn't noticed. *Am I blind?* She thought the singing was good, and she thought some of the sermons were okay, not great, but Pastor Pete was giving it his all, she assumed. She was at a total loss now. The whole lesson was designed around interaction, and without it she was lost. She noticed a few of the girls began to straighten up and look at her. A few more followed the first. Then Joan saw that all but one had straightened up and were looking at her. She began to speak slowly. "Ladies, if I can call you ladies. I have been asked to teach this class, and I take this very serious. Obviously you girls don't take this too seriously. So, I am curious as to why you girls are here.

An angry looking girl who sat spraddled-legged—Joan did not know her name—said, "Momma made me. Duh!" Her response was angry and disrespectful.

Joan waited a moment, then began again. "I am disappointed and appalled at what I see here this morning. Not only disrespect for our Father but a total disregard for yourselves. I feel totally disillusioned by your response to scripture and am saddened to my core that you girls have no more honor for the work that Jesus has done for your salvation than to come here and look like you do and do what you're doing." Joan stopped for a long moment. Then she began to look into the eyes of the girls, to really search them. The more she examined them, the more she realized their loss. These children had no direction, no leadership, no training in the Word at all. They were disenchanted because no one cared for them enough to teach the truth of Jesus to them, no one with skin on anyway.

Joan said, "I want to do a little exercise." They all looked around with that "Oh, brother" look on their faces. She continued. "Raise your hand, palms out toward me. Now I want you to make a fist. Go on, raise your hands . . . this won't hurt. Now make a fist!" Joan raised her voice, then waited. She saw all those hands close into fists. "Now open your hands, palms out. Do it again." They did it again. "Can anyone of you tell me how you did that?"

One of the girls said in a "well, stupid" tone, "See, Joan, our brains sent electrical impulses from our brain down our arm and told our hand to close."

"That is partially correct. Anyone else?" Joan waited. No response. "No one?" Again, she waited. They all sat and stared at her. Then Joan asked as she held her hand up, opening and closing it. "Where do the electrical impulses in your brain come from?"

They all had a blank stare on their faces. Joan concluded, "That is the question that should be asked. Not anatomic operation but where does the electric impulse come from? How is that generated within you? I am here to teach you, but more than that, I am here because I love each one of you and I want to introduce you to the Giver of life. In the book of John, John writes about a woman who had been caught having sex with a man that was not her husband. By Jewish law, this woman was to be stoned to death. Pretty harsh, right? The rulers of the Jewish people dragged her to Jesus while He was teaching in the temple and told him she had been caught in adultery and asked Him what his take on this problem was. Now, this is a very serious crime then and now. What the Giver of life does shocks everyone. He bends down and begins drawing in the sand, but the rulers press Him for an answer. So He stands erect and says, 'He who is without sin among you, let him be the first to throw a stone at her.' Then he bends down again and writes on the ground. When they heard it, all her accusers began to leave. The older ones left first, then the younger. Why did they leave and not stone the woman?"

No answer from the girls. Joan said, "Some think Jesus, being the Son of God, knew their sins and began writing their sins with their name beside it. However, the amazing thing is after all the accusers left and it was Jesus and the woman alone, He looked at her and asked her, 'Woman, where are they? Did no one condemn you?' She said, 'No one, Lord.' Now, girls, listen to what Jesus said to her: 'Neither do I condemn you. Go. From now on sin no more.' Jesus is the giver of life and loves you. No matter where you find yourself today Jesus loves you and will heal and save and bring you to His home, where you will be safe and clean and joy filled."

Joan had no idea why she shared this passage with them, nor why she went into such detail with it.

The bell rang, signaling the end of class.

As the girls stood, straightening their hair and clothes, pushing desks out of their way, leaving the room a wreck, Joan said, "Next week you tell me where the electric impulses come from." She looked out among the girls, whom she could tell were glad class was over, and saw Simone sitting slumped and facedown with her hair covering her face. Joan thought she looked as if she had been crying.

"Remember, I am here for you. If anyone needs to talk please let me know. Okay, dismissed." Simone stood and looked directly at Joan. Joan could see she had, in fact, been crying. Joan stepped toward her, smiling, but Simone quickly turned and rushed out the door.

10

For the grossly impudent lie always leaves traces behind it, even after it has been nailed down, a fact which is known to all expert liars in this world and to all who conspire together in the art of lying. These people know only too well how to use falsehoods for the basest purposes.

Adolf Hitler

Joan was distracted during worship, preoccupied with what she had experienced in her earlier Bible class. She sat at the back for a specific reason . . . to look at her brothers and sisters. She could hardly hear the sermon. But Pastor Pete said something that took her by surprise. He never mentioned specific sins as long as she has been attending. He always seemed to avoid any topic that might cause any one to feel uncomfortable, she guessed that was why he only spoke for fifteen minutes or less, as well. He mentioned the great lie Satan told Eve in Genesis 3 and how that changed the world. Then did what he always did after he mentioned a potentially life changing thought, changed the subject. Don't want to offend, she thought sarcastically.

Before she knew it, people were filing past where she was setting. She gathered her things and turned to join the exodus. Stepping outside into the brilliant sunlight, she squinted noticing a knot of girls standing in the cool shade of a lovely tree and she saw in the middle of the girls was Simone. Head down shoulders shaking slightly and the others seemed to be comforting her. Joan stood on the steps and scanned the grounds where she observed small gatherings of parishioners scattered around talking and planning lunch or afternoon activities. Younger children running and playing everything seemed so normal. She turned and moved toward Simone's knot but as she moved across the lawn, Mary shouted out, "Joan!" She glanced over her shoulder and saw Mary trotting across the lawn on her tip-toes trying not to let her high heels sink in the soft ground and fall flat on her face. Joan immediately became concerned with how Mary was dressed and the amount of makeup she had applied. Mary did not have enough dress on to cover her backside if she stayed upright, much less, if she fell.

"Joan!" Mary made a show of it all Joan thought. "Dear, come with me I want you to meet someone. I am sure you two have meet, haven't you? Well, if you have not, I want to be the first to do the introductions. Pete and I stayed out at his house this weekend and loved it. We do that quit often actually. It is a mansion; you are going to have to come see it and soon, Sweetie." Joan felt awkward with the way Mary was manhandling her and what was up with the short skirt, runway heels and low-cut neckline, jewelry, glitz and glamor look? Mary pushed her right in front of a great looking guy; very well groomed and dressed like a prince; loose fitting white silk shirt and cream-colored trousers. He was in great shape, his dark thick hair combed straight back, his shinny skin all tan and just shinny tan, man was he tan right down to his sandaled covered toes. Joan's eyes were wide, drinking him in, she was instantly impressed and had not even seen his face yet. Gold watch, gold bracelet, and pinky ring adorned this . . . this . . . she was sure he was just a man or maybe . . . she was shaken out of her trance by the sheer excitement of Mary's voice.

"David, David," Mary said, clutching his arm and pulling him around, pressing his arm to her breast, rudely taking him out of the conversation he was smack-dab in the middle of.

"David this is my friend and sister in Christ I told you about." David turned and looked into the loveliest, guiltless, round brown eyes, set in an angel's face of sweet gentleness. He noticed immediately how soft and kind they were. He thought, now I have got to get to know her! He smiled showing his brilliantly, gleaming white teeth. He reached out his hand to take hers as his dark blue eyes turned hard, she could see his pupils dilate with passion and that flash of intense white broke into a strange lustful sneer. Joan stepped back, not taking his hand, as Mary's voice faded in her ears. She was staring into an amazingly handsome face that transformed right before her eyes and was instantly frightened at his ravenous cold stare. She had been gawked at by men and had even felt uncomfortable around a few but this was beyond anything she had experienced ever. Joan had always been able to handle men and had grown accustom to not being shocked by what some of them did or said. Some men without proper influence or those not having Christ in their lives were downright crude. As Joan tried to compose herself Pastor Pete appeared to Joan's right and said, "So, Mary has rounded up the last single in the entire congregation to meet the most elegant gentleman in the whole city. Joan, David is a great guy. You two should get to know each other. The pastor recommends you both to each other." Pete said smiling whispering in her ear letting his voice rise and fall, as he patted her on her back and slid around taking Mary's hand.

"Hey, I know, let's all eat lunch. How does that sound?" Mary beamed with the delight of her suggestion as she looked at each one standing there.

David responded in a flat emotionless tone, not removing his cold craving eyes from Joan, "Delightful. How about my place?"
Joan had such a strange feeling just looking at the guy, she was not about to get trapped in this man's house with stupid acting Mary and the Preacher who was carrying on as if he had already performed their wedding, for goodness sakes! He's a deacon, Joan thought, weren't they supposed to be married?

(Does God send angels at times in one's life when one needs rescuing, a thought we must revisit?)

Joan had no idea how to respond but knew she was not going to go to his house, not the way he was looking at her. The others were already planning the afternoon when Joan heard Simone's husky but young voice cry out, "I thought you loved me!" Then she was gone.

Joan was stunned as they all turned and looked toward the direction of the voice but all they saw was Simone running down the hill toward a waiting car. Joan turned looking at Mary who had a neutral expression standing there holding her husband's hand but also had reached out and was caressing David's bare arm as well. Joan was the only one who was shocked. Not only at what Simone had uttered but with what she saw Mary doing . . . holding her husband's hand and rubbing this dark haughty man's arm like she belonged to him as well.

David chuckled. "Kids? What was she talking about, Pete?"

Pastor Pete moved the group toward the parking lot, "You know kids, she probably has an issue with, who knows what. Mary will talk to her later." As Pete gently pushed Joan and Mary along, a familiar voice moved into range.

"Good morning, everyone; Preacher, you need to work on the length, theological depth and delivery of your sermons." Mr. Booker said smiling, extending his hand, speaking without apology. Then looking at David, "Caught another in your net, Dave?" Not waiting for an answer Booker continued looking at David but speaking to Joan, "Miss Helen and I are going to be sorely disappointed in you if you stand us up for lunch again, young Lady. You are coming over aren't you, Joan?" George Brian Booker Sr. said turning and making eye contact with Joan, looking at her more like her father than a boss.

"Oh yes, Mr. Booker. No, I was just making my way to the car." Speaking quickly, she turned to the others, "I'm sorry guys, I hope you understand. David, it was nice to meet you; you guys have a great lunch. Maybe next Sunday we can get together for lunch or something." She never once looked at David and did not shake his hand. As she was turning to leave she heard David say, "I'm going to hold you to that Joan." His voice had a harsh, cruel, disappointing tone to it. It unnerved her.

Being the girl she was she shouted over her shoulder waving a hand over her head, "I said maybe!" emphasis on maybe.

Joan was the one trotting across the lawn now . . . *well at least my skirt won't flop up and show my unmentionables*, she thought. She felt his eyes on her or at least she thought she did; she wouldn't doubt it in the least. *Creeped me out!* She thought.

There she was, standing by their car patiently waiting for the most important and Godly man in town, Helen was a truly sweet wife. And here came Booger as Helen called him, smiling that impish grin, Joan loved so much.

Helen Rose Booker was the epitome of a Godly woman, kind, trustworthy and wise. As Joan approached, Helen said, "Goodness, sweetie, you looked as if you had seen a ghost when you meet Mr. Clark. Did he say something unpleasant to you?" George Booker walked up, "Booger, you might need to have a meeting with that young man!"

George Brian 'Booger' Booker, true to his character, passed on any negative comment, "Let's get some lunch and if Joan has anything to say about him, she can say it over a good hot meal. Sound good Joan?"

Joan glanced over her shoulder and looked in the direction of the threesome she trotted away from minutes ago confirming her suspicion . . . David was staring in her direction, "Yes, sir," she answered Booger, while still looking at David, Pete and Mary, "lunch sounds great."

Joan followed the Booker's to their home in a silent car. Alone, she mused over the events of that morning. She was putting two and two together. Simone was crying in class. Then she blurted out in front of the building to David, "I thought you loved me!" Joan saw the apathy all the girls had in class and the coldness of their attitude toward Biblical teaching. They have absolutely no relationship at all with Christ. No wonder the stat's Joan had read say that 80 percent of all churched kids leave the church after college and never return. They do not know the Savior! She confirmed her thoughts with how all the kids dressed at church. The boys with their pants down around their hamstrings and the girls, dresses so short you can see their panties. All the spaghetti strap blouses, exposed bra straps and one can even see the cups and at church of all places, for goodness sakes! Half of them look like they are going to a Goth party the other half looked like strippers. THIS WAS UNBELIEVABLE! Tats, body piercings, black clothes and crazy makeup, even some of the boys showed up wearing makeup! Joan knew things have changed since she was a teen but goodness this was like a nightclub on Sunday morning.

She kept her thoughts to herself as she ate with the Bookers.

11

Night vision was a beautiful invention. The man was sitting on the only stick of furniture in the room and he was sound asleep. His snoring was the only thing louder than the air conditioner. His head was laid back on the back of the couch, mouth gaped wide opened. Cole suspected that was why he was in this room all alone. He was in a sitting position with a pistol on his lap and both hands slack at his sides. Cole saw two empty quart beer bottles by the man's feet, one standing and the other lying on its side but no beer on the floor. Clint shouldered his shotgun made hand signs to the others. Hatch stepped to the man's left and Scottie moved to his right side, Cole was prepared to trap the man's mouth as soon as Clint removed the weapon. Clint reached down and gently lifted the pistol off the man's lap, he didn't move a muscle. Cole took his position in front of the man; stepped between his knees to get closer to his face and to keep the man from kicking him. At one perfectly timed moment as if the three had practiced this exact move a thousand times, grab the man. Hatch and Scottie took the man's arms and pinned them to the couch, while Cole slammed his hand over the man's mouth and pressed his knee deep into the man's chest. He exhaled all his air, legs flew out straight as his eyes popped open, wide with shock and fear. He could not see any one in the totally dark room. All he heard was "Silencio. No movimiento!" whispered into his ear. Then he felt the press of the shotgun's cold steel muzzle against his forehead. He was a Mexican bandit . . . he knew what was happening. Of course, he thought it was another gang steeling from him. He didn't realize it was a professional recovery team from America. The man knew he was dead. He began to whimper and again, "Silencio . . . shhhh!" He quieted. Cole wrapped his mouth with duck-tape and took a couple of wraps around his head for good measure. Then put tape over his eyes. The other two hog-tied him tight, so tight the blood was being cut off to his arms and legs. He strained against his restraints but instantly stopped . . . the pain was too intense.

One down.

Cole and his team move into the hallway just off the first room. Three doors off the hall were standing open. One at the end of the hall was shut. They moved down the hall, one by one, they cleared the rooms. The kitchen was the first room on the left. The men moved in tandem. Like one solitary man moving down the hall. No one spoke; each knew the drill and knew what the other would do without orders or explanations. Second room cleared. As Shotgun peered into the next to last room, he held up two fingers. The group stepped into the room saddled up to the twin beds. Assessed the situation for weapons and then with absolute vengeances crushed down on the two sleeping bandits. You could hear bones pop; neither could breathe much less move. The strength and weight of the team was too much. They could not even cry out. Tied, taped and disarmed the bandits just lay there. Cole took out his phone and dialed the priest's number, "Hola, Beto. Buenos noches. Como esta?"

"You can stop pretending you can speak Spanish, Cole. I know dat's all you know." The Priest, as Cole called him, was not a priest, not any longer. He still loved Jesus, make no mistake but found he could move more freely outside the confines of the Catholic Church's political structure and because of an incident that totally embarrassed the Church. He had killed a man steeling a young woman. Roberto Ernesto Rodriguez, known to all as the priest, or simply Beto, was spending his life reuniting stolen children with their grieving fathers and mothers. As Beto, he was often called, liked to quote to Cole, "It is he who will go as a forerunner before Him in the spirit and power of Elijah, to turn the hearts of the fathers back to the children and the disobedient to the hearts of the righteous, so as to make ready a people prepared for the Lord." Then Beto would always say, "Dis is you, mi hermano. You are Elichah." Cole scoffed at this thought but knew he had a purpose on this earth which he believed was to protect the innocent. *If this pleased God, so be it. But why was he even doing this if 'God so loved the little children,'* a question that had plagued Cole for years.

Cole continued. "We've secured the safe house. Call Goose and he will give you his location for the transfer of the packages." Someone clicked on the light in the hallway. Cole heard the last bed room door open and the little girls gasp and begin to cry out.

All the N/V goggles were off and the men were trying to look as innocent as possible which was impossible. Hatch and Clint were saying, "Calma, calma. Vamos llevar a casa. Vamos a ver madre y papa." Cole thought it best for him and the other two to stay back until the girls calmed a bit.

"Beto, we have three presents for you and your men."

"Tank chu for chu gifts, Cole. We will unwrap dim when we bring dem to la casa. Okay?"

"Sounds good to me."

Snake came running down the hall. "Cole, we got company." Cole hung the phone up without saying goodbye.

12

"Now the Serpent was more crafty than any beast of the field which the Lord God had made. And he said to the woman . . ."

Moses

Monday was another Pimsler day and Joan was at her desk trying to concentrate on work when her office phone rang. Answering the phone, she knew the voice instantly even though she had heard it only once in her life.

The voice was strong, deep and alluring, "Miss Joan?" He knew it was her as soon as she answered. Like a thirsty man who cannot wait for his fill of water neither could David wait for Joan to come to him.

"Yes, this is Joan." Her voice was weak. She was caught off guard and was unsteady in her answer.

"You know who this is." It was not a question.

She was quiet, she did not respond. The voice confused her. She felt threatened but the voice was smooth and pleasant to her ears. It excited her and called to her, seducing her . . . she had never had this experience before from just simply listening to a man on the phone. It unnerved her.

"Yes, I know who this is." Afraid to say his name, like saying his name would commit her to an unknown agreement or cause her to fall into a trap. Nevertheless, at the same time she was intrigued and found herself wanting to answer, to experience what he was calling her to.

"I was disappointed when you didn't come to my house for lunch. It hurt my feelings. You know even Peter and Mary thought you should have come." His voice was even and the tone inviting and satisfying but left her wanting.

She did not want to apologize to him! She wanted to hang up the phone or tell him to never call her again. She was frozen. She noticed she was trembling from fear, no, maybe from a little fear but more from anticipation, longing to hear his words. This is so confusing, her mind swirled.

"Beautiful Joan, are you still there? Of course you are. You're waiting for me. Talk to me Joan." In a whisper David breathed out, "I wish to please you."

Joan trembled, her heart fluttering at his words, but her mind reciting scripture, *"with her many persuasions she entices him; with her flattering lips she seduces him. Suddenly he follows her, as an ox goes to the slaughter, or as one in fetters to the discipline of the fool; until the arrow pierces his liver!"* Proverbs 7:21-23. I guess it can be a man or a woman enticing the fool, Joan thought.

Like a teenager caught by her parents talking to the forbidden boy, she blurted out, "I'm sorry, I can't talk right now. I will have to call you back."

The voice, smooth as silk, "Promise me, promise me, Joan."

"I promise." She hung up. Sat still as death itself, starring at the phone. In her head she heard herself promise that man that she would call him back. How stupid; how stupid of me! Trapped!

Out loud she said to herself, "What was I thinking. Call you back. I am not calling you back!" Her phone rang again. She jumped in her chair. It rang again, then once more. She was looking at it apprehensively, picking it up, "This is Joan . . ." timidly waiting to hear that voice again.

"Hey, you okay?" Charlie said. "Are you in trouble with Booker? What are you doing in that office of yours, anyway?"

"Oh, Charlie," first time she had ever called him Charlie. "I, I'm just working. I had a long weekend and am a bit tired. What can I do for you?"

Charlie, never letting a good opening slip by, "Well, how about lunch?" He waited, holding his breath, literally holding his breath.

"Don't you have some documents for me?" She asked smiling to herself, knowing that this voice was as innocent as a lamb compared to the other she had hung up from.

"Yeah, but I am not bringing them to you right now."

"Why, Charlie?" She said with relief in her voice laced with humor.

"Because, uh . . . I'm at lunch. I'm eating at Stacy's. I am going to order a spinach and grilled chicken salad and that strawberry tea. They have those little ginger bread muffins fresh out of the oven, hot and tasty. You huuungryyy yet?"

She took a minute to respond making him wait, "Okay, you got me. I'm hungry. I'm going to call Tammy and see if she wants to go to lunch too. We'll be there in fifteen minutes or so."

As she hung up the phone she heard Charlie's protest about Tammy. She dialed Tammy's extension.

Charlie was actually in his office at the time of the call. He jumped up, grabbed the folder he was to deliver to Joan and ran out the back door before Joan and Tammy had time to come down the hall. He hit the door and ran down the side walk one block and stutter-stepped around the corner into the alley, through the screen door sliding to a stop at the hostess station. Held up three fingers and breathlessly waited to be seated. As they seated him he could not believe his good fortune, Joan was actually going to eat a real meal with him. It was like a first date and everything . . . except for Tammy being there? He wondered why she wanted Tammy there any way. Women were so confusing.

Stacy's was the spot for the Town's professional people to meet for lunch. The restaurant was hidden in an alley way. The entrance was a battered screen door that led through a narrow, bricked passageway between two buildings; to a patio area with plants and trees and flowers surrounding tables which were covered with umbrellas. The tables had linen table clothes, candles and crystal glasses with heavy silverware. Stacy's was owned by Allen Pierre Lungwen. A true connoisseur of fine food; of which he wore most of it around his midsection. He was on a perpetual diet and always told all the available ladies who dined at his restaurant that he was losing weight in hopes of a different outcome but it seemed that the only thing that changed was his middle. He was a moody but very rich man. The restaurant business was a very lucrative business in Pimsler.

Mr. P, as he was affectionately called by his patrons, also had an inside area that had 24 tables; but most wanted to eat outside, although the inside was much more intimate and private.

The ladies arrived and true to his personality, Charlie jumped straight up and waved a big here I am . . . no . . . over here, to the ladies who were sufficiently embarrassed right at the beginning of his "date." They ordered and ate having a very pleasant time. Joan was impressed with Charlie's manners and his humor. He was a polite and genuine man with an ease that she had not expected. He carried the conversation well and Tammy, who had never given Charlie the time of day, seemed taken with Charles. Joan thought, *You sly dog, Charlie.* Charlie's interest had shifted a bit during one short, delicious lunch. Joan knew he was interested in her but he was certainly eyeing that cute little brunet Joan had brought with her. With a cunning smile Joan knew her troubles were over with Charles. As she sat and watched the two talk of nothing, Joan felt a cold hand slide across her shoulder. She shuttered. Then the voice!

"You are as pretty as the morning sun, Joan." Any other voice and Joan would have said thank you. This voice brought an empty chill.

"How's lunch?" David asked.

Joan sat still and was visibly struggling with herself not to look at him. She really didn't want to answer him either. She angrily thought, what was he doing here? Had he been following her? Was he watching her?

"Joan, have you forgotten me already?"

"No, David, I have not forgotten you." Joan's voice was stiff. Charlie turned his attention to Joan and then looked up at David.

"I am meeting a few people for lunch. I see you have already eaten, what a pity." David looked at Charlie continuing his conversation without missing a beat, "If you would have told me you were going to be here I would have offered a much more . . . say . . . expensive and satisfying lunch than this one." Joan flushed and turned her gaze to David but before she could respond, David finished with the trio, "Ah, here's my party. Please excuse me." Looking at Charlie, David said, "Look at yourself, pal; she is way out of your league." Smiling the devil's smile, he disappeared into the restaurant.

Charlie's offense glowed like a beacon. Even Tammy asked, "Gosh, Joan, who was that jerk?"

Joan did not know how to answer. She was flush and angry, first, at the thought that he might be watching her but she dismissed that almost as soon as she thought it, secondly, the flood of things from church the day before came back to her mind. Simone's statement, Mary and Peter pushing her to go with them. Moreover, the girls in class, now this too, she was unsure what to make of it all. It could be just innocent coincidence.

"Hey, Joan, are you okay?" She heard Tammy say.

She looked at Charlie, seeing compassion in his eyes and knew that he was a true friend. Kind, caring and loyal, he continued to look to see if this attractive woman was in fact all right.

"Yes, I'm all right, Tammy. I'm sorry for that rude interruption. If you guys are ready I need to get back to the office." Joan stood watching Charlie grab the bill.

"You go on, Joan, Tammy and I will get the bill and see you back at the office." Joan smiled, looked at Tammy, who was in total agreement.

"Thank you, Charles. I appreciate lunch," she turned walking out of the patio area, both of them forgetting about the folder.

The next couple of days were uneventful except for work and the new sweet office romance going on. Tammy was floating about the office delighted with her new relationship and Charlie was absolutely dumbfounded. He could not keep his eyes off of Tammy. Joan watched, chuckled and offered an ear to both of them. They both were so taken by each other, typical of new love. It always started out so consuming. Joan hoped it would continue. If it didn't she knew Charlie would be right back at her door banging away!

Joan's intercom beeped and she answered, "Yes."

Mr. Booker voice crackled over the intercom, "Joan, are you busy?"

"Yes, sir but I can take a minute. What can I do for you?" Joan answered crisply and was exactly the type of answer a boss loved to hear.

"Tell me what I need to know about this Tammy and Charlie thing, please. I can't seem to get anything out of Charles except that hooked fish look, bug eyes and all. And Tammy isn't any better." He added.

Joan chuckled, "Mr. Booker, give them a few days and I am sure the new will wear off. They didn't know each other existed until Monday. We all ate lunch together and boom it happened. I am sorry if this is causing a problem. I can speak to them if you like."

"So, as I suspected, you did this, smart move Miss. Joan; smart move."

"It was purely by default. I brought her to lunch with me so that I would not be alone with Charles, then 'bada boom, bada bing'!"

Mr. Booker laughed. "Well, we will give them some time. Who knows, they might be perfect for each other, only God knows. I know if you had a hand in it, it will turn out for the best."

"Thank you, sir. I will keep an eye on them and remind them of their responsibility while at the office." Joan assured him.

Life went on at the office with the talk of Tammy and Charlie at the top of the list for the juiciest office gossip. Joan turned her mind to her Bible class.

13

0311 hrs

While Hatch and Clint got the girls ready to move, Cole stepped to the front windows in the room they had entered. He peeked out and saw two Mexican Police cars, one in front of their van and the other behind it. All those hours on surveillance and he had not seen one cop anywhere, now two show up. What are the odds? The hall light was shining into the front room, creating a sickly yellow glow, but allowing Cole to see well enough to discover, taped to the front door jam and the door itself, two small rectangular plastic boxes. An alarm; probably went to the main man, who dispatched the cruisers. It was obvious that these two were on the criminal side of law enforcement, dirty cops. They were checking the van with their flashlights. One kept looking at the brown door Cole and his team were behind. Cole knew they had seconds, only.

He hollered over his shoulder, "Shotgun!" Clint rounded the corner from the hall.

"You got that thing loaded with those bean bag rounds?"

"Yes, sir, a few."

"I'm going to get their attention and you take them both down. Get the kids up here, we're out of time. Let's move."

As soon as the girls came into the room they were hustled close to the wall adjacent to the front door. He ordered them to squat down. Hatch turned the hall light off and all fell into darkness. Cole walked out, leaving the door open.

"Que paso, amigos'!" Both the officers turned and pulled their pistols immediately. "Plumon, PLUMON!"

Raising his hands, Cole said, "Whoa, boys, whoa. It's okay . . . esta bien, esta bien. No problemo, it's okay!" All the while he was moving away from the door holding his hands in the air. Cole eyed the two smaller men and knew, if they had not been in possession of the weapons, he would have taken them down with ease. With no weapons, just his hands.

"Alto! Alto!" They screamed. Pointing their pistols at Coles face, totally concentrating on him. Cole watched their eyes and head movement . . . Cole knew they had tunnel vision on him. Never once did they look beyond Cole's form.

Cole stopped just where he needed to be. One officer had this back to the door and the other had his side to it. Clint stepped through the door and the shotgun went off with an ear shattering boom, boom. The first officer hit crumpled immediately having been hit twice, not by design but effectively knocking the weapon from his hands and slamming him to the sidewalk. The other ducked, stumbling and spun to his right, looking over his shoulder, taking his eyes off Cole. Bad mistake. Cole took advantage of the second policeman's tactical error and moved out of his line of fire. The second police officer lurching behind a car parked at the curb, swinging his pistol toward the direction of the shotgun blast, but not knowing where exactly it had originated from. Shotgun stood behind the cover of the door jam, concealed from view by the blackness of the room, knowing the cop had no shot. The officer was stumbling around trying to get his site picture and to discover where the shots had come from, while struggling to remain behind cover preparing to return fire. When suddenly shooting pain ran up his leg to his hip, Cole had stepped forward and stomped on his right leg just behind his knee, driving his knee into the pavement and bouncing his face off the trunk lid. Cole simultaneously grabbed his pistol hand from behind and instantly swept the pistol from his grip, snapping his trigger finger. The officer yelled a curse through the pain. Then for good measure, rather than killing the man, Cole grabbed a hand full of greasy Mexican Cop hair and slammed his head into the trunk of the car he was using for protection, repeatedly. Cole looked up and saw the team exiting the building ushering the girls into the van, as the officer slid to the pavement, leaving a blood trail down the trunk and bumper of the vehicle. Cole bent, taking the officers handcuffs from the pouch and cuffed his hands behind his back. Snake ran to the cruiser parked in front of the van and backed it up so that the van could get by. Exiting the car Snake pulled the mic out of the radio, taking his knife he cut two of the tires flattening them. Then walked by the officer who Shotgun had shot, looking down at him, the team heard Snake say, "That hurt tough guy?" as he bent and cuffed the second officer.

Scottie did the exact same to the other police car. Snake took the officers hand radios, *no calling the dispatch*, Snake thought *that would be cheating*. Cole threw their pistols on the roof of the building across the street just in case, as Hatch gathered the shotgun shells and the bean bag rounds from the sidewalk. They jumped into the van and were off; heading to their prearranged rendezvous with the priest and Goose. Hatch was driving, looking in his rear view he saw the two police officers, one not moving lying in the street between two parked cars and the other rolling around on the sidewalk, obviously in a great amount of pain.

Cole shouted out, "Everybody here?" Cole could hear sirens in the distance and the police radios screeched with activity, not because of the two dirty cops but because of the two shotgun blasts. Cole surmised if they get into it with the locals it will be because of the shotgun not because they stole back the girls.

Each team member responded. Then Cole turned and counted the girls. Thirteen girls crammed in the back of the van. Eyes wide and tears flowing, fear and panic on their young faces.

Cole called out, "Which one of you is Callie James?" No answer. "I'm taking you back to your mom, Callie, please believe me." Cole was digging for the picture and the handwritten note he had been given by her mother.

A frightened and weak small voice said, "I'm Callie," as she dug her way out from under and around the other girls. Cole's first thought, Thank God, thank You God. He turned and said to Callie, "You want to come up here with me, sweetie?" She instantly began clawing herself out from under and climbing over the others to get to Cole. She sat in his lap, holding his shirt in her little fist and began to cry, BC, instinctively rocked back and forth, "Shhh, now, everything's okay now." His voice choked with emotion.

14

Woe to those who call evil good and good evil; who substitute light for darkness and darkness for light; Who substitute bitter for sweet and sweet for bitter.

Isaiah

David found life in Pimsler, Colorado too easy. He loved Pimsler. He too saw the beauty and enjoyed the sunsets. Even the blind can see some things. What David saw was all the money he could make bringing innocent victims to his house. Without their knowledge or consent he videoed their activity and then sold it to his friends in the porn industry. Unfortunately, the Preacher and his wife were regular victims. So was poor, young, beautiful Simone. He had many other pursuits but he loved this industry with his whole heart.

His producers were chasing him for more material and David was contemplating how he could deliver. Their insatiable appetite at times was so demanding that he felt over worked . . . but oh, how he loved the work.

David was at his palatial mountain home mussing over his producers request for more film when his doorman called to him and said there was a young girl at the door wanting to see him. David jumped up and almost ran to the foyer. He turned the corner and there standing in all her not so innocent beauty was Simone Donny. Amazing how he was presented with his answer about new film material.

"Hey, sweetie, how are you?" His lips were wet and his voice was smooth and apologetic. He could tell Simone was angry.

"Hey, I was going to call you today. Are you okay?" David had such compassion when he needed it.

"You liar!" Her voice echoed through the foyer. She was angry.

"Whoa, honey. I have never lied to you." He reached for her but she drew back. "When I told you I loved you (liar, he loves the money she can bring) I meant it. But then again, you have to remember I am thirty-three (liar, forty-three) and you are sixteen, honey." His voice strained out the words, as he leaned in closer to her, asking, "Do you want me to go to jail? Look at all I'm giving you . . . does that not prove I love you?" (Again, liar, he knows sin cost money).

"If you loved me you would marry me." She quipped. She could not see anything but her hurt over David flirting with her mother and wanting to go to lunch with Joan.

"Come here, Baby." David cooed. She slowly crossed the floor and could not resist taking his out stretched hand. He pulled her close to him brushing her hair out of her face; she felt the electricity course through her young body, this is all that matters, she thought. He touched her face and wiped a tear away. Like a father he said, "There, there now, let me make it better. I have been dreaming of you all night and was hoping that I could see you today." (Liar!)

"No, you haven't." Then she followed with her deeper desire, "Have you, really?"

"Of course. I picked up a present just for you." His deception knew no bounds.

"Oh, David, what is it?" Simone had almost forgotten her anger, as she squeezed his firm sides.

David responded with marked excitement, holding her shoulders pushing her back to arms-length, he looked up and down her body, "You have to promise me you will model it for me." He said tilting his head to the side, letting is eyes play with her's.

"I will, I promise. Oh, Davy, thank you. I love you." Simone said giving herself so completely to him it was almost hard to believe.

"Hey, thank me when you see it. You might not even like it." David thought how stupid these women were. She is just like her Mother, give her a cheap bracelet and she will do anything I ask. David, pulling her close, holding her tightly against him, he could feel her young, firm body, and she responded with arms wrapped around him looking up into his face. He walked her to the elevator and pushed the number three on the dial pad. The doors opened and closed and the elevator lifted them to the master bedroom. Simone thought how cool it was to have an elevator in a house. She nestled closer to him.

The room was full of light with the curtains drawn back electronically every morning at seven. The windows covered the entire North wall of the room. Colorado in all its splendor was exposed to their view. David crossed the white plush carpeted floor to a remote control and pushed a button and the curtain partially closed. He turned and looked at Simone in the dim lighting and wondered why he had to play all these games. Why could he not just pull off her clothes and have his way with no fear, like he does with so many others. *Patience, my son*, he said to himself, *in due time Simone will bend to my control.* Then he will be through with her and she will be just another commodity that he will sell for tens of thousands. But right now he just stood and stared with lustful greedy eyes letting the monster build inside until he took her.

"Look in the box on the bed." His voice had a strange cadence to it. It was light, seducing and quiet.

Simone slowly moved to the bed picking up the box. She looked at him and he could see the mixture of fear and excitement in her face. He could see her hands trembling. She pulled back the paper covering her present. Lying on top of the lingerie was a diamond necklace. Simone gasped looking at David and then back down at the diamonds, then back at David. Chills ran through her entire body as she grabbed the necklace and held it to her neck running to the full-length mirrors that were on three walls and directly over the bed.

She squealed with delight and spun in circles around the room, holding the necklace to her throat, "Oh, David, David, David . . . I love it, I love it. I love you." David didn't care in the least if she loved it or not. He wanted her to put on the lingerie, NOW! But knowing he had to play the game of love he held his emotions in check. Lying down on the bed, kicking off his shoes, he whispered, "That's not the only gift, Simone. Look in the box again." He could not contain his desire for this girl and he knew if she was listening she could hear it in his voice.

She skipped to the box again, reaching in she removed the black shear top and the "T" back matching panties. Her heart skipped a beat and she suddenly felt an excitement that she had never felt.

"You want me to put this on?"

"Yes."

"Here?"

"Yes."

"Right now?"

"You said you love me, didn't you?"

"Yes, I do love you." As she clutched the clothing to her breast, bending forward, displaying an embarrassed smile. While covering her face with the lingerie, she began to tremble uncontrollably from the inside of her body. Like her organs were shaking out of control. She had never felt this before.

"Well? Are you afraid? Have I not shown my love for you? I want to see my bride to be in all her beauty. Is that a bad thing, my love?"

"Bride to be?" Her voice cracked, her mouth went dry, her eyes wide with wonder. "I . . . I'm nervous. I don't know . . . I'm not afraid of you at all David." She ran across the room holding her gifts in her hands as the cameras followed her every move. She jumped on the bed, throwing her arms around him. His wolf like cunning told him she would need just a little more coxing before she obeyed. He kissed her as she lay on top of him. It was a quick little kiss. He pulled his head back looking in her young eyes and then kissed her again. This time it was a long, hard kiss full of passion and she kissed him back. Pulling him close wrapping her body around his, telling him with all her youthful strength and confusion that she wanted him. She would do anything he asked of her because he loved her and she knew he loved her. Her visions of life ever after danced in her foolish head. She was a child, a child that needed someone, something. She thought she needed David and she mistakenly thought he needed her too.

"Will you try on my gift?" His eyebrows raised looking down his nose at her, lying on his back with his shirt unbuttoned now, showing off his hard-muscled, tan chest, teasing her.

"Here? In front of you?" Her heart beat hard in her breast, as she reached out and touched his bare chest. Her fingers tingled from the touch of a grown man. Her heart beat harder and she thought he would hear it or feel it beating. It beat for him and only for him. She looked back at his eyes full of lust, not love, not compassion nor protection. All Simone saw was David's eyes, his eyes, surely he was as excited as she . . . surely she was looking at love? Surely? She pulled back, running her hand down his hard stomach, smiling at him, visibly shaking now. She laid down the gifts and began to slip out of her shorts, kicking off her pink, flowery, little-girl flip-flops.

15

The large white van pulled next to a smaller version of the eighteen-passenger van. It was shorter and had only two seats in it. The back was open and empty except for the medical supplies, two small food and water boxes, extra ammo and a few blankets. As they exited the bigger van, Goose stepped from the smaller one, "Everybody survived I see." He yelled, as he walked to the van and looked in the window.

"What the heck? Where did all these come from? Unbelievable! What are we going to do with them?" His voice was pitched and his eyes wide as he confronted Cole.

"Well, if you keep up the hollering we will be turning them over to the Mexican Police and we will be going to a Mexican prison."

Goose had a so what look on his face as if he had been in worse places than a Mexican prison.

Cole continued, "Priest contact you?"

"Of course. He'll be here in ten or so."

"Priest will be taking the girls. We had three perps for him but the mafia side of the Mexican Police showed up and we had to leave them. They are swarming all over the place looking for this van and all of us right now." They all could feel the pressure of the E and E, it was palpable. Cole didn't need to mention it was time to get out of Dodge, now!

Car lights were seen careening as they flooded the dirt road they were on. Both vans were back in the trees and bushes, hard to see but not impossible. The car stopped in the road, the team had already deployed around their location, in the event a police cruiser showed up. They were ready. The car sat silent for a long moment. The car lights went out and the driver's door opened, fingers were tight on the triggers, the barrels pointed with deadly accuracy at the vehicle and the occupants.

"I can see you, Cole." Came the familiar voice of the priest.

From the bushes a little to the priest's left, unseen by the Priest but heard, "Yeah, and we can see you too, Padre." Snake crawled out of the bushes and walked to the man, Cole said, was a man after God's own heart.

Cole came to the priest looking at the vehicle the priest was driving, "Didn't Goose tell you, you would be transporting some passengers?"

"He deed, si."

"Well, how are you going to get all them in that car?"

"It's a station wagon and we're Mexicans. We can fit twenty in that car comfortably." Priest said laughing at Cole.

Cole laughed too, "Bring it over we need get out of here. The policia are scouring the city for this van and us. I had three perps but the police showed and we had to leave them. I'm sorry I know you wanted to interrogate them but we really didn't have the opportunity to transport them and the children too."

"Si, si, no worries. We will catch dem later. Gi'me de address and I will keep a watch on la casa they used."

"Well, I'm sure they will be moving now . . . especially since the house has been compromised. But here are the directions, description of the location and the bad guys." Cole handed him a small black notebook the kind that flips open from the top. The Priest slipped it into his breast pocket.

As the two walked, Priest looked back and signaled his vehicle to follow. The passenger slid across the bench seat and got behind the wheel, putting the car in gear. Cole's team had the girls out. Callie James sat in the back of the smaller van wrapped in a blanket, eating an energy bar and drinking gator aid. The other girls had bottles of water and were waiting to load into the priest's vehicle. The station wagon came to a stop close to the van and the door opened.

Priest put his hand on Cole's arm, "Cole, chu have never met my wife?"

"I thought Priests weren't supposed to get married?'

"Well, she corrupted me and anyway I'm not a priest. Mi amor, venir aqui. Cole, encontrar mi esposa." Cole was speechless. She was stunning. Her smile captivated him. She moved effortlessly across the rocky ground. She held out her hand and said, "Mucho gusto, Senior."

"No, the pleasure is mine, señora." She dipped her head, smiled and moved to help the girls.

Priest turned to her and told her in Spanish to move the girls to their car and prepare to leave.

"So, she's the one?" Cole asked.

"Si. She is de one. If I had not killed de devil in the man, the man would have killed her. Unfortunately, de man died with de devil. If you live with Satan you will die with him. He is in the fires of hell now. A Dios mio; how horrible that would be my friend." Cole shook his head in agreement.

"Speaking of horrible things, which way are chu heading when chu die, jeffe . . . up or down?" Even though it was dark as pitch, Cole could see Beto's intense eyes staring straight into his. True to form Beto was fearless in life and in the business of saving souls.

"We don't have time for a Bible class right now. Get these kids loaded. I'll take a rain check on the Sunday school lesson."

"Chure, chure, someday will be too late. I will be speaking de Lord's Prayer for de muerto . . . de dead . . . usted." Beto, saddened by his friend's refusal to talk about his beloved Jesus but was undeterred in his pursuit of Cole's soul.

"You dang Mexicans are so morose. Load up those girls!" Cole walked to the small van and looked in on Callie.

"How you doin', little sister?" Cole's voice was soft and fatherly.

"Fine." A standard answer from kids Cole thought. Her voice did sound a little stronger.

"Vaya con Dios, mi hermano." Beto turned to helping his wife load the girls into the station wagon. Seconds later the car was out of sight. Cole stood leaning against the small van, watching his friend drive away thinking . . . how many Mexicans can fit in a station wagon?

0357 hours

It was three minutes to four and the morning was chilly on Cole's skin. The team loaded up, headed to highway 280 and would follow this southwest to where it intersected 150 south; destination, El Dorado, Mexico, twenty-five miles South of Culiacan. Six miles South on 150 the highway would "Y," they would take the right "Y" which was highway 5. This would take them all the way into El Dorado. Once in the village they would intersect Mexico Blvd, follow it to Guayabas, turn right and take the second left, that street had no name. Follow it for about a half mile to Camino a Las Arenitas turn southwest and get to the river. They would follow the river road for 9 miles and at the dead end, hide the van, clean it out and leave the keys so the owner could retrieve it. Take a short hike to the river and uncover a CRRC 520 Zodiac. Load the Zodiac and prep for a 50-mile boat trip. The Zodiac came with extra fuel bladders, a rigid aluminum floor and a roll up hull for speed and smoother sailing. They would stow the weapons in water proof collapsible bags, change clothes and eat prepared meals as they loaded the Zodiac. They were looking at a three- to four-hour trip down the river, then out to the Gulf of California. Not a pleasant thought, but thirty to forty miles into the gulf they would meet up with a sport fisherman, unload the zodiac, deflate it, then load and stow it until they arrived at a second rendezvous, where they would be transported to a waiting aircraft.

16

"And although they know the ordinance of God, that those who practice such things are worthy of death, they not only do the same, but also give hearty approval to those who practice them."

Paul

Simone did not know whether to laugh or cry as she drove home. She had been gone all morning and her parents were going to quiz her so she needed to get over the events that took place earlier. But she could not. David had been so loving to her but then was angry and cruel. It did not make sense. Did he love her or not? She was not only confused about his love but she questioned her own love. She questioned why she went to him. Why she let him have sex with her. She could not call it love; it was painful and embarrassing. It was humiliating and he didn't even let her take the necklace with her! She began to cry. She was angry and indignant, not only emotionally but she was hurting physically. Once he had her in the bed he punished her and made her cry out in pain. She was so confused and felt so lonely; she just wanted to get home and take a shower. For the first time in her life she felt actually dirty, both inside and outside. Like the filthiness was in her mind and heart. She needed to wash the filth off. She began to cry harder. Her tears were tears of shame and regret. She did not know what to do. She had no one to talk to, she felt so alone. She remembered Joan's story of the woman caught in adultery, how shamed that woman must have felt when Jesus told her about her sin. Simone's mind cried out, can I be saved? The tears fell so hard she could hardly drive the car. Her chest was convulsing and the injuries David had inflicted throbbed, reminding her of the ugliness of the acts he made her perform. She covered her mouth with one hand as she steered the car with the other . . . sobbing in humiliation and guilt.

She was trapped and didn't even know it. David had plans for her. Wicked, deviant plans and he knew she would come to love all he would teach her.

17

"Beloved, let us love one another, for love is from God; and everyone who loves is born of God and knows God."

John

Friday came and Joan was glad, she was looking forward to the weekend. It was lunchtime and Joan was in her office touching up her Sunday Bible study for the girls. She was unusually excited about it. She had been working on it during her lunch hours and it was coming together pretty well. She remembered she had left off with the thought of 'Where did the electric impulses come from.' Joan was putting together a class outline:

I. She thought she would spend a few minutes talking about the creation of man and the electrical impulse. Then teach on the love of Christ out of 1 John.

II. John's testimony about Jesus in 1 John 1:1–4

III. An understanding of how the light will not allow darkness to be a part of God verse. 5

IV. Discuss the five conditional phrases of vv. 6–10

V. Conclusion: the only God that seeks people

Joan still needed to fill in the meat of her class outline that she would do on Saturday. However, for now, she had the jest of it down. Joan as always sat back and began to pray over her lesson. It was a simple prayer. Not a particularly strong pleading to God through her Savior Jesus. But then, right at the end she began to feel a weight placed on her shoulders not actually hands but an emotional heaviness, a fear for the girls in the class. Joan stopped and sat still, then slowly slid off her office chair to her knees. She knelt on the floor for a time not moving, not speaking. Her eyes were closed; she was motionless and silent before the Lord. Waiting; feeling the pressure of a great foreboding for the girls in her class. She began to name them individually; each one she mentioned she felt the Lord needed to look into their life. As she moved through the list, she came to Simone Donny and understood that she was to get up and go to Simone. She had no idea why she felt so compelled to leave right at that moment and find Simone. She was to go, now! Joan did not even know where Simone lived. She found herself leaving the office, as she passed the girl at the front desk she told her that she would be right back and to take messages for her.

Joan left the parking lot, not knowing which way to turn but turned left and traveled through down town Pimsler. Finding herself on the opposite side of town, in a neighborhood she had not once been in, found herself turning into a driveway of a house that she had never even seen before. She was confused, as she exited her car and approached the front door, ringing the bell.

Joan stood and looked around. She thought how strange, this was not like a trance but a knowing where to go. She knew this is where Simone was.

The door opened and a woman Joan had not met before answered the door. Pleasant looking woman, she was smiling at Joan, "Hi, are you here for Simone?"

"Is Simone Donny, here?" Joan was in shock.

"Yes. We've been praying for you to come." She was very matter of fact in her statement.

"Oh! I was praying as well and I felt I needed to come to this house?" She hesitated and was uncertain with her words, the woman could tell. Joan was afraid this stranger would think she had lost her mind.

"Simone is here. Please come in." Joan entered not knowing what in the world was going on. The woman led her through her home straight back to a bedroom. As she moved down the hallway, she heard sobbing and deep anguish. The woman stopped at the door and turned looking at Joan, "We do not know why she has come here. She has never liked my daughter. Simone has been very cruel to her many times. But when we saw her, we could not turn her away. I hope you can help her. She has just been crying nonstop since she has arrived."

"Has she said anything to you or your daughter about why she is so upset?" Joan asked.

"No. She just came to the door and rang the bell. She asked for Cynthia and when she saw her, she threw her arms around her and began to cry, saying 'I'm sorry,' over and over."

Joan asked, "You are Christians?"

"Yes, we are. Forgive me. My name is Cindy Wak and my daughter is Cynthia. Simone has been here for over an hour and has not told us anything. We actually know her mom and dad but Simone has refused to allow us to call them. Poor thing is in such pain!"

Joan opened the door believing the Lord Himself was guiding her. "Simone?" Joan said quietly poking her head in the room. Simone jumped off the bed and came to her holding her arms out in front of her like a little girl, crying.

Children can always see Christ in people. Satan is the only one that has to disguise himself.

18

"And if you do not do well, sin is crouching at the door, and its desire is for you, but you must master it."

GOD

George Booker had had about enough of Pastor Pete's 'preaching,' if that was what you called it. George had been an elder of the Community Church but was voted out when he did not conform to the new direction that the leadership had been convinced of by Pastor Pete.

George pulled the church doors opened and walked into the building heading for the office complex. He had slowed allowing his eyes to adjust and then picked up speed through the hallway leading to the offices. He opened the door stepping in.

"Hi, George!" Bonnie the receptionist was one of those that handled the office well and loved her job. She also could keep her mouth shut, unfortunately an unusual trait for most people who heard as much as she had over the years.

"Hey, Bonnie; the Preacher in?" George had things on his mind and was a bit off center.

"Sure. You want me to ring him?"

"Nope, I'll just announce myself."

"Okeydoke, got some things on your mind, I see." Bonnie had seen George in the "need to see the Preacher" mode before. George had actually hired her when he was in a leadership position. He knew she was perfect for the job and he was seldom wrong about people.

George walked around the desks in the outer area and approached the pastor's study. Knocked on the door and opened it, stepping in, "Pete, you got a minute?"

Pete looked over his computer monitor and didn't reply, just nodded.

Pete stood up from his desk and moved to a table across the room motioning to George to sit.

Pete, being as cordial as possible, "Would you like some tea or coffee?"

"No, thanks, Pete. But I would like to start this meeting off with a word of prayer."

Pete looked puzzled, "That won't be necessary, George." Pete retorted, a little put off to the request of bringing God into this . . . meeting.

"Well, I'm going to pray, I need my Father's wisdom here." George bowed his head and silently asked God to give wisdom and discernment to them both, then began straight away. "I am truly concerned about the direction of the church." George said as he took his seat. "I am seeing some things that are quite alarming and I wanted to speak to you about them." He had been here before and knew that all truth given with gentleness with this man fell on deaf ears.

Pete smiled a condescending smile, "Well, George, we all have been here before. The church leadership made the decisions and I am afraid whatever you want to change, can't be changed, except by them. We know your feelings."

"As I am sure you are aware; I have been in front of the other men. They have told me to speak to you. I am going to voice my opinion again and hopefully we can come to some harmony on a few issues. If not, I will adjust." George full well meant to fight for the souls in this gathering of believers before this man destroyed them.

"Okay, George, I'm all ears." Pete was not going to listen to this very long. George was an out of date believer and had to understand that the Bible was a good book but it was as out of date as George was. Pete knew this as well as all the leadership. Pete thought, *Get with the times, George.*

"I want to know if you believe Christ is the only way to salvation." George waited.

Pete blew out a breath of air in exasperation. Eyeing George, "First thing you must understand George is that I believe that statement but you have got to admit, it's a pretty harsh statement. If I were to blab that from the pulpit, half the congregation would walk out. And frankly, George, I have come to understand that there are other ways to reach out to our Great God."

"Define for me, if you can, 'the other ways'?" George was now preparing himself for a divine battle. He had prayed as he came into the building and had asked the God of heaven to give him the necessary words needed to defeat Satan. For call this what you will, those who do not represent Jesus Christ in this world only have one other master to serve.

"Life is a complicated matter and each person in this complicated existence has certain beliefs that they are comfortable with and believe in. If we were to push on them a single way to salvation, well it would be chaos for them. Let me put it simply for you, Brother," Pete was patronizing him and George knew it, "take for instance the Alcoholics Anonymous. They know that all the people that enter their doors are more than likely not Christians. So how do they approach this 'god thing,' by instructing all those that go through the 12 steps to find a 'god' according to their own understanding. It, their 'higher power,' if you will, could be a teddy bear or their 1957 Chevy or whatever. And yes, it can be Christ if one so chooses. But to say that it has to be the God of the Bible? Well . . ." Pete paused for affect, "It puts too much constraint on the one trying to pull himself out of a bad situation. Are you following me George?" Pete sat up in his chair and was trying to look down on George physically, to take him off balance.

"Yes, I see what you're saying. So first Christ is not the most important and it is up to man to create his own god concept so that he can pull himself out of his problems? So relatively speaking, any god concept will do as long as they are here worshipping, uh . . . comfortably?"

"Well, yes. You see once we have them here they are able to sort things out a bit and discover that Jesus is the way, as you put it." Pete thinking he had finally made a dent in this thick head.

George eased back in the chair, crossing his legs, appearing to relax a little, "Well, hypothetically, what if a Hindu decided to worship here but refused to give up his religious beliefs. Would this not be an insurmountable conflict? You know . . . Jesus and elephant boy?'

"Not at all George, you must understand that there are some very good points that the Hindu religion makes. After all truth is truth no matter where it comes from. I have heard you say that many times. Right?" Pete was smiling at George.

This man is a buffoon, George responded, "Question . . . speaking of truth, is there no absolute truth? Is all truth relative to people's own belief system, no one God, no absolute truth?"

"First off, I believe in the same God you do. I believe he is a tolerant and benevolent Father who offers his hand to all and all that take his hand will be saved. Regardless of your belief, values, lifestyles or perception of truth . . . all beliefs are equal and all truth is relative to your situation." Pete quoted a Pastor named Jeffress but took his quote way out of context. Pet continued, "You see George we as Christians must be tolerant of all others or we will never be able to win anyone to our church. Then where would we be?" Pete actually thought he was getting through.

"So, Peter, we don't have to worry about the realities of scripture, is what you're saying? Our God is so great and benevolent that He can overlook . . . say . . . idol worship? Is that what you're saying?" George was trying hard not to burn holes through Pete with his eyes.

"Well, George, idol worship, really? Come on who worships idols today?"

"The Hindu's do and you want them in worship with us."

"Well, I didn't say that, George!" Pete was getting tired of this conversation.

George was contemplating his next move. "Pete, you say you believe in the same God I do but that Jesus is not the only way. You say that you believe the Bible is the inspired word of God. Are all those statements correct?"

"Well, yes, within limits, of course." Pete was trying to prepare his defense.

George ignored his answer, "Luke writes of the historicity of scripture, in other words scripture as fact. He says things like, 'many have undertaken to compile an account of the things accomplished among us.' Luke also says, that eyewitnesses and servants of the word handed down to us those things they saw and heard, I am paraphrasing; but then Luke says that he, Luke, investigated everything fully from the beginning in order that the man he was writing to could be assured of the truth of Luke's letter in order for the recipient to trust the things he learned about Jesus Christ. And this is where it gets interesting, Pete; from the first chapter to the third chapter of Luke's letter, Luke mentions people, places and events with dates that can be traced and proven true or used to prove that Luke was a liar. No New Testament contemporary disputed Luke's claims about the things he wrote."

"What is your point, George?" Pete felt he was wasting time here.

"My point is, no one in Luke's time, contested Luke's letter as untrue. The leadership of the day just wanted all of them to quit preaching about the Christ! They never denied the Christ nor His miracles. Then in Luke 9, three of the disciples were at the transfiguration and heard a voice out of a cloud state, 'This is My Son, My chosen One, listen to him.' If there was no contesting the first part of Luke's writing, then none contested this part either. It stands to be true, then that God spoke from a cloud about His Son and that we need to listen to Him, don't you agree?"

"Yes, I would if in fact that happened. But you know time and distance can have a lot of effect on antiquity." Pete said.

"W. F. Albright, you know who he is?" George paused and expected an answer.

"Should I?" Pete said with ignorant frustration in his voice.

Exasperated with Pete, George continued, "W. F. Albright states and I quote, 'No other work from Greco-Roman antiquity is so well attested by manuscript tradition as the New Testament. There are many more early manuscripts of the New Testament than there are of any classical author, and the oldest extensive remains of it date only about two centuries after their original composition.' Lee Strobel, in his book, reports the latest account of Greek Manuscript as follows: papyri, 99; uncials, 306; minuscule, 2,856; and lectionaries, 2,403, for a total of

5,664 manuscripts! Do you get my point? There is no other book in history that has the amount of evidence that supports the Bible, none! And you are having a problem with the factual truth of it!" Pete began to speak but George held up his hand and stopped him, "You state there is no absolute truth, right?" George asked.

"Correct." Pete was looking straight at George.

"Is that your absolute statement of truth, Pete?" Pete ground his teeth and moved uncomfortably in his chair at George's question.

"Pete, did the sun come up this morning? True or false?"

"The sun did come up this morning."

"Will the sun come up tomorrow morning?"

"Yes."

"Can we agree on the statement that the Sun has come up every morning for thousands of years and it will come up tomorrow as truth?"

"Yes, I suppose."

"Can we say that as an absolute truth?"

"Yes, George, we can say that as an absolute truth." Pete said through gridded teeth.

"Well then, there are absolute truths, your statement and my metaphor. We discover truths based on evidence that leads intelligent people to surmise from that evidence TRUTH! Correct?"

"Correct." Pete sounded a little beaten.

"Scripture records the life, work and words of Jesus Christ. Listen to this, 'I am the way, the truth, and the life; no one comes to the Father but through me' (John 14:6). No other leader of any of the great religions of the world were fore told about hundreds of years before they were born, Pete. None of them! Not Mohammed, Confucius, Buddha, only Jesus had over 400 prophecies about his coming. All were fulfilled in his life, everyone. What are the odds of that? I'll tell you, again Lee Strobel's in his book, THE CASE FOR CHRIST, says that if just 48 of the 400 prophecies came true in Christ's life the odds were 13 trillion to one. From evidence, we can discover truth . . . absolute truth! Tell me your take on what Christ said in the book of John, Pete?"

"Which part of John, George?"

"The part I just quoted to you out of John 14:6! Is He the only way?" George raised his voice an octave.

"Well, I suppose you want me to say because of the evidence that you have produced, Jesus is God's Son." Pete was looking down as if ashamed in not believing this statement.

George looked at Pete and suddenly felt anger mixed with pity. "It's not what I want you to say Pete . . . is it what you believe?"

Pete was quiet for a long moment, "George, I am not sure what I believe. I don't like the God of the Old Testament and I am not sure of the God of the New. I do know that His principles of how we are to deal with each other are what we should do. But a place like Hell? I am not sure at all about that. I do not think a kind God would send innocent people to an eternal Hell. The miracles are just way off the charts for me as well. I just don't know." His voice trailed off to a whisper.

George was staring at him in unbelief. "Pete what happened to you? What happened to your faith, your Biblical knowledge? What is going on? If it is not the Christ that saves, who? You need to seriously think about stepping down. You need to regroup and find your faith again."

Pete jerked his head up and George could tell that he had hit a nerve in Pete, "Step down!" Pete's voice was loud and angry. Again he said with force, "Step down! This is my Church! I built this church and I tell you who is going to STEP DOWN! You get out of my office now!" Pete's voice boomed through the walls and into the outer office. George was looking but the man he was seeing was not Pastor Pete.

Pete stood up pointing to the closed door and shouted, "Get out! Now!"

George Brian Booker stood holding out his hands toward Pete, "My heavenly Father if I have found favor in your sight at all . . ." Pete screamed again, "Get out of My Church!" George continued undeterred, "Open Peter's eyes to the truth of your Good News. Turn his . . ." Pete ran out of the office and shouted at Bonnie, "Call the Police, Bonnie, now!" . . . "Mind and heart back to You and allow him to again believe. Send your Holy Spirit to him and convict him of his errors and sins, remove him from his position and take him into the wilderness to teach him that only You are his Sustainer and Savior. Amen."

George walked out to a fuming Pete and a totally confused Bonnie, who sat holding the phone receiver in one hand with her other on the dial pad, looking between the two men in complete shock and confusion.

"Don't bother Bonnie; I am on my way out." George walked by Pete, then turned to face him, "Pete, God is going to instruct you as He does to all those He loves. Best to prepare yourself son!"

Pete lost control of himself and screamed at George Booker, who refused to be bullied by Peter Donny or Satan himself. Pete's face was red almost purple as he moved toward George threatening him with his entire body, then suddenly turned and pushed all the items on the closest desk off onto the floor. Bonnie jumped up and moved to the far end of the room away from the two men.

George looking at Pastor Pete calmly stated to her, "Bonnie dear, get your things and take the rest of the day off."

Pete spun and stormed out of the room slamming his office door.

George turned to leave and saw Bonnie standing in the corner of the room gripping her handbag, her eyes as big as saucers. George walked over to her, "Come on Bonnie, I've done all the damage I can do here." He helped her get her feet moving toward the front door.

As they walked out of the building Bonnie said, "I've been here fourteen years, George, and I have never seen anything like that! I have seen a change in the leadership and have not known what to do or who to talk to about it. Pastor Pete is not what he used to be. He has changed."

George hated that it had come to this, "Yes . . . that . . . was not pretty. I am sorry you had to see that but sometimes Bonnie, you have got to bring the demons out so God can deal with the man." G e o r g e Booker wondered, as he walked to his car, what God was going to do with this place? Pimsler had more bars than churches. The homosexuals and lesbians had a large, loud and vulgar presence in the community. There were Planned Parenthood groups teaching in the schools and even had their counselors, not just handing out condoms in the school, but actually instructing the children on how to perform sex acts, ON OVER HEAD PROJECTORS! The children were taught that sex before marriage was normal and that 'alternative life styles' were just that, an alternative. Evolution was fact although no one could prove a thing about the theory. Drugs were rampant. People applied for an exemption from the state claiming a medical need in order to grow and sell their marijuana. Life in Pimsler was upside down. No morals, no shame. Each man was doing what was right in his own eyes.

George knew the judicial system in town was bent with judges always leaning toward the most lucrative offer. George almost began to weep over his home town. If the churches were not weakening the cause of Christ in town, they were out right hiring unrepentant publicly practicing sinners to lead worship, teach Bible classes, and lead singing. George was gripped by fear. Not fear of the enemy but fear of what God will do if things do not change quickly.

19

Baja California, 1930 hours: somewhere
in the vicinity of La Paz, Mexico.

The airstrip was not an airstrip but the only one worried about the dirt road the plane was setting on was Callie. The truck that transported the team to the airstrip had left and all the gear was stowed ready for takeoff. The group was sitting under a wing waiting for Goose to finish the preflight. As hot as it was, it was still much cooler there than in the plane.

Everyone was relaxing except for Clint. He had strolled to the top of a small hill that hid people and plane from anyone traveling down the never used road. He was setting on his haunches like a bushman; Cole could see his back, always on guard always checking. Well, if it was not Clint it would have been Cole, Hatch or Scottie. Even Blake the Snake was a good conscientious protector . . . if nobody else stood up for the job. Cole was proud of his guys. And rewarded them faithfully for all the risks they endure with him. However, they can't stand bullies either and that is all these people they fight are . . . worthless, dangerous bullies.

Callie was singing a little song and was squatting in the dirt playing with a small stick she had found. He watched her and was amazed at her resilience. Traumatized as she had been, here she is humming, relaxed and seemingly oblivious to the kidnapping and the rescue.

"Hey, Callie." BC called to her.

She stopped and looked at him. Her sweet face turned up to see his big head staring back at her and she smiled at him. "You're going to be seeing your mamma soon. What do you think about that?" She was small for an eleven-year-old but Cole could tell she had grit.

She stood up, threw her stick down, walked over to him and sat down on his lap. She took his big old head in her tiny hands and kissed him right on the end of his nose, "I think it's great! Thank you, BC." Just as a-matter-of-fact as that. Cole started to laugh as she stood up and began to walk back to her stick.

She turned with a cute flip of her hair, placing her little hand on her hip at the same time and said, "What's so funny big boy?" Cole burst out laughing and said to no one in particular, "My, my, are you going to be a handful!" She plopped down and smiled the cutest smile at Cole. A smile that said I will never forget you; I love you Cole, then went back to her stick and her little song. Cole stopped laughing, checked his emotions and cleared his throat. There is no greater honesty than a child's. How can some people do the things they do to these little people. Whether it is abortion or steeling them for the sex slave trade? How! His blood was boiling and it was entirely too hot for that angel to raise its head today.

Goose had flown the 1959 Beech E 18 S twin engine; fitted with extra detachable fuel tanks; down a day and a half ago. The Priest had some locals who he knew and trusted, to assist Goose in getting the equipment across the gulf and the Zodiac up the river. They delivered the van to Goose and he communicated his location to Cole when he arrived in Culiacan. All things considered, this was one of the smoothest extractions the team had performed in a long time.

"We be ready to fly!" Goose shouted sticking his head out the side window of the plane. "Clear," he yelled and waited a bit, then flicked the switch and the engines coughed and came to life.

Cole stood and whistled for Clint. The group began to board and Sweet Callie ran to Cole, raising her arms to him looking up with that expression that only little girls have . . . pick me up Daddy, please! Cole hoisted her to his chest and hugged her tightly, twirling a turn or two with her throwing her arms out saying, "Do it again BC, do it again!" He had tears in his eyes mixed with pure love for the children and absolute hatred for those who do harm as he passed her through the door.

What is wrong with the world?

"You shall love the Lord your God with all your heart and with all your soul and with all your might. These words, which I am commanding you today, shall be on your heart. You shall teach them diligently to your sons and shall talk of them when you sit in your house and when you walk by the way and when you lie down and when you rise up. You shall bind them as a sign on your hand and they shall be as frontals on your forehead. You shall write them on the door post of your house and on your gates."
Deuteronomy 6:6–9

What's wrong with the world, you ask?
We have forgotten to teach the children about the Lord God Almighty.

20

The Lord said to Moses, "You are about to lie down with your fathers; and this people will rise up and play the harlot with the strange gods of the land, into the midst of where they are going, and will forsake Me and break My covenant which I have made with them.

Then My anger will be kindled against them in that day, and I will forsake them and hide My face from them, and they will be consumed, and many evils and troubles will come upon them; so that they will say in that day, 'Is it not because our God is not among us that these evils have come upon us?'

God

Joan had been holding Simone for well over thirty minutes without Simone speaking of any cause for her pain of heart. Finally, she began to calm down. She whimpered a little, then sat back looking at Joan.

"Honey, what has happened?" Joan began sympathetically.

Simone, still gulping air; a little unsure of the trust factor with this group of women, "I have been with a man and I feel terrible about it." She began to cry again. "It was not at all what I thought it would be!" Simone, sobbing, she was almost hysterical again.

Joan held her, gently rocking back and forth, "Can you tell me who it was?"

"Nooo," Shaking with her answer.

"Was it a grown man, sweetie?" Joan was almost afraid of the answer.

"Yes, but I love him. I don't understand anything!" She yelled the anything part and shook all over as she began to sob again.

Joan's mind immediately went to David. She remembered the incident last Sunday. Joan was not sure if she should ask at this point.

"Honey, come on, let's get you up and get you home, okay?" Joan said as she gently began to stand with Simone still in her arms.

Simone stood and began wiping her face with the back of her hands and wiping her hands on her shorts. Cynthia handed Simone a tissue.

"Thank you, Cynthia. Thank you for letting me in and everything."

"I am sorry you're hurting and I hope you can get all this straightened out. If we can help," Cynthia hesitated an instant, "we will anytime, just tell us how we can help, okay?"

"Okay, thank you." Simone was sincere in her thanks, as reached to hug Cynthia goodbye.

She and Joan walked outside to Simone's car, "Simone, you need to tell your parents what has happened. They will know what to do and they will help you, all right?"

"I will try. It's going to be hard." She almost began crying again.

"Is this a friend of theirs, honey?" Joan was looking into her eyes.

"Yes!" The tears came back on and she was sobbing again.

Joan reached out and just held her until she gained control. Joan knew who it was! Anger flew through her body. She was having a hard time not shaking the kid and getting his name out of her.

"You are going to tell your mom, as soon as you get home . . . aren't you?" Joan had her by her shoulders and was looking into her face, wanting a confirmation.

"Yes, I will, I promise." Simone pulled away and opened her car door. Then stopped and asked, "Did the Waks call you? How did you find me?" She was still sniffling.

Joan was not sure how to answer her, "Well, I was praying about my lesson for this Sunday and I got this strong feeling that I was to find you. I left my office not knowing where I was to go and just ended up here. I pulled into the drive and knew you were in this house, crazy huh?"

Simone wrinkled up her nose with a quizzical look on her face and said, "Yeah!"

"Simone, when one of God's children needs help He tells other children of His to go help. He loves you Simone, you need to know that."

"Thank you, Joan. I was mad at you last Sunday and I am sorry for that."

"Mad at me? Why?" Joan guessed why but needed for Simone to say it.

"I thought you were going to go with my parents and David." Simone looked up at Joan's face and added, "But you're different and he wouldn't like you. You're better than he is." She shut the door and started her car. She pulled away from the curb and disappeared around the corner. Joan was thinking about all this crazy stuff that's happening? She was not prepared for this to take place in her perfect little town.

As Joan walked to her car, she pulled out her cell phone and dialed the Booger's number.

21

"Whoever wishes to become a friend to the world, makes himself an enemy to God."

James

David knew that he needed to protect himself from any blow back from Simone. Although he had handled a hundred or more young girls just like he had handled Simone. However, he was never friends with their families and most of the time they were runaways or one of his minions had kidnapped them. He knew this could have some disastrous consequences.

Dialing Pete's number, he knew the perfect escape.

"Hello!" Pete said it rather sharply.

"Hey, brother. You angry with me?" David thought Simone could not have told so soon?

"David! No not at all, man. I'm sorry. I had a rather difficult day today."

"What happened, pew sitters come in and jump on you?" David said laughing.

"Well, yeah. That is exactly what happened. It was that sorry George Booker. He chewed me up one side and then down the other. Said I was a lousy preacher! Can you believe that?" Pete said with malice in his voice.

David thought this could not be more perfect. "Say it sounds like you need a short get away. How about you and I getting away for a night and a day, just the two of us? You know just us guys, a little escape; what do you say?"

"Man, I would love it. What do you have in mind?"

"I don't know. I got a G5 full of fuel. We could go anywhere. Come on, let's do it, me and you, pal!"

"Sounds great and I need a break from these stupid people. They have no idea how hard I work. Let me call Mary and tell her, you know women; that's all I need to have her on my back too."

David laughing to himself, "I know. You can tell me all about it on the plane. See you at the airport, partner."

Simone went straight home. Walking in seeing Mary standing in the kitchen and said, "Hi, Mom. Where's Dad?"

"Hi, sweetie," Mary said as she turned to greet Simone. "You know how hard he's been working lately, right? Well, David asked him to go on a boy's only get away with him." Mary looked at Simone and could tell she had been crying.

Simone turned and ran from the room crying again.

"Simone, honey. They will be back in time for church on Sunday. What's wrong?"

From the other end of the house Simone screamed out, "NOTHING!"

The plane soared high in the beautiful Pimsler sky. The flight plan was set West Southwest, destination . . . Las Vegas Playboy Club, the VIP treatment, a little booze, girls and more girls, the kind of girls that a man, any man, can't resist. David was in an especially good mood, laughing and joking all the way to Sin City! And Peter L. Donny had no idea the dark pleasures he was about to experience. Setting in a leather Captain's chair being served by a spectacularly beautiful flight attendant, listening to the plane whine through the blue sky; watching the sun's rays bounce off those silver wings; knowing that only a few men have these life opportunities and he was going to enjoy every one of them . . . thanks to his best friend. With the proverbial fish hook set deep into Pete's jaw, Pete's best friend was reveling in the destruction of another human being. Proudly turning a man to be like . . . himself.

22

"Where there is no guidance the people fall."

Proverbs

Early Saturday morning Joan was pulling in front of George and Helen's country home. It was a low ranch style house made of brick and cedar, beautifully landscaped, setback off the road almost hidden in the pines. It reminded her of Mr. Booker, well thought out and practical.

She rang and George answered the door, greeting her as only a kind and committed gentleman would do.

"Come in, Joan. Would you like some coffee?" She had never seen him in anything except a suite and tie. He was dressed in a jogging suite and tennis shoes; he didn't look himself.

Joan smiled and responded positively to the offer, "I would love some Mr. Booker. How's Mrs. Booker this morning?"

"She's fine but won't be if you keep calling us Mr. and Mrs., you do know our first names, don't you?" He chuckled.

"Yes, I do, I just thought, you know, well, you're my boss and all." She stammered a little.

"Not today, I'm not. I am your brother in Christ and we are handling a crisis for our Savior! He has made us for this day." They heard Helen in the kitchen holler out, "Settle down George. There will be plenty of time to preach after we hear what's going on." They both laughed and walked into the kitchen.

Joan felt like she was coming home when she entered the Booker's home. She was family and she knew it. They ate and laughed and drank the best coffee, smooth and delicate, very satisfying. The trio cleared the table and the conversation turned serious.

"Well, missy," George started out, "Tell us what's going on." They were still at the breakfast table, Helen was bringing more coffee; Joan thought she could drink this coffee all day.

"Well," Joan dipped her head a little toward Booker and raised her eye brows, "George, you both know about last Sunday and what happened then, and my class and the girls . . . all of that. I don't want to

83

hash it all over again but something very strange happened yesterday that led me to a girl in big trouble."

Helen joined in. "Well, tell us, Joan, Please!"

George retorted, "Sweet Pea, this ain't no murder mystery. Give the girl sometime here."

Joan continued. "I was praying about my Bible class and thinking about all the girls and all that I saw in class. When all of a sudden I had this weight or pressure on me," Helen gasped, "It was like a physical pressure, I can't explain it any better than that." Helen was making these little ah and ooh sounds, nodding her head up and down. *She's going to have to stop that*, Joan thought. George put his hand on Helen's arm and Helen settled down. Joan thought *'it must bother George as well.'*

"What happened, then?" George asked.

"I got up and literally drove to where Simone Donny was, without a clue where she was before I found her. It was absolutely freaky, ya'll."

Both, at almost the same time asked, "Why?"\

"Why was it freaky?" Joan was now really confused.

"Yes." Helen said.

"Well . . . because . . . nothing like that has ever happened to me before, that's why."

George picked up his Bible and opened it to the book of Acts chapter 8, "Let me read something to you Joan. Starting in verse 26, let's see . . . here it is; 'But an Angel of the Lord spoke to Phillip, saying, 'Get up and go South to the road that descends from Jerusalem to Gaza. So he got up and went; and there was an Ethiopian eunuch, a court official of Candace, queen of the Ethiopians, who was in charge of all her treasure; and he had come to Jerusalem to worship, he was returning and was setting in his chariot reading the book of Isaiah. Then the Spirit said to Phillip, 'Go up and join this chariot.'" George put the Book down and looked at Joan, "You see Joan when someone is searching for truth God will always provide an avenue for that person to find the truth of God. Even Sunday school teachers can be sent by the Holy Spirit to a needy person God is listening to. Scriptures like this put an end to the unbeliever's statement about the lost souls in Africa . . . God will take care of all those who seek Him, period. So what happened then?"

Joan began to relay the story about Simone's encounter with a man and the trauma Simone had experienced and as usual George was the one that brought up 'the who' question.

"Who do you think did this to her?"

"Well, she would never say but I think it was David Clark." Joan replied.

"Our David Clark the deacon?" Helen squeaked the words out in a high pitch voice from derived shock.

"Yes, our David Clark the deacon," Joan responded.

Helen looked at George, sat back in her chair crossing her arms across her chest and said with that I told you look on her face, "I told you, you needed to have a meeting with that guy!"

George ignored Helen's comment for the moment. "Joan did Simone state his name?"

"No, not out-right but she did say something interesting. She said as we were leaving the Wak's home, that she had gotten mad at me because she thought I was going to go to lunch with David. Then she said he wouldn't like me anyway because I was better than he was." Helen reached across, patting Joan's arm and smiled agreeing with the statement.

"Well, if it was not David, why would she bring him into the conversation? And with last Sunday's comment about his love for her, my money's on it being David but we can't jump to conclusions. I want to make sure it is him before we do anything." It was George's turn to set back in his chair now.

"I told her she needed to go home and tell her mom and dad what happened. I don't know if she did but if she did surely they will follow up? Don't you think?"

"Pete and Mary are way off base as far as theology goes but they are still parents with a moral responsibility to Simone. If she tells them, I think Pete will go through the roof." George stated, then followed with, "What do you think Sweet Pea?"

"Booger, I think we need to pray about this and ask God to guide us as surely as He guided Joan yesterday." They all held hands and bowed their heads and Booger led them in a moving prayer for wisdom, strength and courage to defend the innocent and to receive an extra measure of strength to love God even more.

23

Some mortals, against all odds, will choose the highest good over the basest wickedness that other mortals bring into the world through following evil. In the battle for souls, men must determine the true course. For in my estimation it is men that God uses as his weapons to turn the world back to the path of righteousness. Jesus says follow me and walks into battle against all those that stand against Heaven; and us, His warriors, shout the battle cry. When we see no struggle for souls we have lost our own. It is when we see the battle and only when we see it, do we know right from wrong, victory from defeat, righteousness from damnation.

The Author

Simone stayed in her room for most of the weekend, something she has not done for years. She was always gone, every night if she could be. However, this weekend was different and Mary knew it.

"Simone," Mary said knocking on her door, "Simone?" She cracked the door slightly, "Simone, dear, you have been in here for hours. What's wrong, baby girl?" Mary had sympathy in her voice.

Mary looked into the room and saw Simone setting on her bed Indian style. She said nothing in response to her Mother's call.

Mary entered the room and sat on the corner of the bed, "Simone, will you please tell me what is going on? This is not like you. Something has happened and I want to know!" Mary was concerned and it showed. "Please Simone, has someone said something or done something that has hurt you, honey? Please, can't you tell mother. This is breaking my heart."

Simone looked at her Mother and Mary saw a tear roll down Simone's cheek.

"Honey, what has happened?" She pleaded in almost a whisper.

Simone's bottom lip began to quiver as her eyes filled with tears. Then the dam broke and the flood of information came spilling out. Not in a healthy way but in a brutal gush of pain and anguish. As much as Simone wanted to love and give herself to David, she had neither the emotional capacity nor the mature understanding to do so. So Mary received all the information including an explicit description of David taking her virginity. Mary sat in shocked disbelief at the story unfolding in her ears. Mary fumed over the graphic description and how long this romantic pursuit David had had for Simone had gone on.

Mary's jealously was struggling to come out and punish the girl. To scream at her, telling her she had no right to be so beautiful, no right to be so young and no right to be with David! Mary held her tongue and pretended to care while she plotted a course to David's door to confront him with this betrayal. For David promised Mary his love.

Consequently, Mary held Simone in mock sympathy and told her it would be all right. That Daddy would be home soon and he would take care of it all. She rocked back and forth masking her feelings of hatred for this beautiful girl. All the while Simone believed her, found comfort in her lies and in her motherly embrace. But Mary had another plan, a plan that could only come from one who had forgotten the God of heaven. A plan to do harm and not to do good.

24

"But you, beloved, ought to remember the words that were spoken beforehand by the apostles of our Lord Jesus Christ."

Jude

Late Saturday night, David and Pete landed at the Pimsler Municipal Airport. Both were exhausted and smelled of sex, booze and cigars. David suggested that Pete come to his house first and shower and change. Pete was feeling a strange loneliness; it was as if he had forgotten something or had left someone behind. Like when he went off to college and left his family for the first time, a strange emptiness that he could not fill. As soon as his foot touched the tarmac, he was washed with even a greater emotion of sorrow and desolation. Not loneliness but a lost-ness, a darkness engulfed him and he almost began to cry. It was the heavy feeling of oppression, as if an anvil were on his chest. He had a hard time catching his breath.

David saw his victim struggling, "Hey man, you okay?"

Pete looked a bit panicked, "yeah, I'm fine. I guess I'm a bit jet lagged." Pete's mind went to visions of the night before at the Playboy Club. He grew weak, what had he done! What had he DONE! David introduced him to the most beautiful women he had ever seen, who acted as if he was the only man they wanted. Like he was exceptional and only he could please them, only he could satisfy their hunger, their lust. He felt their wet lips against his ear whispering empty words of love, sexually arousing him. Words he could not resist. He shook his head as if his brain was an etch-a-sketch board, trying to clear his thoughts. While he played in the club, he thought he never wanted to forget the beauties that stripped for him, danced for him, seduced him but now back in the real world those same beauties were clawing at his heart of hearts. His body trembled and his heart pounded, he lost his breath again, his knees went week and he stumbled across the tarmac as he walked to the car.

David grabbed him by the arm, "Whoa, hoss. You sure you're okay?"

Pete saw David for the first time, "What have I done, man?

Dear God, what have I done?"

David at first looked confused but then began to laugh a loud, deep, vicious laugh, "You had a bang-up weekend, man." David released his hold on Pete and danced around him shouting, "A weekend that less than a half of one per cent of the population could have had, a weekend with absolute beauties that do anything for their man, a weekend that most men would die for!"

That was it. That was the feeling . . . death! Pete felt dead inside. Pete heard a moan that started deep inside of him, a noise that he was not in control of; a groan that was building up in him . . . forcing its way out. It was in his throat! Pete clinched his jaw shut, held his breath but he could not keep it in.

Oh, Lord, he did not want his friend to hear this but it broke out of his nostrils and he blew phlegm out of his nose and then the noise came out; a deep wail, a bizarre sob that had a distressful, painful, animal cry that escaped his lips. He fell forward onto his hands and knees vomiting. Convulsing in his sorrow, choking and sobbing, vomiting the grief out of his body. Mourning his own death. He cried kneeling before David.

David's voice was flint hard, "Get up! I said GET UP!" He waited a beat, then reached down and jerked Pete off the ground. "You wanted this. You wanted to experience my life. What? Now you aren't man enough to handle it? You're pathetic. Tell me one part you did not enjoy? Now all of a sudden you regret everything. I'll tell you something cowboy, you better get a grip before you go home. And don't forget about tomorrow." David let out a cruel laugh, "Preacher boy! Get in the car." David knew he had accomplished his goal of self-protection. Pete would not dare confess what he had done and would live in fear of David telling all . . . forever.

David's driver started the limo and the pair crawled into the back. The stench was so pungent they had to roll down the windows. Pete had his head laid back on the seat and was staring at the ceiling of the car. David had gone quiet, lost in his thoughts of his night and day with the beauties and how he had watched his friend follow them like a lemming, right over the cliff into the abyss.

25

"But whoever causes one of these little ones, who believes in me to stumble, it would be better for him to have a heavy millstone hung around his neck, and to be drowned in the depths of the sea."

Jesus

During the discussion with the Bookers, Joan had learned of the unprecedented number of female run-aways that plagued Pimsler. The Bookers had explained that the town had a huge pregnancy rate higher than any other city in the state and one of the highest per-capita in the country. Runaways and pregnancies; she had asked them if it was only girls that ran away or if boys did too. Yes, Helen said many boys ran away from home as well. Helen thought it was because of the weak church, permissive school leadership as well as a loss of cohesiveness in the family unit. The divorce rate in Pimsler was higher than the national average and the drug scene was an open discussion at every city council meeting. But with the majority of the city council smoking medical marijuana, control was limited with the city ordinances. Not to mention the strong feminist community and constant bombardment from the homosexual community. Joan realized; what the people in Pimsler did not ever discuss was what happened to all those babies that so many girls carried and never delivered? That was the big secrete. Joan asked herself, and why so many girls went missing? Where were they going and why? What was so bad about Pimsler?

Sunday, The Lord's Day, she knew she should be excited but there was a dread over her. She gathered her things, left the comfortable security of her home and headed out the door for the church building.

On the drive, Joan could not help but think of the last two weeks. She wondered if other girls in the class knew David or were wrapped up in illicit activity. She was scared for them for so many children thought they had a handle on life, thought they knew all there was to know about life but had no real clue. They learned life from friends that had no idea what was really happening or from adults that taught life from a totally selfish perspective. Often times leading the kids down a path of darkness, that was one way . . . down!

As she turned on to the street the Church sat on, she was overcome with how this building was a perfect example of what she thought a church building should look like. Red brick, slate roof, two tall copper covered steeples, white ornate wood trim, with ten steps leading up to the ten-foot-tall white double doors, stained glass windows lined both sides of the sanctuary. The lawn was deep dark green, huge pine trees in the yard.

Flowers blooming in the flowerbeds, a swept parking lot, back dropped by a dark blue Colorado sky . . . so beautiful and serene, everyone smiling and greeting one another. Hugging and shaking hands like everyone was coming home for the weekend and all who were at home really wanted to see those coming home. She parked her car and was gathering her things, when Simone appeared. She waited patiently for Joan to exit the vehicle.

"Good morning Simone, how are you, honey?" Joan genuinely cared for the girls and had true compassion for Simone.

Simone smiled, "I am better. I still have some things I need answered in my head but I suppose that will come in time. I just wanted to say thank you . . . and . . . I don't know. Just thank you, I guess."

"You're welcome. Did you have a chance to speak to your parents yesterday?" Joan felt it was not her place to ask but she could not help herself.

"I did, I spoke to Mom a little. Dad was out of town with David until late last night. He was not feeling well when he came in. He said he thought he had gotten food poisoning or something? He looked awful. But I guess he's feeling better this morning. He's going to lead worship."

"Oh, that's terrible, I am glad that he is doing better, though. We had better get inside. You are coming to class this morning?" A question every teacher asks.

"Yes, can I help you carry something?" Simone offered with a smile.

"Sure, here you take these little booklets." She passed them off and both headed for the building.

In class Joan wanted to sing and pray with the girls but their attitude seemed the same as last Sunday, all except for one's. So Joan let the singing go and started the class with a prayer. When she looked up Simone was setting in the front row. Joan thought how nice.

"C. S. Lewis said and I quote," Joan said, "'I believe in Christianity as I believe that the sun has risen; not only because I see it but by it I see everything else.' I believe with the same strength of truth he believed."

Joan continued her class introduction, "Has anyone figured out where the power comes from that moves through your body and makes your body respond to your desires?" Joan waited. Only Simone was looking at her. The others were afraid to look her in the eyes, she was sure they thought if they made eye contact she would call on them. She waited . . . no answer.

"Well, we'll cover that at the end of the class. Right now please take a Bible and open it up to 1 John chapter 1." She waited . . . not even Simone reached for a Bible.

Oh, well.

"When you meet a person, tell me how you get to know them." She waited.

And waited, determined to wait until, they became uncomfortable.

Simone answered, "You hang with them. You talk to them, ya know?"

"Yeah, you go to their crib and stuff." Christi said; the most gothic looking girl in the class and the last one Joan thought would ever speak.

"That's right Simone . . . Christi. John the author of this letter we are studying is a real man who really lived during the days Christ lived. That is an important point that I will prove in a later study but right now I want you to take my word about a few things. First, the Bible is a factual book. The whole Bible."

"Really," said Christi, "I thought it was like, ya know, Greek Mythology or something. All made up and stuff."

"No, not at all. The Bible is totally a book of historical truths based on the life of one man, Jesus Christ. The Old Testament tells of his coming with more than 400 prophecies, from his virgin birth to his crucifixion. And the New Testament tells of his life on the earth as the Son of God and what He did for us. This is where John comes to tell us about how he got to know Jesus and what he thought of Him."

One of the girls quizzed, "Virgin birth? How does that happen?"

Joan chuckled. "If you hang with me I will tell you a great story about how it really did happen. Now let me read to you out of 1 John chapter 1. 'What was from the beginning, what we have heard, what we have seen with our eyes, what we have looked at and touched with our hands, concerning the word of life, and the life was manifest and we have seen and testify and proclaim to you the eternal life, which was with the Father and was manifested to us—What we have seen and heard we proclaim to you also, so that you too may have fellowship with us; and indeed our fellowship is with the Father, and with His Son Jesus Christ. These things we write, so that our joy may be made complete.' Does it sound like John hung with Jesus at his crib?" The girls all laughed.

"It does; doesn't it? Listen to what he is saying . . . in verse 1, John uses the word "beginning.' This has two possible references; one is John wants his readers to know that Jesus is eternal. That Christ was not a created being like us but was as John wrote in the Gospel of John chapter 1 verse 1 that Jesus was co-equal with God the Father. On the other hand, it could mean that he, John, was with Jesus from the beginning of Jesus' ministry. I think I will go with the second one because it fits with the context of the following verses. Everybody with me so far?" She paused a beat.

"You know if you guys grab a Bible it would help you to understand it a little better." Joan waited. Simone reached under her chair and slid a Bible out from under it. Another couple of girls followed suit.

"All right!" Joan was suddenly charged. "Now what John wants these people to know is what went on with him as he followed Jesus around for three years. Just like you and your high school friends, you guys hang out and get to know each other. Well, so did John and Jesus.

Listen to how John describes getting to know Christ . . . we heard Him speak . . . we examined Him with our own eyes, studied Him, looked closely at Him; put Him under a microscope. Then touched Him with our hands, they hugged him, prayed with Him and ate with Him and knew the same people He knew. Do you understand the point here? John is saying I knew him as well as the people he is writing, know John!" Joan prodded.

"You see; John uses words like 'heard' in the perfect tense which means not that the disciple just heard Jesus speak but expresses an act in the past with lasting results. John knew Jesus so well that he is still hearing Jesus speak to him. Not literally but John uses that word to strengthen his point to the people he is writing. Again John uses a Greek word for 'look' that expresses a continuous contemplation of an object which remains before the spectator. So they looked for a long time to make sure Jesus was what he proclaimed to be! Do you see how exciting this is! We are reading a firsthand account from a man that actually saw GOD on earth.

"Now John continues with the word 'touch,' John is trying to explain that he handled Jesus much like a blind man discovers a new object that he has not come in contact with before. The blind man holds the object and feels the texture and the shape of the thing or like a person who is in a dark room and is trying to find his way out. He is groping around, feeling the walls and bumping into things until he finds the door. So John is saying I got to know Christ with all my senses. I got to know Him intimately, like a good friend, no like a great friend, no like my best friend.

"John then says in verse 2, 'the life was manifested to us' referring to Christ. John is saying as they got to know Jesus he was revealed to the disciples to be the Son of God. Over a period of time Jesus explained to them His incarnation. John says 'we have seen' meaning they witnessed, EYE WITNESS and are still witnessing, as a witness would do in a court of law, to all that Christ was on earth. Again John uses the word we translate as 'proclaim' to express a report. It is interesting to know that John uses the word to witness or to testify as if in a court of law in reference to Jesus but then he uses 'proclaim' which indicates the authority of a commission and both words rests on the authority of eyewitness accounts. John is using these terms so that there is no possibility of a mistake concerning the life to which John is making reference to; that that life was revealed by God in the historical person of Jesus Christ. Girls, it is important also to understand that John was one of the three disciples that went with Jesus when He was transfigured on the mountain and spoke with Moses and Elijah. This is important in that John and the others wanted to build an altar for all three (Jesus, Moses and Elijah), which was not what God had in mind! So in this cloudy mist in which all six men were standing a voice came out of the cloud that said, 'This is my Son, My Chosen One, listen to him!' Now remember John is speaking to people that know that he walked with Jesus and has by his testimony and the testimony of others reported the same historical truths. No denying this. He says God spoke to him and two other men. Those two others have said the same things. But it goes further than these three. There are a host of people in that day that had been raised from the dead, healed from blindness and all were talking about Jesus doing those miracles.

Therefore, John is saying, I heard this, saw this and then in Matthew 28 Jesus says to the disciples after his death on the cross, go and preach to the entire world. Because of this command from Jesus, John is bringing into account all the teachings that he was taught and others who taught believers previously and saying this is what I am referring to when I saw the Life manifest to us!"

Joan looked out at the girls and they all seemed to be absorbing what she was teaching, "Verse 2 actually brings in the idea of the eternal side of Jesus. John says, 'the eternal Life which was with the Father,' John is trying to bring home the fact that Jesus was a man on earth and was with God from eternity and that the people could trust John in John's description of these events. That this Jesus was mortal, physical not merely an assumed appearance. Jesus was a flesh and blood man, who was God's Son sent to earth to save the world.

"Now listen to this. John wants all the people to understand the significance of the first 2 verses which is seen in the third verse, 'so that you too may have fellowship with us.' Who did John have fellowship with?" She waited for the girls to process the answer."

Timidly one girl ventured a guess, "Jesus?"

"Correct, Jesus and God the Father! This is what John is calling them to—a heavenly fellowship with our Creator. John is saying the whole purpose for his writing is to call people to fellowship with God! John does not want to stop there; he is going to explain the result of this fellowship, which is joy! John's joy, he is experiencing daily because he has a strong relationship with Christ and the people John is writing to, their joy for believing and accepting John's words as truth, leading those that hear and obey into a deep and abiding, saving joy with Jesus and His Father."

Simone barely raised her hand, "Joan can we have this joy today? I mean, if we believe in Christ can we be joyful?" It was obvious to Joan, Simone was still suffering with the 'David' experience.

"Yes, we can. That is what verses 5–10 are all about. How this joy is developed and incorporated into our life. Let's look at verse 5: 'This is the message we have heard from Him and announce to you, that God is light and there is no darkness in Him at all.' Why do you suppose John went from fellowship and all this nicey-nice stuff to God is light and there is no darkness in Him; AT ALL." She put emphasis where it needed to be and lowered her voice to imitate God speaking.

The girls laughed at Joan's pan-a-miming but did not answer the question.

"Because, these people are having trouble in their fellowship with God and each other; John is going to help them get past their life struggles and enter into a deeper relationship with God. He does this by explaining to them first that the God of Heaven and Jesus Christ are all light. What do you think light equates to, what is the meaning of light and what is the meaning of darkness?"

"Light is good and darkness is bad?" The Goth girl understands more than she lets on.

"Wow, Christi that is totally correct! Verse 6 says something somewhat scary, 'If we say we have fellowship with Him and yet walk in the darkness, we lie and do not practice the truth.' John is going to introduce to us five conditional phrases. Now these are important for all of us to know. When you are with your friends at their house, are there things you can do and things you can't do while in their home?"

No answer again, Joan wondered if she had lost them. "Well, let me explain a little. Let's say your best friend invites you over and as soon as you get there you go into her mother's bedroom and began going through her mom's closet, trying on her mom's clothes. Then when you got through with the clothes you just threw them on the floor, then went to her mom's jewelry box and took out all the expensive jewelry, putting some in your pocket and tossing other pieces on the floor. What would your friend do?"

One of the girls in the back of the room said, "Throw the bum out!"

All the girls laughed. It was good that they were relaxing some.

"Of course you would! So you have conditions on your friendship.

Right?" Joan was leading them.

"Right." Most of them answered.

"We call that, social etiquette. We all set boundaries with people even if we do not know we are doing it. We accept some behavior and reject another type of behavior. Jesus does the same thing. Except being God He has a right to set the type of behavior He universally accepts, whether you believe in him or not and the type He will not accept. Notice in verse 5, John says there is no darkness in Him at all? Well, that means we cannot ever be in the presences of God. Because we have all sinned, which is darkness and we all have fallen short of His standard which is light. In verse 6, John continues with the thought that some are saying they have fellowship with him but are not living according to Jesus' standard. These people John calls liars and they do not practice the truth that Jesus has said is His standard for fellowship with Him because they are not walking in the truth of God's standard. Are you all following me?" Joan knew this can be a difficult concept if she didn't go into some detail. All heads shook up and down.

"Great. So, John continues with the idea of how we keep in fellowship with God. He says 'if,' a conditional phrase, we walk in the light as He Himself is in the Light we have fellowship with one another and the blood of Jesus' His Son cleanses us from all sin.' What is John saying to you with this sentence?"

Simone was first to speak, "Well, I think it says you have to be perfect to be in fellowship with God." All the girls nodded in agreement.

"If that were the case nobody could enter into fellowship with God. Look at this phrase, 'the blood of Jesus cleanses us from all sin.' What does that mean?" She waited again. "Let's back up a minute. In verse 5 John says God is all light in Him is no darkness. Where is the darkness found?"

Everyone sat still and ventured no answer.

"On earth." Joan said in a matter a fact way. "The Bible tells us that the prince of the air is Satan. You see, girls, we are living in the spiritual darkness that John talks of on this earth. That is why there is so much pain and suffering. That is why John wrote his letter. The struggle is, as John wrote in the gospel of John, that 'light has come into the world and the world did not understand it.' The Reason the world did not comprehend it or understand it, is answered in John 3:19, 'men loved the darkness rather than the light.' Men will not come to Jesus because their deeds are evil and the light of Christ will expose them. That is the last thing people want to be exposed for, is the evil they do. People love darkness.

"So now look at the phrase 'the blood of Jesus cleanses us from all sin.' This is the most important verse I can think of, because this verse tells me of the complete love of Christ. Our struggle is to not sin . . . period. How do we walk in the light since we all sin, daily? We walk in the light by believing in the only Son of God and His saving grace through his sacrifice of Himself on the cross, taking away our sin forever! Even if we continue to sin."

"Look in verse 9 of 1 John; this is how you stay in the light, 'If we confess our sins, he is faithful and righteous to forgive us our sins and to cleans us from all unrighteousness.'

"Ladies have you ever done anything that made you ashamed? See, we as people have a sense of right and wrong inherently in us. We know we need help to quit smoking or cursing or lying or sleeping with a boyfriend. I know the world tells us that that activity is all right. But why do you hide or lie about it if there is no problem with it? You see the Prince of the power of the air is shrouding you in darkness and is telling you that it is ok, just stay close to him and he will take care of you. Stay in the darkness where it is safe and no one will know your sin. Turn to Genesis 3. Two things I want to point out and then I will close the lesson. First, you all know the true story of Adam and Eve. They ate of the tree of knowledge of good and evil, recognizing only after their disobedience, that they were naked. So they hid themselves from God. Every day Adam and God walked in the garden at evening. God came to the garden and called out to him, 'Adam where are you? Adam!' Do you think God didn't know where he was? Of course he knew! God was giving Adam a chance to come to the light . . . God his Father. But Satan fooled him and cheated him of his relationship bringing Adam and Eve into darkness. Adam said to God, 'I heard the sound of you in the garden and I was afraid because I was naked, so I hid myself.' Never before had Adam been afraid of seeing God and he had been naked all his life! God said, 'Who told you that you were naked? Have you eaten from the tree of which I commanded you not to eat?' God gives Adam another chance to confess his sin but he hid in the darkness and Adam blamed his wife. Now the second quick point: the story of Cain and Able. Of course Cain killed Able and tried to hide his brother from God and everyone else. Listen to what God said to Cain, 'Then the Lord said to Cain, why are you angry and why has your countenance fallen? If you do well, will not your countenance be lifted up? And if you do not do well, sin is crouching at the door; and its desire is for you, but you must master it.' How do we master this sin at our door? We believe in Jesus Christ and confess to him our sins and He is faithful and just to forgive us all of our unrighteousness as we struggle to master those things that God disproves of.

"God loves you all and will not let darkness have you unless you reject the love Jesus is offering. We all sin and sometimes we must talk to someone about our sins in order to get past them, I am here if anyone of you needs to talk. I love you all, bow with me in a closing prayer. Our precious God and Savior, I ask for you to touch the ones in this class that need your loving forgiveness. I ask for you to convict them of their need for You in their young lives and if some have not accepted Your Son as their Savior, open their heart so they may ask your Son to come in and cleanse them from all unrighteousness, in Jesus name, amen."

The bell rang but the girls didn't jump up as they had done last week. Joan walked to the door and hugged each one as they walked out. As Simone came to her, she whispered to Joan, "Can we talk a little later?"

"Anytime you need, Simone. You tell me when and where and I will be there, okay?"

"Okay, I will call you. Would this afternoon be all right?"

"Sure, just give me a ring, anytime today is fine." Joan knew she had a heavy heart and was struggling with the David thing. Joan could not even say it.

Joan had planned to talk to Mary during the break between class and worship, but she could not find her anywhere. Joan walked by the pastor's study as the pastor was coming out of his office.

"Good morning, Pastor." Joan said cheerfully, just like you were supposed to on Sunday morning.

Pete turned and said, "Morning Joan," but did not even make eye contact with her. He didn't even slow down just pushed on by like he was late to the service.

"Pastor!" Joan said a tad frustrated at him. "I was wondering where Mary was this morning?"

"She didn't make it, not feeling well."

"Oh, I'm sorry." Was all Joan was going to get to say. Pete was already around the corner and gone. Gosh, Joan thought, I have never seen him so abrupt. But she knew he had been with David.

Joan walked on into the assembly where the Choir was warming up with some beautiful music.

She wondered what happened to Mary. Well, she would ask Simone if her mom was okay, when she talked to her later in the day.

Mary was missing all right. She had told both Simone and Peter that she was not feeling well and thought she would stay home. She also told them that it would be nice if they both would spend a little father- daughter time together.

So Mary suggested they go out for Sunday lunch and maybe a drive up into the mountains. Pete was to sin sick to argue and Simone needed to talk to her dad about her problem anyway, so both agreed.

Mary had other plans and today was as good as any other in her mind. Pete and Simone would be gone for several hours. Plenty of time for Mary to drive to David's and confront him about his activity with her adopted daughter.

26

Big Bend Country: Sunday morning

Callie James' family was waiting at the ranch airport near nowhere. As a matter of fact, it took the James' family a full two days, a total of 27 hours' drive time from their home in Northern California to where they were to meet Cole and his team. He also advised them to tell no one; especially any law-enforcement; the less people who knew where they were going and the reason for their travel the better for all.

The Big Bend country was a vast, rugged place. A dangerous place, if one did not understand how to survive in such a wild place. Ranches were huge and ranchers were still highly patriotic and one or two knew that Cole and his Unit's business was a business that many people needed but he did not need the advertisement. The few Ranchers who Cole dealt with were more than willing to allow him to come and go as the group pleased. Also, they had needed Cole's services themselves once upon a time.

Cole and his men were preparing to board the plane again, when he looked up and watched the car drive away with little Callie James waving out the back window. Everyone was happy, Mom and Dad, all Callie's siblings and most of all Callie. She held on to Cole for a long time, so long that Cole thought he was going to start crying with her as they said goodbye. He did not necessarily get so attached to anyone in such a short period of time but Callie had a uniqueness about her that pricked Cole's stone heart. It was a hard goodbye.

"She was special wasn't she?" Wayne had walked up to Cole's side. Leaning around, Wayne looked at Cole's face, "What? Are you going to start crying over all these people we bring back?" He said it good naturedly following with, "Nobody saw me but I cried by the plane a little while ago. Maybe when we get back to HQ we can all have a good cry, you know one of those set in a circle and hold hands and cry like old women at a wake, cry?"

Cole turned and walked toward the plane and in a low growl said, "If you touch my hand I'll gouge your eye out!"

Wayne laughed walking to the plane, "Gosh, Cole, I love you too man."

The plane lifted off and the team settled in for a long flight home.

Cole thought, now what? What's next? Where are we going next? He could not help it; it was part of his DNA. Setting still was not a natural expression of his personality. Actually, it was the worst thing he could do. Setting still at home was worse than surveillance and everybody hated surveillance.

Once in the air all the men started to grab their cells and call the ones close to them. Cole watched as Hatched called his wife of 27 years. His kids were grown but Cole knew he would call his daughter and son before he was done. Clint had a woman in his life as well but he refused to allow anyone to meet her yet. Blake pulled out his little black book and started going down the list of available beauties. Cole could hear Goose on the horn with his bookie. Near death experiences and the first person Goose called was his Bookie. Cole chuckled to himself thinking of how diverse they all were but how cohesive they were at the same time. Cole remembered when Scottie brought them all a tee shirt that said 'IF YOU BLEED WITH ME TODAY; YOU WILL BE MY BROTHER' . . . that is what they are, brothers to the end. He looked at each one as they slept or talked on the phone or to each other and thought 'Bone of my Bone, Flesh of my Flesh; just like King David's mighty men. A wave of loneliness came over him. He pulled out his phone and hit speed dial. The phone rang . . . "Hello?" Distant, yet so close to his heart, "Hey Sis, how are you." The only family he had left. He loved her so.

The first words out of her mouth, "When can you come to see me! Are you all right? Everything okay? No bullet holes or broken arms?" She was laughing and cheery as always; so glad to hear from him. She knew what he did for a living and knew that one of these calls might not be his voice she heard.

"Well, just so happens I might have a day or two to spare."

27

"And just as they did not see fit to acknowledge God any longer; God gave them over to a depraved mind, to do things which were not proper."

Paul

It was still early on Sunday morning; Mary had wanted to get to David's before he had a chance to leave for town. Pete and Simone left early so Pete could get a lesson together for their worship time. Giving Mary the opportunity to arrive relatively early at David's.

Her car pulled up to the front door of the mansion. It was unusual that the front gate was left opened but Mary did not think too much about it. She climbed out of her car and stomped up the steps to the main doors. She rang once and walked straight in yelling out as she entered, "David! David!" She was angry and frustrated but mostly she was excited to have the time to be alone with David. She heard a muffled cry coming from behind a door just off the foyer to her left. She had not been in every room of this mansion and the door she was heading toward was one she had always thought was a closet. But being the woman that David had promised half his kingdom to, she marched to the door and stormed in as if she had already collected on the offer.

Shock and fear consumed her instantly. The sight was so abnormal she was frozen in place. She could hear her mind screaming for her to run but not one muscle would respond to her commands. She was immobilized and stared as David, stripped naked, stood walking away from the child he and two other men were holding down on a couch. As Mary's mind began to recover, she scanned the room. It was sparsely furnished. In one corner was a very large and expensive looking camera on a tripod, with large lights attached and a white sheet looking thing reflecting the light back to where David was coming from. In the corner behind the couch, she saw several other girls standing naked trying to cover themselves with their hands and arms with horror stamped all over their faces. The room reeked of a heavy musky odor and everyone looked as if they had been up all night. Mary notice white powdery substance on a small table with razor blades and short straws lying beside it. There were liquor bottles on the floor and clothes scattered around the room. It was a mess but no one seemed to care. As she was trying to make sense of this, she felt David's strong grip clamp down on her arm. She turned and was consumed by a face that terrified her.

"David. What's going on here?" She stumbled over her words trying to make sense of a face that once was familiar and the nauseating chaos that now consumed her entire being. Up to this point, Mary was fully aware of her sin in this adulterous relationship. She knew she was sinning against God and herself, but she never felt the consequences, she didn't care. She cared now; pleading she asked, "Please, David tell me what you are doing with these children?" She searched his eyes. He did not answer; he just glared back through avaricious eyes.

She screamed, "LET GO OF ME!! Tell me what you are doing in here! Who are these girls and where did they come from?" The girls started to cry loudly and began to beg Mary to help them. The other men stood releasing the girl on the couch who instantly turned and crawled over the back of the couch and gathered with the other girls. The men were looking at David as if waiting for orders. Mary could hear herself yelling but could not make out her own words. The girls crying became screams for help. One of the men suddenly turned and slapped one of the girls to the floor shutting up the others instantly. They began whimpering and bent down to comfort the one who had been knocked down. The other men were naked as well. Mary began to pull away from David. He clamped down harder. She began to fight and scream. One of the men grabbed her from behind; she was repulsed when she felt his naked body next to hers.

"Let me go! I am going to call the police. Let me go. David, David," She suddenly calmed and in a frantic whisper she continued, "Let me go and I will leave and I will not tell anyone. You can go on with what you're doing and I will just go. Okay? David? Just let me go, okay?" Tears were welling up in her eyes and she was beginning to tremble. David didn't answer.

She looked at David as he spoke to her for the first time since she entered the room, "Oh my sweet Mary, it's too late to let you go, honey." She burst into a violent struggle screaming, "LET GO OF ME!" But the man behind her had wrapped his arms around her and had lifted her off the floor. He squeezed her so tight she could not draw a breath. She began kicking but to no avail. Tunnel vision set in and she felt herself slipping into unconsciousness, "David, please David let the girls go . . ." she said as her last bit of breath passed her lips. The third man came close to her and Mary's eyes went wide as she recognized him. She was falling into darkness as she heard the man say, "She recognized me, man. We can't let her go. She knows me; she looked right at my face!" She slumped in the man's arms unconscious.

"Take her to the basement and tie her up tight! I don't want her running all over the place screaming she's going to the cops." " Y e a h , since the cops are already here." Said the man Mary had recognized. Captain Don Henry of the Pimsler City Police Department had possessed his own bad habits years before David had arrived in Pimsler. Both men were amazed at how likeminded professionals manage to find each other. David, a professional film producer and director and Captain Henry believing he was a fantastic actor. Both men loving the movie business and making a bundle of cash while entertaining themselves with the benefits.

The two men picked Mary off the floor and carried her out of the room, while David went back to the girls. "Well, girls we're going to have to start all over. That woman interrupted the whole show!" He was laughing. David had no worries about these girls. No one would miss them, all run-aways, all street urchins, no home, no friends, and no family. Even if they had family they had given up looking long ago. The girls were the lost and faceless children of America. David went and re-ran the digital camera, making 'hum' sounds and laughing under his breath while he watched the video feed. Then suddenly, "I like it, girls! I think we can spin this to be a great side story. Mary can be one of your moms. How's that sound to you guys?" He said that as if the girls were enjoying their part of the production and in agreement with the sexual torture he had planned for each of them. He turned and punched a button on the intercom. A voice answered immediately, "Yes, sir?"

"Carl, you and Sunny get down here and keep an eye on these girls for me while I go check on Mary and the boys." He ordered. Minutes later a large, hairy, barrel chested, balding man with pig eyes and strangely large ears entered the room followed by a rail thin, sinewy red headed woman covered in fading tattoos and large ugly piercings. She had hard green eyes engulfed by pale red sagging facial skin; which made the piercing holes look large and gapping. David knew he didn't really need his hired help to come and watch these girls, the room had no windows and only one door that locked from the outside. But David looked at all his people as one big family and he wanted to keep them all happy. David put on a robe as the two employees entered and said, "Don't hurt them. You can play but do not hurt them! Do you understand?"

"Yes, sir." They both understood. David exited the room; following the two men and Mary.

28

"If we confess our sins, He is faithful and righteous to for gives us our sins and to cleanse us from all unrighteousness."

John

Simone had called and was on her way to Joan's. Joan thought she sounded a little anxious but dismissed it until she answered the door.

"Hi, Simone, I'm so glad you could make it." Joan, more often than not, always had a cheery tone to her voice and was always genuinely happy to see people. Even in the worst of times and unknown to Joan, it was quickly becoming the worst of times.

Simone was visibly upset, "Hi." She said flatly, arms folded across her chest and face was turned down with her hair covering her. She was flushed and squeezed past Joan without making eye contact.

She walked into the middle of the living room and stood in the center, all closed off. Then she started her conversation, "It was David!" She blurted out the words as a clogged hose suddenly spews water.

"David? David Clark? He was the man that raped you?"

"Yes!" Her voice was thick as she struggled to compose herself.

"Did you tell your mom and your dad?"

"I told Mom but when I started to tell Dad he didn't want to hear anything, he said he didn't want to talk. So I didn't tell him." She spit out angry words.

"What did your mom have to say?"

"Wait for your dad to come home and he'll take care of it!" Simone said exasperated turning away running her hands through her hair.

"Where's your mom now, Simone? I think it is best that we get together and talk as a group." Joan knew she could only take this so far before she needed Simone's parents involved. "I don't know." She said defiantly, still not making eye contact with Joan, "Mom said she was sick this morning but when Dad and I came in from church she was not there and has not come home. We don't know where she is."

"Well, sweetie, sit down and let's see if we can figure this thing out, okay?" Simone went to the love seat and sat down on the edge as if she was ready to bolt out of the house any second.

"I'm going to brew some tea; do you want anything?" Joan was trying hard to break Simone out of this funk so she could get all this off her chest.

"Yes, I would like some, thanks." Simone snapped, staring off into nothing, "I wonder where Mom could be." She said more to herself than Joan.

Joan called out from the kitchen, "Well, why don't you call home, maybe she's there now." Simone took her phone out of her back pocket and dialed her mom's cell number. It rang, then went to voice mail.

"Mom, it's Simone, call me. Where are you I need to talk to you please, call me? I am at Joan's. I talked to her about David and what he did to me. She thinks it's best for the three of us to get together and talk about it. So call, what are you doing . . . where are you . . . why aren't you answering your phone?" Simone's frustration was out of control and was passed the point of caring about who knew what David had done.

29

"But these, like unreasoning animals, born as creatures of instinct to be captured and killed, reviling where they have no knowledge, will in the destruction of those creatures also be destroyed suffering wrong as the wages of doing wrong."

Peter

Don and David's chauffeur, Martin, had duck taped Mary to a chair. Martin had put a towel around his waist but Don liked the freedom. They were standing over in a corner waiting for David to give the order. They both knew what was going to happen to Mary and were excited about getting to perform for the camera but no one had told Mary.

The room swam as Mary opened her eyes; a fog seamed to surround her, her head pounding as she rocked back in the chair; it was then she realized she couldn't move; dread flooded her entire being. It was a painful feeling that clamped down on her insides. Her eyes were wide with fear as she clawed at the chair with her fingernails trying to free her hands. She had no idea what was happening. She struggled against her restraints with no gain. Her mouth was taped shut and her hands were taped to the chair along with her legs and feet. She was confused and stunned as to why these people were doing this after all she knew they weren't going to kill her. They had to let her go at some point. This is ridicules she thought. "This is crazy! Let me GO!" She screamed through her tape lips, both men turned and looked at her as if she was nothing more than lint. They continued to look with empty eyes that said nothing, just looking through dull, lifeless eyes.

The door opened and David walked in and bent down in Mary's face, "Mary, Mary quite contrary . . ." He reached out and yanked the tape off her mouth with a jerk. She screamed out in pain.

"Oh, that must have hurt? Huh, Mary?" David said without a hint of emotion in his voice or on his face.

She turned her face up and looked at him, "Why are you doing this,

David?"

Over David's shoulder one of the men said, "Her cell's been going off. Whoever it is left a message."

David didn't turn or even acknowledge them in anyway; he just stood looking at Mary. Then tilted his head to the side and asked, "Mary, did you tell anyone you were coming here?" He waited for her answer. She looked down and said nothing, realizing this might just save her from any more pain.

He stood a minute longer, "Of course you didn't. You came here to see me. Didn't you? You wanted to make sweet love and steel away for a time before you had to go back to reality. Didn't you?" He waited a beat, "So no one knows you are here. Good!" He half turned and smiled at the two behind him.

"Martin can you get her keys and move her car to the garage for me, please Sir. But come right back, Don's going to need you in a little bit. Thank you." His voice was dripping with the sound of sweet gentleness.

"Pete knows I am here. I told him I was coming here to talk to you about Simone and what you did to her." The words slid out almost as if she did not expect them to.

"I don't think so. Pete can't do anything anyway and the last thing he would do is to confront me, especially after our little trip to Las Vegas, baby! WOW! What a time we had." His voice grew loud and aggressive as he danced to his delightful memories, "You should have seen your husband. You would have thought he grew up chasing the women. He had a blast, Mary, but enough of Pete." Mary sat starring in unbelief at him feeling a new pain. *Pete had been unfaithful to her?* Her mind swam. "So, Simone told you of our little tryst, huh? Who else knows?" His voice was hard again. He reached out and grabbed a hand full of hair; shaking her head hard. She could feel hair being pulled out.

"Who . . . else . . . knows?" He said through clenched teeth.

"No one! Please, David you're hurting me." She pleaded from the pain.

"Good girl, Mary." He patted her on top of her head like one would pat a dog, wiping hair from his hand on her head.

"Are you sure Simone has not told anyone else?" David asked again.

With great fear in her voice, "I told her to tell Peter. But I don't think she did." Mary realized that she just put Pete and Simone in possible danger, "Don't hurt them David. Don't hurt Simone. Please!"

"What? You don't even like her. You told me that yourself. Now you want to protect her? What a laugh you are."

Don said, "We going to do this all day, man?" Anxious to feel the consuming joy of evil rise in him.

"Hold your horses' big boy. Your times coming. Don't worry." David said over his shoulder. "So you don't think Simone has told anybody else, right?"

"I don't think so." Mary began to cry, "What are you going to do to me? David, I won't tell anyone! I promise, I won't tell a soul. I will keep my mouth shut and tell Simone she can't tell anyone either. Just let me go and it will be okay. Baby, I love you, you know how much I love you. Please Honey, please don't hurt me. I'll do anything you ask."

"Shut-up." His lips curled into a cruel snarl. Mary could tell he had no feeling in him at all. He turned and walked across the room to Don. They stood and conferred in low tones. She could see the police captain nodding to whatever David was telling him. Don handed David her phone and he began trying to retrieve her messages from it but became frustrated.

"This things password protected, Don. I need her password."

Don turned and strode over to Mary. He had not covered himself at all and it was beginning to make Mary nauseous to look at him.

Don bent down and looked her in the face, grabbing her blouse with both hands he tore it open, ripping her bra exposing her breast, "Mary, I want you to tell me how to get those messages off your phone . . . okay."

Mary bent over trying to cover herself and began to cry, "Why? Why do you want my messages?"

Don blew air out of his nose and straightened up. He looked down at her; she had followed his accent tilting her head up looking at him. He extended his left hand and gently held her chin looking in her eyes. Then with the speed of a pro-boxer, he slapped her so hard he almost knocked her and the chair over. She held her breath an instant, then let out a moan that turned into a wail that produced sobs. Not just from the slap but just as much from the confusion and the pure evil she was feeling from the men. Her head swam from the blow, her ear was ringing and the pain was a stinging, throbbing pain. She never had been slapped; she could not even remember being spanked as a child. This was all new, how can people treat other people like this?

"David, what are you doing? Please David don't let him hurt me!" Mary was in full terror mode.

David quickly came to her grabbing her hair again and screamed in her ear, "GIVE ME YOUR PASSWORD!"

Mary in shock rattled it off, squeezing her eyes shut and trying to duck her head out of the way of his voice. He typed it in. Seconds later, she could hear Simone's voice on speaker telling the world where she was that she in fact had told someone else and they were waiting for her to meet with them and discuss the David thing. Both men turned and looked at her and Mary instantly knew she was not going to survive this ordeal.

"Oh, God, please no, David!" Mary screamed through her sobs and tears "Leave her out of this, PLEASE! What do you want me to do? I'm begging you, David, please, please . . ." she slumped over in the chair, head down, and her body heaving up and down weeping.

David turned to Don, "She's all yours man. Make sure you guys keep the camera focused this time, okay?" With that, David walked out.

Don walked to a cabinet and took out a vile and a syringe. Mary sat in silence as she watched Don make up the drug and turn to her, smiling. "We're going to love this baby! You're not. But we are."

30

"They count it a pleasure to revel in the daytime. They are stains and blemishes, reveling in their deceptions, as they carouse with you, having eyes full of adultery that never cease from sin, enticing unstable souls, having a heart trained in greed."

Peter

David filmed most of his female victims in his Hollywood studios; those that came to his house were typically professionals in the porn industry, looking for a weekend away from the Southern California hustle. David would treat them to booze, drugs and lots of money. Not the type of drugs given to Mary.

The little ones upstairs just happened to be prime property, the men who snatched them made a gift of them to David and, of course, David, shared them with Don and Martin, like one would share a stick of chewing gum. A reward of sorts, for all of the hard work done by Don and Martin in building an extensive network of felons while establishing their supply lines of young girls for the porn industry.

Don had been the captain over the city jail for years giving him easy access to men and women with whom he established a criminal relationship. He would do certain legal favors and they in turn would do certain illegal favors. Like kidnapping, drug pushing and even murder. Captain Don had gone so far as to supply the drugs from the Police Department's evidence locker to his 'boys' and 'girls' for their own use and also to sell for him. He gave them some of the drugs and often a cut of the sale. David had taught him that little trick . . . keep the family happy and you will be happy. Don learned that trick quickly, the trick of . . . don't get greedy.

David usually left Don to handle the security matters and so far Captain Don had done a bang up job. Clean and efficient with no one ever snooping around and if any local cops came looking into an incident; Don would cut the investigation short. A beautiful set up. Don had even recruited a few of the other local police officers and sheriff deputies to help on the fringes of the operation, never allowing any one of them to get too close. Don's Boys snagged the kids and David found buyers for them, while the police unknowingly protected the local operation. He sold them all over the world. China liked big-breasted blonds, Mexico liked white girls that were blond as well but they weren't as selective. Southeast Asia and Africa all loved white girls. The slave trade was a lucrative business. David usually kept the girls for a time putting them in porn films, addicting them to drugs. He used them in the porn flicks until they were used up. A few he would turn to become stars or extras. Those loved the business as much or more than he did. Those that didn't die trying to escape or didn't overdose, he sold on the slave market. Those that he knew were not going to bring anything in a sale he turned over to Don or Martin to be used in snuff films. He hoped the boys down stairs did a good job of filming Mary. She was perfect for the snuff film they were making. Although he knew his partners would be up in arms for killing her because she was a good-looking woman. But he knew best, she was too old for the porn films and she had to go and Don would do an Emmy-winning performance.

Lots of sex, blood, and screaming before Don would cut her throat. What David found so amusing was Pete. He could probably walk straight up to Pete and say, 'Hey, man, I just killed your wife after I had two guys rape her senseless. What do think about that?' Pete would not do a thing. What a coward, David laughed to himself. Well, it's time to see what I need to do about the ones upstairs.

He loved his work.

31

How is it that such evil exist? How can people be so cruel? As I write this book our Libyan Embassy was attacked and burned to ashes. The American Ambassador was tortured, sodomized and murdered. How can we say there is no evil in this world? But where there is evil there is over powering good as well.

"The light shines in the darkness; but the darkness could not overpower it."

John 1:5

David decided he needed a break from Pimsler. He went upstairs and ordered the couple, who had been watching the girls, to prepare to move the girls to their Hollywood locations. He needed to check on his porn production business and see how the sales were going. Of course he could get the information from a quick phone call or log on and check his sales that way but he felt he needed to move these girls and dispose of Mary's body, of course. He knew Don and Martin would be awhile so he had some time to consider what he was going to do about Simone and Joan as well. Simone was worth a lot of money. The tape he sent to his partners of him and Simone, they loved. She was exactly what they liked in an up and coming star. But Joan was too old and he knew she just wasn't the type for a porn film but she was perfect for sale or a snuff film. He felt a twinge of angst, it passed as soon as it came. To David, people were a commodity; they were a form of currency, that's all. A dime to be made off of their looks or their death, David didn't care which as long as he made the money. David had been in this business so long and had so many bodies disposed of he was not concerned in the least about the girls upstairs or Mary. After all, no one knew she came here. No one knew they had been seeing each other, not even good old Pete. They will get rid of her car and haul her body out to a deserted canyon somewhere, bury it, and no one would be the wiser. But he knew Simone and Joan were going to be different. A light clicked on in his lovely, wickedly, sick mind . . .

32

The small man thinks that small acts of goodness are of no benefit and does not do them and that small deeds of evil do no harm and does not refrain from them. Hence, his wickedness becomes so great that it cannot be concealed and his guilt so great that it cannot be pardoned.

Confucius

Peter was tormented. His mind was reeling with what he had done and he could not accept the sins he had committed. He was lying on his bed praying and crying all at the same time. He could not understand how he had gotten in this mess. His mind careened from George Booker attacking him to the women at the Playboy Club, to his wife, then Simone and then jump to his congregation. The more he thought about it the more ill he became. Sin sick, driven by fear of exposure, we all have experienced sin that brought us shame, that shame we could not ask for forgiveness nor confess it to anyone. His crying went to uncontrolled weeping, to burying his face in his pillow, to screaming and cursing himself. As God fought Satan for the soul of the man.

His cell phone rang. He ignored it. It stopped but started again, then stopped. A minute later it began ringing again. Pete grabbed it, "Hello?" His voice was weepy and heavy.

"Pete, my man . . . you all right?" *No confession,* Pete said in his mind, "Yeah, what do you need?" Wiping his eyes and picking up a Kleenex to blow his nose with.

"Well, I need to talk to you if you have a minute? I have some news that will be hard for you to hear, brother. Are you sitting down?"

"Yeah. What's the matter? What's happened?" His mind was not tracking well.

"Well, man, I have really messed up. I have wanted to talk to you about this for a week or so but have not had the courage to bring it up."

"Well, what is it? It can't be all that bad, can it? Spit it out, David. Whatever it is, I'm sure we can work it out."

"Okay, then, just remember I am your best friend and I can give a great life to whoever I want, okay." David was feigning deep concern and regret. He spoke as if he was so hurt by his situation.

That response confused Pete. He waited.

"Simone and I have liked each other for a long time. We have enjoyed each other's company and well about a week or so ago she came to the house and well we . . . got a little too close."

"What do you mean 'too close'?"

"Pete, I'm sorry. I do not know how I let things get out of hand but things just went too far and . . ." David waited, listening to Pete's breathing on the other end of the phone. Smiling to himself.

"I really love her, Pete. I mean, I really do!" David said with such conviction. Pete could only see David with the beauties at the Playboy Club. His mind was racing.

"What happened, David? What did you do to her?"

"It was not just me, man. She was in total agreement and wanted to as well. I know I should have stopped it but I love her and wanted to ask you if . . ."

"Did you sleep with my daughter?" Pete was more scared that angry. He had seen David's bad side and it scared him.

"I'm sorry, Pete but, yes, we slept together."

"What are you doing to us? What have you done to us?" Pete realized that this situation was beyond dire. His non-belief exploded into belief in great evil for he realized it was Satan himself manipulating his way in to destroy not just his life but the congregation and his family as well. He knew that he had to be smart. He could not show his hand or too much more of his emotions. This was all foreign to him, how does one fight this, how does one overcome this kind of horrible strength?

David was tired of playing with Pete. What could he do anyway? "Yea, I slept with her. She loves me too. I want to take her to California with your blessing. Regardless, I am going to take her with me whether you like it or not, good buddy. Do you understand that?" His voice turned cold, hard, and sarcastic.

Pete got off the bed and began to pace across the bedroom floor, "Do you have her with you now?" Pete felt totally defeated, wiping his eyes with his shirt sleeve. Trying to think through this disaster.

"No, but I am going to go get her and take her with me. I want you to know that and know that you can't do anything to stop us. You do remember Vegas, don't cha? How would you like the slide show presented at next week's service, brother?" His words were cutting Pete and causing more pain than his present condition.

Pete was quiet for a long moment. "Well, I guess I can't do anything about it now. When are you leaving?"

"Tonight, as soon as I get some things wrapped up here."

"Are you sure she wants to go with you?" Pete's voice was weak. He was standing now, running one hand through his hair, holding the phone to his ear with the other, looking at the floor.

"Sure I'm sure. She loves me, daddy-in-law. We are going to be one great big happy family." David laughed loudly in the phone. "I'm sending Martin to pick her up in a little while."

Fear struck Pete's heart. Pete quickened his paced around the room feeling trapped like a man in a cell. He didn't even like the way Martin looked much less being around his daughter.

Come to think of it, he didn't like any of David's employees, "She's not here right now but I'm sure she will be back soon. I'll have her ready for you." He tried to steady his voice.

"No need, I know where she is."

"You know where she is?" Pete said surprised. "Well, I can go get her and have her pack a light bag for the trip."

"No need, Pete! I will buy her everything she needs and wants."

"Are you going to let me say goodbye to her? At least let me see her before you go, okay?"

"We'll be back in a week or so, don't worry." David felt so powerful at times like these, he loved it.

"David! Her mom will want to see her and if we don't handle this right, Mary will pitch a fit. Neither one of us will have a moments rest. Come on, man, let us see her and talk to her before you take her away." David could hear his absolute frustration and was delighted.

"Mary's not going to care." Whoops, David thought, can't let that out.

"What do you mean? Have you seen Mary today?" Pete, almost in a panic, needed his wife.

"No, man, but what mother would not want her daughter to marry a millionaire? Tell me that?" Saved by my shear intelligence, David thought.

Pete felt suspicious but didn't know why. He always felt something strange around David. He determined to start paying attention to those feelings even if it was too late for him.

"All right, you win. At least have her call us before you guys take off, okay?" Pete sounded exactly the way David thought he would sound . . . totally defeated and controlled.

"I'll have her call. She can say goodbye to you and mommy. Got to go; we'll talk later." David thought what a pathetic human being. He felt confident that all was going his way for the moment. Now Joan, what to do about Joan?

33

"The evil you know is better than the evil you do not know."

Unknown

Pete was on the phone immediately, "Hi, Dad."

"Where are you?" Pete was panicked and Simone could tell. "What's wrong, Daddy?"

"Where are you?"

"I'm at Joan's house, Dad. What's the matter?"

"Let me talk to Joan, now!" He didn't care if he sounded angry or offensive to her. He needed them out of that house and somewhere safe right now. He was not going to let David take Simone anywhere.

"Hi, Peter. Is everything okay." She could tell by Simone's facial expression that something was not right.

"Listen to me, Joan. We have no time; I need you to move Simone to a safe place. I don't care where. You can tell me where later. Just get her out of your house NOW!"

"You have to tell me what's going on here?" Joan was moving to her purse and motioning to Simone to follow her.

"I have done some terrible things Joan," Pete's voice was breaking, "David is a horrible person and he is coming to get Simone to take her away with him. You must get her out of the house to some place safe. He knows she is at your house. Joan, please help me, please." David began to sob.

"I'm going to help you Pete. We are moving right now, don't worry, I'll take care of her. How does he know she is here? Are you all right?"

Pete was crying uncontrollably, "I don't know. Have you seen my wife? I need to find my wife." His voice trailed off in a silent sob.

Joan heard how absolutely miserable he sounded, "I'm sorry Pete, I have not seen her at all today; neither has Simone."

"If you see her please tell her I love her and come home . . . please . . . come home." He wept like a child.

"I will Pete and I will call you when we are at a safe place okay?

Pete, are you there?" All she heard was his sobs, then the phone went dead.

Joan turned to Simone, "You and I are going to a friend of mine's for a little bit until we get this sorted out."

"Why?" Simone asked.

"David is coming to get you and take you away with him." Joan said abruptly. Simone's eyes went wide with fear and like a doll on an elastic string, she jumped up and marched out the back door beating Joan to the garage. Leaving Simone's car in front of Joan's home parked in the street.

34

Life for life . . .

"George!" Helen called from their back door. George was in the yard throwing a ball for his prized Alapaha Blue Blood, a highly protective and aggressive animal. Once the one-hundred-pound animal bonded with its owner the dog would do anything to prove his loyalty. The dog was originally bred in Georgia but had adapted well to the higher Colorado climate. George had his best friend from a 6-week-old pup and the bond was tight between the two.

"Come on Boy. Momma's calling us." George said to his large four-legged companion. The dog loved George and obeyed instantly.

"Who is it Sweet Pea?" He hollered back.

"It's Joan and she sounds upset . . . really upset!" Helen called back from the back porch.

"Okay, I'm coming. I'm not as fast as I used to be you know."

"Well, jump on Smokey's back and ride him in. That way you can get here faster and not be out of breath!" She laughed as she turned to enter the house.

"Did you hear that boy? She's calling me decrepit." George laughed. He loved it when Helen played with him. They batted each other around, kindly joking, keeping the love alive.

George entered the house and picked up the phone breathing a little harder than he should have been, "Hello?" Helen walked by, "I told you, you should have ridden Smokey." She chided, smiling at the love of her life and giving him a pinch on his heinie.

He cleared his throat and started again, "Hello, this is George."

"George, its Joan. I have Simone here with me and we have been talking about her problem. We both think you and Helen need to be involved in this. We are coming over right now. Some things have taken place and I need your help." She rattled it all out at once as she maneuvered her car through traffic.

"We are here, as you can tell. Is the girl all right?"

"Yes, she's fine. Pete called us while we were at my house and told me David was coming to get her. That he knew where she was! He knew she was at my house?" Joan said with puzzled concern.

"Kidnap her! How did he know she was at your house? Did you or Simone tell anyone she was there?"

"No. Not a soul. I wanted to keep this as quiet as possible because of all the potential damage it could cause, you know."

"Is she being followed? What's this kidnap business all about?"

"We're about fifteen minutes away. I'll fill you in on all the rest when I get there. Okay?"

"Okay, we're here. Do you think I need to call Pete and talk to him about this? We will need to call the police Joan?" George was not too excited about speaking to Pete again but for the girl's sake he would.

"Yes, we might. Give Pete a call and see if you can get more intel, he may want the police involved."

"'Intel,' where did you hear that term? That's military lingo." George thought there might be more to this girl than I know.

Joan laughed a little, "My brother, he's a big military type. He uses words like 'intel' and 'I read you 5 x 5,' stuff like that. He's funny." She wished he were here right now. He would handle this without question.

35

Greater love has no one than this; that one lay down his life for his friends.

Jesus

Pete sat despondent on his couch. Not knowing what to do. He could call no one from the church. His sins stymied him and no one would believe him anyway. Besides most Christians would not help even if they knew a kidnapping was in progress. All they would want to do is counsel him. Not moving to help his daughter. The pretty world of Christianity could not be disturbed with the reality of sin or evil. There is no battle with evil, he had heard Christian counselors say that to his face. Ephesians 6; putting on the armor of God to fight the principalities of the air, is not to be taken literal, they would say. Most Christians didn't believe in real evil just the vampires or Freddy Kruger movies, all fairy tales to them. His house phone rang, "Hello." He was exhausted and sounded like it.

"Pete, this is George Booker." Oh no, not Booker, not now. "George, I don't want to talk about my sermon okay. I'm
busy right now."

"I know your daughter and Joan are on their way to my house. Joan has filled me in on a few of the details. Pete, I am truly sorry for this mess with David and Simone." George had true compassion in his voice. "Thank you, George. I appreciate that." His voice was dull and lifeless.

"We are here to help you in any way we can. Do you mind telling me a little more about the situation? I would like to know because even though he might have had consensual sex with Simone, she is still just sixteen, correct? It is a violation of the Colorado State Law. So we might need to get the police involved if a crime has actually taken place. Are you for that, you don't sound so good." George was drawing an assumption and was beginning to be concerned for Pete's mental wellbeing.

"Yeah, she's still 16. I'm not too well at the moment. There are some other things that have gone on between David and me that I need to straighten out, before I can get the police involved. But I honestly do not know what to do about them." George could tell that Pete was completely defeated.

"Well, Pete, let's take this one step at a time. We will handle Simone's situation and then we will take care of yours. Okay?"

"No one can take care of mine. However, I don't want him to take her anywhere." He said with emphatic frustration, then continued almost screaming, "This is my entire fault! George, it's all my fault!" Pete gathered his strength. "I am going to Joan's. David said he knew where she was and he was going to pick her up there. I need to tell him face to face to leave her alone." Pete said, not thinking clearly but resolute in his decision. "You're not done Pete, don't talk like that son and I'm not so sure going to Joan's is the best idea. Why don't you come over here and we can discuss this a little further. Okay, Pete, come on over here and let's discuss it?"

"Sure, I'll be over there after I see David. He's my friend and he'll listen to me. Don't worry. Please take care of Simone for me. I'll see you in a little while.

"Uh, George."

"Yes Pete."

"Tell Simone I love her and never wanted any pain to come to her. Would you tell her that for me?"

"Of course I will." George answered with compassion. The line went dead.

36

I was born a long way from home . . . and I am just trying to get back there.

Bob Dylan

Goose keyed his mic, "Pimsler Tower this is Beech E 18 NINER SEVEN TWO NORA requesting landing instructions; over"

"NINER SEVEN TWO NORA, this is Pimsler Tower, wind is out of the west northwest at five to ten miles per hour. You are clear to land on runway 2-7 WEST that's runway 2-7 WEST."

"NINER SEVEN TWO NORA, roger that, Pimsler Tower, runway 2-7 WEST, copy over and out." Goose had the airport in sight and banked left, lined up the horizon and began to ease
the twin engine Beech E 18 S down to the tarmac.

With no planes coming or going, Goose taxied the aircraft as close to the little terminal as allowed and Brady Cole stepped out. Goose had radioed the tower and told them his passenger needed the courtesy car without giving a name. "Roger that. Keys will be in the ignition. Out" was the towers response. Cole said his goodbyes and grabbed his go bag. He was the last one Goose dropped off. He headed to a fenced in area where two loaner cars were parked. He thought he would surprise Joan and then she could follow him back to the airport in the morning and return the car. Goose would be on standby to pick him up first when the next 'job' came up. He heard the Beech spool up its engines and felt the wind from the prop wash pushing the plane down the taxiway. Cole turned and watched the silver '59 Beech disappear into the darkening Pimsler sky. Cole stood surrounded by silence. The tower had shut down for the night. The place was empty and it was getting cooler by the minute. He had just enough light to see the beauty of Colorado as the sun slipped behind the distant peaks. He was glad to be this close to the only family member he had left. He was hoping for a good home cooked meal, warm shower and a clean bed. Hopping around the world he discovered it was the simple things he missed; family, comfort food and hot water. He hefted the go bag to his shoulder and walked to the courtesy car.

37

Whoever fights monsters should see to it that in the process he does not become a monster. And remember when you look into the abyss; the abyss also looks into you.

Friedrich Neitzsche

Pete had arrived at Joan's and was setting on the front porch when Martin pulled up to the curb. It was dark and Joan's porch light glowed a yellow tint, which made Martin's bleached blond hair look a little green in the light. He was a big man, 6'6" 245 lbs or so and had a scar across his left eyebrow. He had beefy hands, strong shoulders but it was the look in his eyes that unnerved Pete. He had never met a man that could look at people with such loathing; as if he didn't care if you lived or died. David had always told Pete that Martin was his body guard as well as his chauffeur and had to be threatening just in case. Pete agreed and dismissed the man's menacing looks and gruff personality. He felt different now as he watched Martin approach him.

Martin walked up to the steps, stopping two or three feet from the bottom step, "Where's Simone?"

"Hi, Martin, Simone's not here right now. Did David come with you?" Pete stood and stepped down a step placing him two steps above the sidewalk, a foot closer to the big man and putting Pete's head about four inches above Martin's.

Martin stood with his arms hanging straight at his sides, swinging slightly, like an orangutan's. His head was bent causing Martin to look up at Pete but without turning his head up, giving Martin a devilish appearance, "Pete, I am going to ask you one more time and then I am going to kick you through that front door and drag her out of this house. Fair warning."

"Well, she's not here Martin. I don't know how much more plain I can be. And I want to talk to David before I let her go anywhere with anybody, especially you!" Pete got animated leaning forward, throwing his arms out to his sides. Pete had never dealt with unscrupulous men before. Had never even had to defend himself and like most people, he didn't think really bad people truly existed, not in his world. Sure, he read the papers and watched the news but none of that ever came home to him. The idea of we can talk this out was what rational and civilized people did. Talk and talk and talk until an agreement was reached and everyone was happy.

Martin eyed him hard, "Is that her car?" Pointing at the black sporty Saturn with his thumb, not taking his eyes off Pete.

"Yes, but she's not here, Martin!"

Martin's foot hit Pete square in his sternum sending him crashing into Joan's front door. Unfortunately it held. Pete slid off and found himself lying on his left side gasping for air. Martin grabbed Pete's foot and jerked him off the porch banging his head on two of the three concrete steps landing Pete in the yard. Pete was dazed; blood began to flow into his right eye caused by laceration from head striking the edge of the concrete step; not to mention he thought he was having a heart attack from his broken sternum. In all his life, he had never felt such physical pain. He was still on his back hearing Joan's front door crash open. He rolled on to his stomach to get up but could not get his feet under him. He had never been hit so hard in his life. He was stunned and confused, his head pounding, bleeding worse from the exertion and the low position of his head. He heard Martin coming down the steps.

His voice was calm and smooth, "Pete, you are going to tell me where she is or I am going to beat you to death." No emotion just the fact that Martin was going to do what he said.

Pete got to his hands and knees just before Martin lifted him to his feet by his hair and threw him toward the front door. Pete landed on the steps, crashing his shinbone into the edge of the steps and skinning all the hide of his right elbow. Pete tried to stand up but was kicked toward the door way slamming his left shoulder into the door jam. The pain was excruciating. He rolled through the doorway onto the living room floor, Martin followed him and his large frame filled the doorway. Martin stepped in and shut the door the best he could. Pete was on his back doing a semi spider crawl backward away from Martin. The pain in his shoulder was so great he thought it was going to pop out of its joint. As he crawled he could feel the blood filling his shoe from the gash on his shin. Martin just stood there for a short moment. Then like Frankenstein he walked toward Pete, lifted him off the floor and slung him into a wall smashing all of Joan's knick-knacks and several shelves off the wall. No sooner did Pete hit the floor than Martin drove his size fourteen boot into Pete's chest again. Pete tasted blood in his throat from the damage he sustained in his chest area.

Martin launched him off the floor by his hair and struck Pete in the left side of his face so hard Pete almost went unconscious. Pete felt like a rag doll in this man's hands as his head slammed into the wall behind him. Pete crashed to the floor again. Feeling a large amount of blood run out of his mouth, he gaged on the thought as much as from the blood itself. Pete was on his back and could see the door being pushed open behind Martin. The man who was standing behind Martin was not quite Martin's size but big enough. Pete knew he had not a prayer of escaping from the beating he was receiving and believed it was going to only get worse judging from the size of the second man. The two monsters against one puny preacher who had never even been in very many arguments; much less fist fights, he waited for the worst and it was coming!

"Hey, what's going on here?" The second man hollered out.

Martin froze, then gradually straightened up and said over his shoulder, "Police officer, sir. This man broke in this house and I caught him in the act of committing a burglary." Martin began to slowly turn with his hands out to his side, looking at Cole out of the corner of his eye.

Cole watched intently waiting for an inkling of evidence of who was who. The room was dim from a small light that had been over turned during the struggle and was shining from the far corner of the room. Cole could not see the big man's face well enough but from his aggressive stance he knew he meant business.

'No problem, Officer, I just didn't see a prowl car outside. May I see your badge?" Cole stood ready.

Martin relaxed, turned to his left and looked at Pete, "Don't move scum bag!" Then spun back fast, swinging his left fist hard in the direction of where Cole's head had been a short second before but Cole had silently stepped to his right inches out of the big man's swing. Martin tried to adjust but it was too late, he was bent over and off balance. Cole struck him behind the left ear driving Martin's head to the carpet face first. Pete jumped up and caught Cole's attention for a split second. Cole moved in Pete's direction with the intent of putting Pete back down on the floor.

"Wait, don't hit me . . . wait, please. I'm a preacher; I'm here for my daughter." Pete said as he covered his head with his arms and slid back down the wall to the floor.

Cole had turned sideways to Martin and had moved four or five feet away from him toward Pete. Martin seized his opportunity and half crouched, half stood, ran out the opened door. Cole turned and gave chase but stumbled and fell on a broken wooden shelf giving Martin just enough time to get to his car and speed away, leaving black marks and tire smoke in the street. Cole had made it to the curb before he gave up the chase. He turned back toward the house and saw Pete on the stoop bent at the waist with his hand on his head trying to stop the bleeding.

"Thank you, I think you saved my life. Are you a neighbor? Did you hear the scuffle?" Pete spit blood out with the words as he coughed, weaving back and forth holding his chest, blood running out of his nose and dripping off his chin.

"Scuffle? That was a major butt-kickin' son. Look at yourself!" Cole could see blood all over the man's face and his light blue shirt had large dark spots in several places. "What was this all about? Who was that guy? And who are you and what are you doing in this house?" Cole didn't want anyone to have too much information on him at the moment. Cole started walking toward the Preacher.

Pete started to answer but was seized with searing hot pain he had never felt before. He clamped his arms around his midsection becoming light headed and being bent over at the waist he stumbled forward off the steps onto Joan's lawn. Pete rolled toward Cole and Cole could see that he not only had blood all over his face and shirt, his pants were tore and bloody as well. Cole stepped toward him and knelt down getting a closer look at the damage the big blond man had inflicted on this smaller man. He saw large patches of hair missing from the poor man's scalp.

"Can you stand?"

The man looked up through one eye because the other was swollen shut, "I don't know . . . my chest is killing me. Martin must have broken something when he kicked me." Pete squeezed the words out through a badly swollen jaw.

"I'll call 911 and get some help for you."

"No!" Pete grabbed Cole's arm but then let his hand fall because of the pain.

Cole didn't like that response at all. "No cops? No Ambulance? Why don't you tell me what's happening and where the owner to this house is, right now?"

"Do you know Joan?"

"Yes. Where is she?" Cole's facial expression had changed from caring to menacing.

Pete looked into the eyes of this stranger through his one working eye and was actually more afraid of him than he was of Martin. Right in front of him, he saw what the book of 2 Samuel described about King David's mighty men, they had faces of lions. "She's with my daughter at a friend's house. We had to move my daughter so that Martin would not take her away." Pete was trying to speak without breathing. His chest flamed with pain with each breath.

"So Joan took your daughter to a safer place to protect her? Where is this safe place?"

"Who are you, again?" Pete asked through lose teeth, swollen and split lips. He tried to gain more information about this stranger. Didn't work, Cole grab Pete by the front of the shirt one handed, lifting him to his feet. Pete's pain increased several levels as he cried out. Cole, one handed, half drug half carried Pete to the house.

"Tell me who you are and what your relationship is with my sister or the devil is going to pay you a visit." Cole sat the man down on the steps. "Do you understand me?" This was not a request, Cole's voice was turning from human to an animal growl.

"I'm Joan's pastor and she is helping my daughter. Something's got out of hand with my daughter and a friend of mine and he wants to take her away. We moved her to George's house and she is there now." Pete was turning into a fearful little blue faced man. Fearing God, fearing the evil he felt from Martin and this man standing over him, fearing for his daughter and fearing for his own salvation. All the while wondering where in the world his wife was!

Cole took his cell phone out and dialed Joan's number. "Joan! What's the address of your present location?"

"Are you in town Cole?" She said with great relief in her voice.

"Yes. What's the address! I want it now!" Cole was worried and demanding.

"28345 East Columbine Road. I can give you directions." She offered hoping to curb his aggression.

"No, I have GPS. Don't worry. Are you all right? Is everything okay, there?"

Yes, I'm with some very good friends and everything is fine here. Why do you ask like that?" She was worried now, he could not possibly know the situation she was in; and besides, Cole didn't talk to her in this tone . . . ever.

"I just broke up a fight between two men . . . in your house! Well, it was not a fight it was more like a slaughter."

"Oh no! Who . . . who was it? Were they in the house?" Her voice raised and shrill.

"Yes. In the house, on the front steps, out on the lawn, everywhere; judging by the blood on the side walk and front porch." Cole turned to the pastor and growled, "What's your name?"

"Pete. I think I have a concussion." Hoping that would stave off any more pain from his new assailant.

"I'm here with a guy named Pete. He says he is your Pastor."

"What does he look like?" She was cautious.

"A beat up scrawny preacher covered in blood." Both men were looking at each other. Pete shook his head and looked away placing his hand on his head again.

"Sis, this guy needs a hospital. I think the assailant broke some of his ribs, he has a couple of lacerations and he might have a concussion. He doesn't want me to call the law. So I am heading your way, I don't want to get hung up here with the police trying to explain this mess if you need me there. You can fill me in as I drive. We can call the Police from where you are."

Cole, walking up the steps, pointed his finger at the preacher, "Stay!" Cole growled. He attempted to secure the door but saw that it was going to need more than a quick fix. It needed major repair. Cole secured it from the inside as best he could, then exited the house via the back door. He came around the side of the house in time to see the preacher driving away hunched over with one hand on the steering wheel and the other on his head.

38

There are mighty men of valor, who need not be ashamed.

David's cell rang with Martin's ring tone, "You got her?" David asked half demanding, as usual.

"No, man, she wasn't there. Her dad didn't know where she was or he wasn't telling." Martin sounded disgusted.

"You weren't persuasive enough Martin. You do understand that that kid can bring the whole deck of cards down on our heads . . . don't you?" David was feeling the pressure of sin's consequences. Of course, he didn't know that, he didn't believe in sin.

"Hey, I beat him senseless and out of nowhere another guy shows and cold cocks me from behind. He stepped over to grab Daddy, and I ran out the door. I'm down a few blocks from Joan's house, maybe the preacher boy will drive by. He might take me right to the girl." Martin was defensive.

"All right, did you get a look at the other guy, his car or anything? Was he a neighbor, did he call the police . . . anything Martin? Anything at all?" David's voice was rising.

"Look, David, he came in from behind and knocked me down on my face. I didn't even get a look at him, man. Okay?" Martin reached up and rubbed his head where Cole's fist left a knot the size of a golf ball.

"You hold tight and if you see either of them call me on the cell. Don and I are heading your way. Any luck we can catch Pete and finish your job for you! Call if you see him . . . do you understand?"

"Yeah, I understand." As Martin ended the call he was right back on the phone dialing David's number again. "I spotted him!" Martin could not hide his excitement, "He's just come off of 16th pulling onto Wild Flower heading west." Martin checked his traffic and pulled out two cars behind Pete's car.

"Who?" David was walking to his car where Don was sitting in a 2012 Land Rover with the engine running waiting for his orders.

"The Preacher!" He yelled, "I am two cars behind him. He has no idea I'm following him."

"Don't lose him! You hear me?" David yelled into the phone.

"I won't!" Martin yelled back agitated with David; pitching his phone onto the passenger's seat.

Unknown to Martin, Cole pulled out a car length behind Martin. Cole had parked his car one house down and across the street from his sister's, just out of habit, it's hard to turn off the job. Cole stepped on the gas and began to catch and pass Martin when Cole recognized the man and slowed letting Martin pull ahead allowing other cars to move in between him and Martin's car.

As Cole watched Martin, it became obvious that he was following a small maroon Toyota several car lengths ahead of Martin's Vehicle. Cole called Joan's number again. "Hello."

"Joan, I have the assailant in front of me and he is following a Maroon Toyota, it's your preacher friend. I think he is going to try to finish the job he started. If he gets the information where the daughter is he'll find you as well. I need to stop this and get the police involved as quickly as I can. Right now we have a breaking and entering, destruction of private property with a possible felony assault. That is enough to hold the big guy and then I can get to you. You hold tight there, and I will keep you posted."

"I'll be here, you be careful, you hear me? Brady Cole, don't let that guy hurt Pete anymore, okay?" Joan's concern was not for her brother but for the preacher. She knew her brother, very well. He hadn't lost a fight since the third grade protecting his little sister from a sixth grader. He took all the big kid could dish out. The big boy blacked his eye and gave Cole a bloody nose. All Cole could say through his tears as they walked home together was no one was going to hurt his sister and he was never going to be beat up again! But what could happen in Pimsler; a quiet and peaceful little Colorado town full of wonderful people.

"I'll be careful." Joan sounded just like their mom did when he was a kid, "Don't worry, see ya' soon." Cole said, then quickly followed with, "Say . . . what's your friend's name you're staying with?"

"George and Helen Booker, why?"

"Just wondering, I'm glad he has a wife." Cole said ribbing his little sister.

"Yeah, well he's sixty-five, a little old for me anyway." Joan response was sarcastically good humored.

"What's all this about, BS?" Cole asked. He had called Joan BS forever. Some thought it was derogatory but it stood for Baby Sister.

"Well, in a nut shell, a guy named David Clark had sex with Pete's sixteen-year-old daughter and then threatened Pete with, as Pete put it, kidnapping her. It's crazy I know but I guess the other guy got involved to help David find Simone." Normal people didn't think like this; it was hard for Joan to get her mind around it all.

"I'm guessing Simone is Pete's kid?

"Yes. She is sixteen, Cole! My gosh, I can't believe all this!"

"Well, sis, if they've already gone to this length to get their hands on her . . . there's no telling how far they will go. They've committed criminal acts trying to find her along with conspiracy to commit kidnapping. Sis, this is major. It can't just be this guy David's love driving him, I wouldn't think. He's adding charge upon charge trying to get his hands on this kid? You are right, he is either crazy or there's a lot more to this that we don't know. I'll call you back in a bit."

"You better. Be careful!" Joan pleaded.

39

"It seems that true courage comes from a rightness of life."

David and Don were racing down the mountain to the location as Martin advised them of direction and progress.

"I thought he might go to Community Hospital but he is turning on Main eastbound, looks as if he is heading out of town." Martin advised the other two.

"Stay with him." David was anxious to catch Pete, to get the information he needed, "This might be a good thing. If he leaves town we can pull him over without anyone seeing anything." It was turning dark and in the mountains, when night fell, darkness took on a whole other meaning.

Cole slowed his car even more allowing several other cars to pass. He could see Marin's vehicle and knew the tail light design, so he knew he wouldn't lose him. Main Street came to an end turning into State Highway 170. Pete was not going to get medical help; he was going to his daughter! This situation was not good! He had to stop all this as soon as possible.

Cole turned on the GPS in his phone so that he could identify his location when he called the police. If he was to guess, Pete was going to drive straight to his daughter's location without even thinking of looking in his rearview mirror, taking the perp right along with him. Cole didn't know how far this guy would go or how many people were involved with Martin, other than this David guy. But Cole knew he was not going to take any chances. Cole was contemplating action when Martin's vehicle turned onto Columbine Road. Cole put two and two together, he knew then he had to do something. If he called the police leaving them to handle these two and go to his sister, that left Martin alone to do as he pleased with Pete before the police could arrive stopping Martin and Martin possibly escaping. Without Cole's eyewitness account of the beating the police might not hold Martin. Too many variables; Cole decided to take Martin out; hopefully without much damage to the loaner he was driving. But considering the loaner a little more damage would not even be noticed.

Columbine was a curvy, winding, gravel road that had major hills and valleys. The darkness was amplified by the trees and mountains.

The only light were the head light beams and they were directional, so if you got out of the beam the ambient light was not much good. As Cole rounded a tight curve, Pete's car was sideways in the road, its front end angled off on the opposite shoulder dipping into the ditch, the driver's door open. No Pete inside! Martin's car was off on the right shoulder with his door opened . . . no Martin. Cole slid to a stop as much from the need to get to the preacher as to keep from colliding with the cars in the roadway.

Cole hit his high beams and stepped out of the car in a crouched position. Immediately moving to the driver's side, rear door and easing out of his go bag his H&K model 23 .45 caliber pistol.

He closed the door gently, pushed the pistol into his pants at the small of his back, then moved to the rear of his car for cover and concealment as well as to see if he could hear or see any movement. Pete's car had stalled. The only sound was Pete's key alarm pinging and Martin's car quietly idling. Cole Punched 911.

"Morgan County Dispatch. What's your emergency?" A women's voice spoke in to the phone, crisp and succinct.

"I am 2.6 miles north of highway 170 on Columbine Road. Two cars have collided with no sign of any occupants. I need a deputy here as soon as you can please."

"Yes, sir, I am dispatching a deputy to your location. Sir what is your name?" The dispatcher waited.

Cole contemplated his response. "Sir, what is your name?" Again the question. He knew the less people knew of him the better for him, "Sir, are you there? I need your name, please." Not a question a polite order this time.

Cole was looking over the trunk lid of his loaner car holding the phone to his head, when he saw movement in front of Martin's car. Dim at first, then Martin slowly materialized from the dense darkness coming into full view. He was smiling and waved his hand over his head. "Over here, I got him over here!" He hollered out as if he was expecting someone. Martin half turned to his right and looked back in the direction he had come from. The car light washed over his broad back, he must have knocked the drivers light out when he slammed his car into Pete's car for only the right headlight was shining. His blond hair reflected the light and took on a glow like you see in a Catholic painting. Cole knew this guy was no saint. Martin turned around again and Cole could see blood on the front of his shirt and right sleeve. "Come on, hurry up." Martin was getting impatient.

"Sir, are you there?"

"One of the people has come out of the bushes. We are going to need an ambulance, dispatch!" Cole hit the end call button.

Cole stepped to the passenger side of the loaner car cautiously walking toward the rear of Martin's car. Cole's high beams were only adding to Martin's difficultly to recognize him. Martin turned again and looked back into the darkness. Martin's car had come to rest with just enough room for Cole to turn sideways between the car and the trees, adding to the difficulty Martin was having in recognizing him. Cole stepped to the front of Martin's car removing his pistol from his pants with his right hand, pointing it at Martin's head, "I want you to lie flat on your face with your arms out to your sides. NOW!" Cole barked. He did a quick scan of the area and saw Pete lying on his left side facing away from the two of them; not moving. Cole couldn't tell for sure but it looked as if Pete had fresh blood on his head staining his collar and pooling on the ground just below his neck. Martin jerked and tensed up but did not obey and did not turn around. He stood stone still, "You again!" Martin said with hatred in his voice.

"Martin, don't let three seconds of courage screw up the rest of your life, get down on your face." Cole demanded watching him intently, with his finger tight on the trigger of the model 23. Cole was standing off to the right of Martin's car in the shadows, making it hard for Martin to see him if he spun with a gun in hand. For that matter hard for anyone to see him no matter what direction they came from. Cole heard a car rolling up and saw head light beams flash across the road as the next car came to join the party. Cole was relieved realizing he could turn this maggot over to the Deputies and get to his sister.

"Oh, Martin, I called the sheriff department this is probably them now." Martin was silent. "Hey, this will give you a chance to catch up with your jail house lover boys. What'd-you-think? Vacation time sound good?" Cole harassed.

Cole heard a car door close, "Martin, where are you?" Cole didn't recognize the voice but Martin did. "We got company. It's that guy that hit me on the head." Then to Cole, Martin said, "You're going to get yours now!" Cole had one of those uh oh moments. Cole eased back farther into the bushes as quietly as he could.

"You move . . . I shoot you in the head." Cole whispered; Martin knew he meant it but as many criminals think, *Does he really have a gun?*

Things went silent . . . Cole then saw red and blue lights appear popping off of the trees and cars and the roadway. The deputy's spot light came on and the darkness disappeared.

Cole heard a Spanish accented male voice, "Hey Captain, what are you doing all the way out here?" Cole heard low muffled voices but could not make anything out. He waited. The spot light went off followed by the red and blues. He heard the crunch of gravel on tires as the prowl car turned around on the dirt road. Cole waited silently. For the first time in Cole's life he didn't know quite what to do. *I'm in*

America where things don't pan out as well as when I'm on an extraction scenario in another country. Cole thought.

"Martin." It was David this time.

"Yeah." Martin hollered out.

"Shut-up, one more word and I will cold cock you, hear me?" Cole's tone had a vicious tint to it. But to do any cold-cocking he would have to leave concealment.

"The deputy's gone bring Pete out here." No answer. "What about that other guy?" No answer.

David yelled, "MARTIN, answer me!"

"Boys, it appears we have us a Mexican standoff." Cole shouted out. Then stepped from the shadows and grabbed Martin by the hair with his left hand, kicking Martin's right leg out from under him. Martin fell on his back with a thud. Looking up at Cole's large bore .45, "Told you I had a gun, boy. You do as I say and you might live through this." Cole checked Martin for weapons, rolling him onto his stomach.

The two saw the flash of movement and heard the scuffle. The police captain moved to the side of Cole's car leaving David exposed in the light.

"Sir, this is Captain Don Henry of the Pimsler Police Department. Can you hear me, sir?" Don pulled his weapon.

Sounds pleasant enough, Cole thought. "What's the PD doing way out here, Cap?" Cole has always been eternally suspicious. "Put your hands under the car." Cole whispered in Martin's ear.

"Well, first, I like to know who I am speaking with, sir. What's your name, if I might ask?" Cole rolled Martin on to his left side, still checking Martin for weapons.

"Cap, let me help you understand where I am coming from. Is that all right with you, sir? Get us all on the same page." Cole shouted back. Cole rolled Martin back onto his stomach, placing his knee on his neck, grinding his left cheek into the gravel road. Then leaning down to his ear, "You are going to be the first to die if things don't go my way, understand?" Martin felt the cold steel barrel pressing hard against his right temple. He said nothing.

"Sure, let's get on that page, sounds good. What's on your mind, sir?" Don sounding so official and professional, faking his desire to work with Cole.

Cole pulled his cell out and dialed 911 placing it on the hood of Martin's car. "911, what's your emergency?" "Point one . . . I know there are two of you. I can see both of you right now. Therefore, until we square this little deal . . . I do not want to lose sight of either one of you so move back into the light, Captain. I need to feel those warm fuzzes, or Mr. Martin here will be cold and stiff. Second, I assume you are who you say you are because I heard the deputy address you and give the scene to you. I do not know what you told him but it worked because he left. So, that creates a dilemma for me. I am a law-abiding citizen and I support the local sheriff, Police, fire and anybody else that is legitimately in charge, if I am not. Right now, I'm in charge. Now this is the dilemma I am having. This man broke into a house beat the crap out of Preacher Pete and now it looks as if he has crushed his head in with a rock and you are calling out to him as if you are his best friend and ally. As a matter of fact, he has made an incriminating statement to me about your tight little group. So, Captain, I don't know what to do? You sent the law away and have assumed control of the scene here outside of your jurisdiction. It seems that you do not want any other law here? Why not, I wonder? I also know that your best friend, who I assume is standing next to you there, has threatened kidnapping of a young girl. And I think this bozo I am holding here is your accomplice. So, I believe you are up to your neck in this mess! How am I doing so far, Captain?"

"Good summation, so far." Don did not care if Cole knew any of this. "Is Martin still with us or have you dispatched him?"

"Well, if you address him in any way his new name will be Comatose. Understand me?"

"Yes, sir, I do. Are you in law enforcement, sir?" The captain was getting a bad feeling about this unknown entity.

"Let's not get too personal, Captain, if that's okay with you?" Cole said condescendingly. The less information the better.

"Well, you have all the cards. What is your proposal, sir?" The captain wanted to bring this discussion to a quick and decisive end by killing this man.

David pulled his cell out, pushed the speed dial number for his house. He held his phone down by his side, seconds later he heard, "Hello?"

"Sir, this is David Clark. May I speak? I might have a solution that will satisfy all concerned." The man on the other end of the phone was listening."

"By all means speak, David Clark."

"Well, here we are, all the way out on East Columbine road. You have my friend and colleague, Martin, held at gun point I am assuming, correct?" He waited . . . no answer. "Well, knowing Martin you would have to have a weapon of some kind or he would have already crushed you."

Crushed me? Awe, that hurts . . . but of course you don't know me. Cole thought to himself pressing the barrel harder into Martin's scull. Again no answer.

Martin heard the 911 operator, "Sir, I have re-dispatched the deputy to your location" Martin was trying to muster the courage to yell out. His face was killing him, not to mention his neck and he was having a hard time breathing. Every time he drew a breath, he sucked in road dirt. He burst out, "He's dialed 911. Their listening to . . ." Cole almost stood on his neck. Martin screamed out just before Cole's fist collided into Martin's right temple. Comatose!

Don decided to end this. Don aimed his nine millimeter and fired three consecutive rounds, popping the rounds into and ricocheting off the car while he moved sideways to the left front of Pete's vehicle. Cole, balled up behind the car and Martin, pointing his weapon toward the ditch and fired once. The .45 went off like a cannon. Cole hadn't decided if he was going to shoot anybody as of yet. Don and David dove for cover. Cole pushed Martin's head and shoulders under the car he was behind giving Cole better control and more protection from flying lead. David shouted to Don as he ran back slipping and sliding on the gravel road behind Cole's parked car. "Tell people you're going to fire that thing BEFORE you fire it next time!" He slid to a stop behind the car and looked over to where Don was behind Pete's vehicle. Don was smiling at him.

"Well, I see you have a weapon, sir. Was that a warning or are you that bad of a shot?" Don chided Cole.

As quietly as he could David called out, "Don! I think the girl is at George Bookers house! He lives right up the mountain here. I'm sending the others to check it out. They can come in the back way, snatch the girls and be gone. What'd you think?"

"Get it done! Tell them to move fast. We are out of time here."

Cole yelled into his phone, "Shots fired; shots fired! Send back up 10–18!"

Oh, crap, he is a cop! Don thought when he heard Cole's cry for help. Don peered around the left front quarter panel of Pete's car looking for a kill shot. All he could see was Martin's motionless legs lying on the roadway. He fired once, just because, striking the fender behind the left headlight.

David had other ideas. He moved back silently to his waiting Land Rover, slid into the driver's seat cranked the engine and hit the gas.

Don screamed, "David . . . David!" Don cursed David under his breath, "Coward"!

Slinging gravel and bits of rubber, David fish tailed backward and up a short hill around the curve out of Don's line of fire and from any other stray bullets that might start flying. David heard Don's shouts but ignored them. David thought, *Earn your money Don, kill that guy!* He needed to get things moving so they could all get out of here.

"Carl, need you to listen." David was shouting in his phone while trying to turn the Land Rover around in the road as he was still backing away from the firefight. He hit his breaks and cut the wheel but the big vehicle slid straight backward. He let off the breaks and the Land Rover swerved hard and fast to the side of the road into the ditch banging into a small cedar tree. David's head jerked backward as he slammed the Land Rover into drive throwing dirt and gravel as it climbed out of the ditch. "Call the boys and send them to George Booker's house. I am going to need about five of them, understand?"

Carl was far from the brightest bulb in the closet, "Where does he live?"

"Look it up!" David screamed over the phone. "I'll be there waiting. I need you to get those girls ready and meet me at the airport. Lock up the house. What did Don and Martin do with Mary's body?"

"I don't know; me and Sonny's been here with these girls."

"Well, go check her out and if she is not wrapped up . . . wrap her up and dump her in that old well out in the garden area. No one will find her there. That things a hundred feet deep."

"Okay."

"Move it, Carl! I mean MOVE YOUR BUTT! We don't have much time!"

David keyed his cell and called his pilot.

"Hello?" Randal Broder was a twenty-year professional jet pilot. He had worked with David for four and a half years. He loved his job and the benefits he received because of David's profession. However, like everyone else, he believed that his time off was deserved and coveted.

"Get the plane ready. I'll be at the airport in thirty to forty minutes." David was sliding around corners and curves on the dirt road stressed out.

"What's going on David? You sound stressed."

"Get the plane prepped! NOW!" David was stressed and the pilot did not have to guess about it.

"David I'm at a cocktail party and I have been drinking. I can't fly now. I could have my license pulled! Can't this wait until tomorrow?" The pilot knew this was a losing argument. David knew he was too deep into David's business and Randal had too much knowledge of all the shady deals David had going on, all the time, to argue. He also knew that he was paid very well to keep his mouth shut, to see nothing and fly the G5 every time he was asked to and go where he was told to go.

"Get that plane ready or Martin's going to be visiting you . . . understand?" David knew how great the greed factor was for all people, you just had to find the right number or the right motivation. Martin was a great motivator for almost everybody.

"Yes, sir" was the only response David received. Randal hung up and called his copilot.

Don looked back, facing his potential assailant, never leaving the cover of Pete's car. Cole stole a look around the passenger side of the car and could see the Land Rover leaving, while he was taking Martin's belt off him and securing Martin's hands behind his back and to the bumper of the car with it. Cole had rolled Martin onto his chest pulling his arms up into an awkward position. Not impossible to get out of but time consuming and that is all he needed, time. Cole moved to the passenger's side of the vehicle. He was looking under the vehicle to see if he could get a shot off without killing the police captain. The curve of the roadway and the car being half in the ditch prohibited the shot. He crept down the side of the car to the rear. Martin's car slightly behind Pete's and from the passenger's side of the vehicle Cole could see Don perfectly. Cole took deadly aim. "Put the gun down Captain!" Cole ordered. Don Henry was an expert shot and had been trained at the FBI academy in combat shooting. He passed the course with flying colors, albeit fifteen years ago; he was presently the department's combat shooting instructor and had several continuing education shooting courses under his belt as well. He also knew he could still save this debacle if he could just kill this intruder; he was motivated. He instantly turned attempting a point and shoot scenario on Cole. He and Cole fired simultaneously . . . strange how people's bodies react to an impact such as a .45 caliber round creates tearing into one's body. Time slowed as Cole watched. As Don was being knocked off his feet from the low crouch he had assumed in his firing position, Cole saw the impact; as Don's hands and feet shot straight out in front of him, feet kicking up road dirt, head dropped on to his chest, eyes were tight shut; he rocked backward. Cole thought he could hear the breath being violently punched out of the body. He could see saliva spew from the open, twisted mouth as the tiny dark hole appeared on his chest. He saw the face relax and the eyes partially open as the head disappeared from sight. The body bounced on its posterior, the arms and legs flailed like a dropped rag doll. Cole hated the visuals that a shooter sees as one's soul is separated from the body.

You never forget them. The body bounced sliding back into the ditch stopping with the legs and feet on the roadway, the head and torso in the ditch. Everything was quiet. No sound at all, not even ringing in the ears. Total silence, the scene played again in Cole's mind's eye in slow motion. Cole stood and walked toward the body holding his pistol at the ready. Don's foot twitched. Cole picked up the police captain's pistol, then bent and checked for vital signs . . . Cole knew before he ever touched the body he was dead; even before Don hit the ground, he knew his life had departed. The hollow point round passed through the man's chest and directly into the heart exploding inside like a tiny bomb killing him instantly. As Cole examined the now dead police captain he noticed his handcuff case. Cole reached down, popped the case open and pulled the cuffs out. He walked over to Martin who was struggling to get his hands off the bumper and slide out from under the car. Cole grabbed the belt and jerked Martin's arms straight up causing great discomfort. Martin yelped as Cole fell on Martin grinding his knee into the small of Martin's back. Cole angrily removed the belt from Martin's wrist. Blaming Martin for the situation he found himself. He stood and drug Martin out from under the car.

"Roll over to the front tire." Cole ordered.

Martin rolled over to it and looked at Cole with a questioning look.

"Now hug the bottom of the tire putting your arms around the tire so I can cuff you."

"You're going to cuff me to the tire with me lying on the road? There are bears out here man!"

"Well, I guess I can shoot you in the knees and leave you here." Cole waited a moment letting Martin make up his mind. The two men stared at each other. "Okay, okay, your right this is a democracy. You vote. I kill you, I Shoot your knees OR YOU GRAB THAT TIRE! WHICH IS IT?" Cole was done. He was sick that he had killed a policeman. He was sick with the thought that he could go to prison. He was sick that his sister was somehow in the middle of this and now he was sick that he was holding a gun and this idiot was arguing with him! Martin grabbed the tire. Cole viciously cuffed his hands together. Martin moaned in pain again.

He had seen the other man called David Clark leave in the Land Rover. He knew these people were here for his sister and the girl. He also knew that the man the girls were with was at least sixty-five years old. Nothing about this had a good ending. He quickly turned to Pete. He was correct, the man had been hit in the head hard but that was not his biggest problem. Pete had been shot in the right upper back Cole thought possibly from a ricochet. Although, Pete was still breathing, his breath was labored. Cole turned to his phone, "Dispatch; dispatch you still there?"

"Yes. Sir, what is going on at your location? I want to know who you are. I have deputies heading in your direction and they will be there in minutes."

"Yes, I know. We have two down; one dead at scene and the other a minister named Pete. His head is bashed in and he has been shot in the back. He is still breathing but his vitals are weak. Please send an ambulance. I have another handcuffed to the front of a vehicle.

"Sir, what department are you with?" The dispatcher was a little relieved in assuming Cole was law enforcement.

"I am heading to 2-8-3-4-5 East Columbine Road. Dispatch deputies to that location as well. I believe there is a double kidnapping in progress. I will be proceeding from this crime scene to that location. I believe the people at that address are in danger." He was not aware that Morgan County had only three deputies on duty for the night shift.

There had been a rollover accident with injuries, two deputies were working the incident; which happened to be over sixty miles away on the other side of the county; one was holding back waiting for further instruction ... from Captain Don Henry.

Cole trotted to his loaner car. As he passed Martin's vehicle he hurriedly looked for his expended brass; he saw it on the trunk lid of Martin's car in the crack between the trunk lid and the car body by the back window. He put the brass in his pocket, then grabbed his go bag from the backseat of the loaner. He heard the dispatcher command, "Sir you stay at the scene. Do not leave the scene . . . do you hear me Sir! Sir!" Cole hit end. Flip the screen to his GPS and looked at distance and direction from his location to Booker's home. He ran back to Pete. Cole dug out of his bag his emergency medical kit. He heard the phone ringing; it was the sheriff department's 911 operator calling him back. He took out his solar blanket and laid it on the ground and as gently as he could, he lifted Pete on to it. He then began to stop the bleeding of the two wounds. The head wound would be second. He took his knife, cutting Pete's collar and down the back of his shirt. Then Cole checked Pete's chest to see if the bullet passed through. It had not. Cole rolled Pete onto his chest and cleaned the wound with an antibacterial wound solution. He grabbed a squeeze bottle of powered blood stop, pouring it on the wound, then placed a trauma pad over the wound tapping it in place with the first roll of tape he could find. He always loved duct tape. He even heard of a couple of guys hunting in Alaska, who had the skin of their plane tore almost completely off by a bear and duct taped it together, then flew it home. It is an amazing product but could be a little too much for this situation. He turned his attention to Pete's head wound. He tried to keep Pete at least on his side, he knew with the gunshot wound there would be internal bleeding and that can be a real problem if Pete stayed left on his stomach or his side for too long. Cole pressed around the head wound to see if there was any scull damage. No soft mushy scull, a good thing. He irrigated the wound, repeated the blood stop and grabbed a trauma pad, placing it on the wound, then wrapping Pete's head in gauze. Cole then did a quick check of the rest of the little man's body for bleeding injuries. ALL the other damage he found was dried and beginning to scab over. Cole stuffed his equipment back into the go bag, stood looking down at Pete, I know when you signed up to be a preacher this was not what you expected. Cole heard sirens in the distance. He walked over to Martin and kicked his foot saying, "No matter what you say, they will think the captain put these cuffs on you. You will go to jail until they figure this out. Once they put you in; I am going to make it my mission to keep you there."

Martin responded with a grunted, "We're going to kill you." Cole seriously thought about shooting the man. Cole checked the immediate area, found the other shell casing and picked it up. Looked at the loaner and knew that it could not be traced to him. It had been Goose who called for it and no names were given, no one was there who could identify him as the one who picked up the car. As long as they did not lift any finger prints off it but his prints were not in the criminal data base and if they called Goose . . . he would conveniently forget his passenger's name. He thought he needed to make contact with Goose anyway. He dialed his number, second ring he heard the familiar disgusted voice of "The Goose,' "Yeah, what do you want. Your sister kick you out of her house already?"

"I don't have time to explain but I am in a tight situation. I need you to load up the bird and get back here as soon as possible."

"What, you up to your neck in alligators Brother? Leave you alone for ten minutes . . ." Goose said with muted humor.

"Something like that. Goose can you break away and head this direction? I really need you and the plane. I would like you to fly in before the airport gets hopping in the morning. Can you do it?"

"CAN I DO IT, Ain't the question! The question is, 'Do I want to do it?' That's the question; Boss man." Goose replied in his thick southern drawl.

Cole responded, "Let me help you with that. Get your butt in that plane and get it in the air heading this direction!" Cole was seriously in need of Goose and that plane.

"Well, since you put it that way . . . aye, aye Captain. What do I need to bring with me?" Goose grasped the severity of Cole's situation.

"Grab your kit, the plane and you, for now. If things get worse I will get the boys to haul out what we need in the checked luggage."
"Roger that. Do you need me to call Hatch?"

"No, just get on the plane and head this direction. Once you get here, I will fill you in. Goose this is serious, brother; I need you to be on your toes. We have crooked cops running the show for some pretty bad hombres, comprende? Don't want to tell all on this line but call before you land. Copy?" Cole had moved from Big Brother to Covert Operative.

"Copy, Boss. See you in about three and a half hours."

"Oh, hey . . . by the way, if you get a call from the police . . . you don't remember my name, okay?"

Goose laughed. "I love it when I got something on you . . . remember that new plane I talked to you about?" Goose's voice trailed off as he hit end.

Cole looked at his watch, 2243 hours. What did my little sister get herself into; what's going on in this place? He looked back down at Martin. He squatted down, took Martin's cell phone and slid it into his own pocket.

"Hey, what are you doing with my cell, man?" Martin protested and then tried to kick Cole in retaliation.

He stood and turned beginning the long jog up the mountain road. He reached into his bag retrieving a flashlight. At a jog in total darkness; *I could trip over a pebble and roll-off the mountain; then I would need the trauma kit.* He clicked the light on.

Cole slung the bag over his shoulders holding the flashlight in one hand and his phone in the other, he speed dialed Joan's number.

"BC, are you all right?" The connection was poor; Joan's voice was surrounded by static. "We're worried sick. What is going on? Where are you? Are the Police with you? We heard gunshots!"

"We'll, BS if you will let me say something I will tell you . . ." He was already out of breath. *I'm too old to be running in the mountains.*

"Okay, you're on speaker. George and Helen are listening."

"We had an incident down the road. What happ . . . d . . . hr explain."

"BC, can you hear me!" Joan was panicking because of the static.

"I need for you to prepare to defend yourselves until I get there." Again the static took control, "Ge-ge you ha . . . otgun will b-best -nsive for you. Get the women in the that be most easily defended. I am on foot I not g my car two others that blocking the road. Besides I not want to disturb the crime scene anymore. I will probably needing use for my defense."

Joan perked up, "Your defense? What are you talking about; what happened? We can't hear you. Say again BC; SAY AGAIN!" Joan shouted into the phone as if that would help.

"Joan! Can you hear me? Joan!" Cole heard the automated digital voice response, "Call dropped."

Cole was running down a steep hill and was going to have to wait until he reached the other side before he called back. He was hoping they received enough of his transmission to do what was needed. He ran on as best he could in the dark with a bouncing flashlight beam leading the way.

He ran listening to the rhythm of his own footfalls on the roadway drumming his mind into past images mingled with the new stains of thought. He again saw the death faces of those he had snatched life from; he had au swayed his guilt in the past by reminding himself that those he had killed were the worst of the worst who deserved to die. They actually chose to die by resisting his recovery efforts hanging onto their kidnapped property; easily dismissing the lives and the images that haunted him at times. *What was happening to him now,* he mused. *Was he weakening? Was he becoming soft to the point of being no good to his team or those he vowed to recover from the hands of evil men?* He ran on trying to out run the ghostly faces that pursued his thoughts. *Had he become what he was fighting against, pure evil?* He remembered Joan reading to him from the book of Mark about a demon possessed man named Legion. This man was powerfully evil, consumed by demons and devils that contorted and controlled his mind, body and spirit. Charged Jesus viciously but fell before Him on his knees without doing Him any harm.

She said Christ never even took a step backward as this demon- man charged. Christ asked him one question, "What is your name?" Everything is wrapped up in the name. Our whole lives are wrapped in our names. Cole wondered, *what is my name? Who am I? What is this life of death and destruction I have led? What happened to that demon man . . . he was seen by the village people to be setting with Christ in his right mind. It's not the violence that disturbs so much but the not knowing who I really am. Who am I? How do I reconcile my life with my actions? Am I my actions or is there life beyond what I do?* Cole silenced his mind a moment, then it dawned on him as he ran to protect innocent lives. Lives that neither caused nor asked for this violence to come in. *I must set with Christ. I must hear what he has to say. I must tell him my name.*

He ran with vigor and purpose as if he had a hand on his back pushing, comforting him . . . easing his mind's pain as he ran up the mountain. He had to set with Christ and know.

40

Unlike most in the world, some men and women love evil, others just unwittingly participate in it.

David was a quarter of a mile or so from the Booker's residence having come from the opposite direction. He came to a sliding stop when he saw a motor cycle and an old Ford pickup truck off on the side of the roadway. There were five burly men between the bike and the truck; two setting on the tail gate, two standing and one setting on the bike. David stopped beside the small group.

"Whatcha got?" The largest one, called Little Dave, approached David's Land Rover. Not named after David Clark and not little at all. Six foot six almost seven, David had previously seen jailhouse tats on parts of his body; he knew for sure they were on both arms; from his shoulders all the way down to his fingertips, back up his neck and the left side of his face. His hair was long, to the middle of his back, which he had pulled back into a ponytail revealing a large pirate looking earring in his left ear. He and the others were wearing leather jackets and pants, with heavy black boots. David could tell they came to jack people up. David had actually ask Little Dave once why he was so into crime and doing bad things . . . his response was, "I'm just like you Davy, I love it."

David's window was down . . . he leaned out, "I got two beauties that I need snatched just up the hill."

"Cool." Little Dave said in a deep bass voice with zero emotion. "Where's Cap'n Don?"

"He should be here in a bit. He's takin' care of another matter an intruder that needed terminating."

Little Dave gave a quizzical look, "Terminating? Why can't you people just say 'killed'? That's what Cap'n Don does best, he just kills people." The others chuckled in agreement

David thought he was above all that kind of verbiage, "Yeah, well . . . okay. He is out killing people. The deal is; just up the hill is George Bookers house, I will guide you to it. There are probably four or five people in the house and I need you guys to kill all but two younger women."

The one called Ax-handle Charlie spoke from behind Little Dave,

"So we're after young women? How old and what do they look like, Slick."

David hated to be called Slick, actually, he hated Ax-handle Charlie but he was not going to say that to Ax-handle's face since his specialty was beating people to death with an ax- handle, "Well, Charlie," David drug out the 'liiie' part of his name, "They're the two best looking women you have ever seen." Charlie's eyes narrowed as he stood up from the tailgate and walked toward the Land Rover.

Little Dave put his hand out to stop Ax-Handle and in his deep bass voice said, "David, be careful how you talk to Ax . . . ok . . . He don't like you much. Ya know what I mean?" Little Dave leaned in close and allowed David a look into the eyes of a stone cold killer.

David could smell the alcohol and pot he had been drinking and smoking earlier. David's tension level went up ten notches. He remembered why he let Don handle this part of the business, "Okay, I . . . I'll watch it." David cleared his throat, "Now, once we got 'em I need to get them to the airport ASAP. And get them loaded on my plane; everybody good with that?"

"Got ya check book, Mr. David? This ain't gonna be cheap. We don't normally deal with you, straight up, ya know."

"Yes, sir, I know."

"Yes, sir!" Ax laughed loud echoing through the mountains, mocking David.

"Little Dave, I do think Mr. David here is sceered o' you."

Little Dave was looking at Ax, then turned to David but still speaking to Ax, "Naw, Ax, he's scared of you, my brothah!"

At the moment, David was scared to death of all of them. He knew money was not what these men loved the most. If one felt offended, all would attack like a pack of wolves and tear David apart, money or no money. They love doing bad things even to the hand that feeds them! "You guys want to do this or make fun of me? Captain Don will be here any moment or as far as I know, he is up the mountain waiting on us right now. So let's go and get this done . . . okay?" David, hoping to forestall any negative outburst from these guys with the threat of Captain Don's disapproval, and also being as cordial as he knew how to be at the same time.

Laughing, Little Dave said, "Come on boys, load up."

41

"No Greater love has any man . . ."
Jesus

George had understood enough of the transmission to act on it. He went to his gun case and took out two pistols putting a 1911 Colt military issue .45 cal. in his waist band and handing a model 60 five shot Smith & Wesson .38 +P to Helen. He took out two shotguns giving one to Joan, a pump 870 with a shortened barrel, still legal but designed to create a wide pattern of destruction. All the weapons were loaded.

George quizzed, "Joan, you know how to operate that shotgun?" Joan racked the slide and slammed it home charging the weapon; "Yes, sir" was all she said.

George eyed her, surprised at her ability with the 12 gauge, "Okaaayy . . . Joan I want to show you something." George took her to the back of the house into a large closet. I would like for you, Simone and Helen to get into this closet. If anyone opens this door without first identifying himself, shoot them. Understand?"

"Perfectly." Joan said it with hardly any emotion. Joan was also not showing any fear at all.

"Have you done this sort of thing before?" George was prompted to ask.

"No, Why?"

"Oh, okay. Just . . . wondering. I will be in the front of the house with Smokey. If things get too bad I will retreat back to here."

"Make sure you call out before you open this door!" Joan said.

"I am not going to let you face bad people alone George Booker!" Helen was adamant.

"Sweet Pea, I am not going to put you at risk. I can handle this you know that. I will hideout so no one can see me. I promise. Don't worry. If there is any shooting, do not come out of here until Joan's brother arrives or I call out. Okay. Sweet Pea." George said, looking in her eyes, pleadingly. "You have got to do this, for me, okay?"

"Oh, Booger, are you sure? Don't go out there by yourself, please honey, stay here with us, Booger. You're too old to do this sort of thing. Stay here." Helen said as she held the front of his shirt. She had loved him too long to lose him now, she thought.

"Cole will be here any minute. I have to wait for him in the front room. Don't you worry. I've been through this sort of thing before, you know that. I was not a cook in the Marine Corps after all!" George leaned in and kissed her. Then gently began to push her into the closet closing the door behind her. Helen teared up then said, "You show them what an old Devil Dog can do, Booger!" He smiled and shut the door.

George turned all the lights off in the house. He turned the outside lights on. The house had an open design to it. The kitchen, dining area and living room were all one big room with the den off to the side toward the garage. But from the kitchen one had a panoramic view of all three rooms. All the rooms had large floor to ceiling windows again giving one a command of all movement outside the house. There was only one blind spot, a large double sided fire place between the living room and the den. It was fifteen feet long and 8 feet wide. This was only a problem if the intruders knew it existed. Which they did not!

"Sit, Smokey boy. You'll tell me if anybody comes from the back of the house, won't you boy." Booker patted the big dog on his head. The inside was completely dark with the outside of the house surround by light. So, Booker could see out well but no one could see in. He was at a great advantage if an intruder entered, they would be silhouetted against the outside light with eyes that were not adjusted for the inside darkness of the house. He laid the double barrel Browning 12 gauge shotgun on the kitchen island he was standing behind, he patiently waited.

Cole dialed Joan's number again . . . no answer. *Didn't even go to voice mail?* Cole picked up his pace. He felt a strange joy. As if he had discovered a great secret or treasure. It was an odd feeling of relief and wellbeing he had never felt before.

42

"Tyranny brings ignorance and brutality along with it."

Rev. Jonathan Mayhew

Martin lay in partial darkness. For a big tough guy his mind was creating visions of bears and mountain lions chewing his feet off. Not to mention wolves. He heard a rustling behind him. He stopped breathing. He lay perfectly still. He knew Pete was out and had been ever since he had bashed his head in. It crackled and scraped on the ground. Being hand-cuffed to the tire kept him from being able to even look over his shoulder. He could not see anything in front of him because the tire obstructed his view, so, the only direction he could see was off to his right. He was lying in front of the left front tire, facing it. His feet were directly behind, hands wrapped around and cuffed on the opposite side of the tire. And he could not move; not even slide to the side. Whatever it was, was right behind him! The muffled noises it was making and the dragging sounds were unnerving. He heard it moan and then it moved closer. He knew it was eating Pete and would soon be coming after him. All the car lights were on but they were no help to him from this angle. Martin pulled his knees up under him and tried to slide under the car.

"Martin is that you?" Pete's voice was groggy and weak. He had struggled to his feet. He still could not see out of his left eye and his pain sensors were screaming at him from every part of his body. He was weak from blood loss and dehydrated. He knew he needed a hospital. He was disoriented.

"Yeah, Pete, it's me. Say, can you go get the keys from Don and unlock me, please?" Martin was sounding innocent and helpless.

"Where's Don?"

"He's lying over in front of your car. I think his keys are in one of his pockets."

Pete looked in the direction of the car through the fog of his right eye and saw Don's legs out in the roadway a little ways. "What's wrong with him?"

"I think he's dead, Pete. Hurry and get the keys, man, c'mon."

Pete had never seen a real dead person before. Not one that wasn't in the mortuary. Not one that was just lying about on the road. "How did he die? Oh no, I didn't run over him did I?"

"He was shot, man, just get the keys, stupid!" Martin was yelling now. His aggravation had reached its short limits.

Pete stared down at Martin for a long moment weaving back and forth; then drew back and kicked the man as hard as he could. Martin yelled out in anger, it was not that hard of a kick. Pete kicked him again as he regained his memory of the last few hours of life with Martin in it. Martin returned the attack with floundering kicks of his own but they all missed the mark. Pete staggered back away from Martin's violent kicks looking around for a rock. He found a nice one about the size of his fist.

"Lay still Martin, I only got one good eye to aim with."

"What? What are you doing?" Martin felt it and knew what Pete had done. The rock struck him in the middle of his back right on his spin. If Pete had had all his strength about him it might have done serious damage but as it was it bruised him and lacerated his skin. He picked up the rock again and aimed as well as he could, this time it struck Martin behind the left ear, exactly where his big knot was that Cole had given him earlier. The rock made a hollow thud sound splitting opened the golf ball size knot given to him by Cole, the sound sicken Pete. It was a sound that only the desperately cruel enjoy. Martin's body flexed strangely and then laid still, Martin did not make another sound. Comatose again; twice in one night.

"You like that Martin, that feel good, Martin? . . . Martin?" Pete bent down and saw gobs of blood on Martin's head. He kicked his leg. No response. He kicked his soft lower abdomen area. No response.

Pete grabbed his head and walked in a tight circle, "Oh no, I've killed him. Oh, nooo!" Pete looked at the man again, "Martin. Martin! Answer me!" No response. Pete felt cold and totally confused. He reached down and grabbed the solar blanket, wrapped himself up and began to walk off into the woods. Tears streaming down his checks, he felt like vomiting as his thoughts raced to the worst scenarios.

43

"Tyranny degrades men from their just rank into the class of brutes."

Rev. Jonathan Mayhew

David and the five men stopped short of the drive; dismounted from their vehicles and began to walk up the drive.

Smokey's ears perked and George heard a low deep growl from the wary animal. George picked up the shotgun, pulling both hammers back, still and patient.

The men walked up the circular drive and at the point where the drive 'Y's off to go to the garage, George saw two split off from the group and head toward the garage side of the house. George prepared himself with a prayer to his Great Heavenly Father for protection from evil and strength to protect his family. Smokey stood and George reached down to pet his friend and felt all the hair standing up on the big dogs back. Smokey's head lowered and his shoulders stiffened. He crept around the corner of the island bar they were behind, his growl low and deep in his chest. George had never heard his dog like this. He was glad but it was unnerving to see this loving animal so vicious sounding. The dog quietly disappeared.

44

"There is nothing great or good where tyranny's influence reaches."

Rev. Jonathan Mayhew

Martin woke to the voice of Deputy Raul Ortega. Ortega was removing the cuffs from his wrist, "Marteen, what happened mon?"

Martin rolled away from the car tire and sat up, dizzy from the blow on his head, "That preacher clubbed me with a rock."

"What preacher and what happened to de Boss?" Ortega asked pointing with his chin toward the late Don Henry.

"Well, Ortega it looks like he was shot. You being the cop should have figured that out." Martin was angry with everyone especially one he had a bluff on. He felt sick and leaned to his left and vomited on the ground. His head pounded and he an offal metallic taste in his mouth. He felt terrible.

Ortega stood and backed away from Martin and the odor, knowing two things; one, without Don Henry there was no longer a desire to be part of this happy group of criminals and two Martin had a severe concussion and Ortega did not care, "Yeah, Marteen, I see dat. How did it happen, stupido? If I don't know that I can't help you or anyone else. Now tell me what chu know!"

"I need some water man. Do you have anything I can clean the blood off me with? Did you see Pete Donny around here? He's been beat in the head with a rock. I need to find him. He can blow this whole deal." Martin was trying to take inventory of his injuries, rubbing his head and wrists.

"I tought we were after hees daughter and dat Joan lady?" Ortega said Joan more with an "H" sound than a "J" sound.

"We are, man! But we are after him, too." Martin's anger was rising with every word he spoke. "He knows too much. And what the heck took you so long to get here?" Martin scooted away from the vomit.

"De Boss told me that he was going to take care of dis and not to worry. He didn't do such a good job, huh?" Ortega said it as more of a statement than a question. He walked to his prowl car and dug out his first aid kit leaving Martin setting on the ground leaning against the tire he had been cuffed to.

45

"It is appointed unto man to die once and then the judgement."

Hebrews

The other four were walking directly toward the front of the house like John Wayne in 'Rio Bravo.' "Well, boys, you ain't The Duke and this ain't Rio Bravo!" George raised his shotgun and aimed. He held steady waiting, both eyes open. He was listening for the first sound of entry. He had always heard if you are going to shoot an intruder make sure they are in the house before you pull the trigger.

Silence.

A face was looking in the plate glass window.

It was David Clark! George knew David could not see him. He stood statue still. He was watching David. The glass window to David's left shattered in a million pieces and flew all across the room followed by one of the lawn chairs. Seconds after the chair the first of the four ran through the empty window frame. He was a huge man dressed in black. His hair was flying all around his head and shoulders; he screamed an Indian war whoop as he rushed through the window. Another window crashed followed by a chair and a man who shot off his pistol as he entered. George took aim just as another window was struck with a chair but didn't break. George fired and the big man went down. He turned and fired again, the second man screamed in pain and fired as he fell backward. George felt a white-hot pain shoot up his side as he was pushed back against the refrigerator. The shotgun went clattering to the tile floor. A third man came in firing wildly. Rushing the area where he had seen George's muzzle flashes originated. The bullets pelted the refrigerator around George's body. George pulled his pistol and fired several rounds at the dark silhouette rushing him. He screamed out and collapsed forward striking his face on the edge of the stone counter top. George moved toward the den and the hall way that led back to the closet where the love of his life was waiting for him. George staggered a step farther when he heard Smokey attacking. The brutal growls and horrifying screams were unsettling. Gun fire was going off and men were yelling and crashing over the furniture as they defended themselves in the dark against his brave and vicious companion. George turned and there in the darkness the second man was standing hunched over spitting out words of filth and venom, "I'm goin-a kill you now!" Just as his head slammed forward and the man sprawled out on the floor.

"Shots fired, mon! Get up and move the car we got to head up the mountain!" Ortega shouted out.

Martin still groggy got to his feet as he heard Ortega put the patrol unit in gear and pull around the loaner. Martin pulled his car forward and to the opposite side of the road, behind Pete's car. He got out and moved as fast as his dizziness allowed to the deputy 's unit. Ortega floored it up the mountain. No siren . . . no red lights. They were not going to arrest anyone. Their mission was to save David's Pimsler operation.

"George! It's Cole Williams. Joan's brother. Don't shoot." Cole yelled into the darkness as he crouched behind the over turned kitchen table.

"My dog . . . my dog! They're killing my dog." George cried out.

Cole picked his way into the house bumping into furniture and tripping over lawn chairs, sliding on broken glass, passed the dead men on the floor, into the den where a horrendous struggle was going on. Cole entered the room gun at the ready but all he could see were shadows, then a flash and a boom. In that instant Cole fired, one man fell dead. George flicked on a light; Smokey turned and rushed Cole with an intensity of a charging lion. "Smokey, SMOKEY!" The dog turned obediently to his master's voice; coming to his master he began to comfort George as only a man's best friend can do. Cole moved through the house and assessed the dead and dying, moving weapons away from even the dead, lifeless fingers. Those in the living room all were gunshot victims. In the den one was gunshot with multiple bite wounds; the other, who bled to death, from having his throat ripped out. Cole turned looking at the dog that was covered in blood. Then noticed George slumped on the floor at the end of the island in the kitchen. Cole approached George but Smokey came off the floor growling moving between his beloved master and the man he didn't know.

"Cole, the girls are in a closet down the hall in the back bedroom. Get my wife please." Cole headed into the hall. "Cole, call out . . . they're armed!"

Cole hollered from the hall to the women. Seconds later Joan ran around the corner into the hall throwing her arms around her big brother. Helen ran passed to her husband and Smokey the hero dog. Cole turned with Joan in one arm and dialed the phone with the other,

"911, what is your emergency?"

"I am waiting for your deputies to arrive at the address I gave you earlier. Where are they?" Cole boomed into the phone.

"Sir, we have a deputy on scene at the moment. Where are you?" Smokey began barking and ran out through one of the windows. Helen called him back inside. Cole was standing looking out when he saw a muzzle flash and heard the bullet impact the wall by his head. Cole yelled, "Lights off . . . lights off now! Get down, get down!" Everyone hit the floor. Cole yelled into the phone, "Dispatch sent an ambulance to the last address I gave you. We have a wounded man. He is shot and is in need of emergency medical aid. We have shots fired here and need back up." Other bullets began zinging around the room impacting areas to close for comfort. Cole peeked above the bar and fired a succession of rounds in the direction of the muzzle flash, then slid across the floor to where Joan was crouching behind the island. Cole grabbed the shotgun George had been using. "What have you people done to these guys?" George laughed at Cole's question. Cole was not laughing.

"BS, George said you were armed, get ready to return fire."

"Cole, I left it back in the closet. I thought it was all over." She began to tear up.

"It's okay, sis. Here take this shotgun." He handed her the weapon George had been using. Cole continued his instructions, "The guys shooting at us are going to have a hard time seeing in here until you shoot this thing at them. Once you do, they will see the muzzle flash if you didn't hit them." He did not want to use the word 'kill,' he knew his little sister was a Christian and did not want to upset her to the point that she would not shoot the weapon in order for him to get a bead on them and take them out. "So once you shoot, I want you to drop behind cover, then move to the other end of this island and fire again. Understand what I want you to do?"

"Yes"

"Okay, get ready. First, we're going to do a mad minute. Or maybe ten seconds."

"A mad minute?" Joan asked. "What the heck is a mad minute?"

"See that big tree that has the bench beside it? We are going to fire at it. That is where I saw their muzzle flash. Aim just to the right of the bench at the base of the tree. Got it?"

"Yes."

"Joan take these two shells and reload the shotgun" Joan took the shells from George and inserted them into the double barrels closed the breach raising the weapon to her shoulder.

"On three . . . one, two, three!" Helen stood up and fired her wheel gun with the rest of them causing Cole to jump sideways looking to see who else was shooting. Once the firing stopped, Cole ordered all to reload. He turned to George, "George how's the wound?"

"I think it passed through." Straining out the words.

"Where are you hit?"

George took Cole's hand and put it on the wound. It was low on the right side just above his hipbone. Cole felt around on his back. There was an exit wound . . . a large one. "Helen, get some clean damp towels. We have to stop the bleeding. George I need to see what color your blood is coming out of the exit wound." Cole turned and saw Joan looking at him. "Hey, you watch out there for the bad guys. If you see them move, tell me. We all can't be surgeons here." Cole tried to see but it was too dark, "George I can't turn a light on right now. Tell me how you feel."

Helen came back with the damp dishtowels, "Perfect, Ms. Helen. You are going to have to . . ." Joan's shotgun went off with an ear-splitting boom. Cole turned pulling his pistol, "What was it? What did you see?"

"I don't know! Somebody wearing a uniform?"

"Did you hit him? If he's a deputy, he's here to help us BS!" Cole's voice was strained, he peeked over the island. "Helen put hard pressure on both wounds. You have got to stop the bleeding first. Then get some tape and tape the rags on him. Okay?" Helen didn't answer she was too busy attending to George.

"I'm sorry. I fired before I recognized him." Joan felt terrible, thinking, *What if I shot him*?

Cole hollered out, "Deputy! Deputy!" No answer from the deputy. Cole moved to the other end of the living room behind a large couch to get a better view of the outside area. He knew if he was shot at here he had zero protection. But it did offer concealment. He peered out the windows and saw a blond streak move low across the far end of the yard where it dipped down the mountain. No shot. He watched carefully. He saw it again and then he saw the face and the shirt. Cole aimed but no shot again; *'I should have shot that guy back on the road, infuriating!'*

Martin waved his hand as if directing another. Movement caught Cole's eye off to his left it was the sheriff's deputy responding to Martin's direction! He aimed again but had no shot! *'This whole place is corrupt,'* Cole thought. *'What is going on in this town? Cops protecting the bad guys, bad guys have even worse bad guys working with them.'* Cole was confused but was determined to protect those in this house.

The stench of death began to fill the rooms. Five men lay dead like broken manikins, one barely had a head left. The floor was slick with thick, spilled body fluid mingled with blood. Cole knew for Joan and Helen it was a surreal experience to see the devastation inflicted on other human beings, to smell the blood and see the destruction of

Helen's home but both seemed to be handling it better than Cole expected. He knew once the lights came on it would be different. It's one thing to know there are dead all around you, it is another thing altogether to see them.

Joan shouted out, "Simone! Get in here now!" No answer. "Helen where's Simone?" Cole could tell she was more afraid for Simone than agitated about her not being in the room with them.

"I thought she followed us in here?" Helen said looking over her shoulder into the darker hall.

"It's been so confusing . . . I don't know if she did or not. Simone! Answer me right now!" Joan was afraid the girl could have been shot. Cole jumped up and made his way back by the trio, "Watch out side, these guys might rush us any moment. I'll go see if Simone is in the back."

With Cole's admonition George said, "Helen, hand me the pistol. I need you to go to the gun case and get more ammunition for these weapons. All the shells are in the bottom drawer. Pistol shells are on the left side and the shotgun shells are on the far right. Do not turn a light on Sweet Pea. You will have to find them by feel."

"Okay. Hon, you stay still." She could not help herself, she bent down and kissed his forehead, "I love you my hero."

"I love you too." He whispered. "Before you go Sweet Pea, help me to the corner so I can help Joan watch."

"Oh, Booger, you can't do that, honey."

"You quit that and move me over there, now." He hated being forceful with his wife but sometimes the man of the house had to demand a thing or two. Joan and Helen drug George to the edge of the island. Smokey followed growling at nothing and everything. This experience was as traumatic for the dog as it was for the people. He sat with his back against the island. Smokey sat beside him sniffing George and reassuring George he was there. His field of fire was not great but he could watch one side while Joan watched the other. His side was on fire and with each movement he felt as if he was tearing it open even more; his breathing was labored but he didn't feel like he was dying or even in any danger of dying. He was weak and hurt . . . living on adrenalin.

Cole eased his way farther into the house back to the closet where the women had taken shelter. He was glad there was carpet on the floor. As he passed a room he felt a cool breeze blow across his face and arms. He looked in the room and his eyes fell on the broken window. He froze for a split second, his breathing stopped and his hearing strained to recognize the sound. Footsteps, no, foot slides; some one's feet were sliding across the carpeted floor. Darkness engulfed this part of the house. Cole slipped his weapon into his pants at the small of his back, if it was Simone he didn't want to be the one to shoot her. Cole squatted in a corner of a doorway and began to take shallow breaths. He waited. The sliding came closer. Cole could feel the warmth the other body radiated. They were right on top of him. What is that odor? Old Spice? This is not Simone! Cole readied himself. Cole surmised the intruder would be holding a weapon out in front of him at the ready. Cole exploded up twisting his body to face the intruder; with his left arm extended feeling the intruders left knee first, then his belt, and then the triceps muscle of the intruder's upper arms as each passed Cole's upper arm area. Cole was moving fast and hard driving up against the intruders out stretched arms, into the body, lifting the body of the man up and across the hallway. Slamming the man's right shoulder into the sheet rock wall, the man's weapon discharged. Cole drove his right knee into the man's left thigh muscle. The man moaned and weakened. Cole's right hand cupped the left side of the intruder's face with his fingers wrapped around to the right side while he pulled his left arm back, wrapping it over the top and around both the man's outstretched arms pulling them into Cole's left armpit. Cole had pulled the man's head back, then pushed it hard with the heel of his hand against the wall stretching the man out. Cole slipped his body in front of the intruder's body, still with the man's arms trapped in Cole's armpit with Cole's arm over the top and wrapped under the man's arms. Cole instinctively kicked the man's left knee, knocking it out from under him; partially collapsing the man onto the floor. Cole then stretched his own torso up dislocating the man's right elbow simultaneously striking the man on his left collar bone with a right hammer fist, instantly shoving his right hand back into the man's face with the heel of his hand. He shrieked in pain dropping his weapon. Cole's right arm went from pushing the man's face to a quick and devastating elbow strike to the side of the man's head. Cole felt the man go limp and begin to slide down the wall. Cole drove his knee into the man's face hearing the crunch of facial bones.

"Cole!" Joan cried out. BOOM! Her shotgun went off again.

"What did you see, BS?" Cole shouted back as he was dragging the man into the kitchen area.

"I don't know . . . something." She raised her voice in frustration.

In the distance sirens could be heard usually a welcomed sound. Cole was not sure if it was the sound of friend or foe. He was worried.

Cole drug the man into the kitchen area, laying him on his face, he began searching him.

George spoke in a shocked tone, "Where did he come from?"

Joan turned and said, "They are coming out of the woodwork! Cole how many more are there?" Cole could tell she was almost over the top with fear. Cole did not answer and he was glad that this man proved to be an interruption; he did not want to tell everyone that Simone was nowhere to be found.

Cole moved his hands down to the man's waist. It was the deputy; he had not come here to help them but to kill them. He found the man's handcuffs. Took off the deputy's Sam Brown duty belt hooking the cuff's through the back of his pant belt insuring that if the man woke he could not slip his feet through his cuffed hands and do damage to any of them. He checked the deputy for any hidden handcuff keys or weapons not finding any he quickly drug the man out in front of their firing positions.

"Now, BS, you have a live person in front of your firing position. Do not shoot him. If he wakes talk to him and let him know where he is and tell him not to get up or he will be fired upon. Understand?"

"Yes, Cole!" She was disconcerted with all the chaos and instructions. "I understand everything you say to me. I speak English too, you know?" Cole heard George laughing.

"Ain't nothing like brothers and sisters. Gotta love 'em."

"I know BS, I love you. I'm sorry but this is important and you have not done much of this, ya know." Cole said apologetically continuing his commands. "Now listen to me. I am going outside to see if I can circumvent their idea of coming in here and us getting into another gun fight at close quarters."

"Cole, don't you dare!" Both women spoke at the same time. Helen had reentered the room her hands loaded with boxes of shells.

He ignored their protest. Cole had moved back into the hall. Turning back, he asked, "George, you good enough to handle this end?" Cole knew he could not be in both places at the same time and he knew he could do more good outside right now.

"Good enough, 'Semper FI' my friend!" George heard a low 'Uh RAH,' from the hallway. Both men smiled, nothing like having Marine on your six.

Joan suddenly felt guilty for having snapped at her brother. "George I should not have snapped at BC like that. I'm sorry."

"Hey, he understands. He just wants to protect you Joanie girl. It will be all right. He'll be back in here in a minute and you can tell him yourself, okay?"

"Okay." Joan responded weakly like a little girl that just got in trouble . . . She loved Cole . . . he was her brother but he had been her Father as well. Actually, he was her whole family.

46

"To stalk men by night's cover, takes an uncommon man."

Cole crouched by the broken window that he assumed an intruder snatched Simone from. He examined the surrounding area for movement or noise. He waited. Cole eyed his path to the nearest shadowy area and glided through the window with ease. Stopped in the shadows and looked back at the house wishing he could secure the window. Again he waited, listening; feeling the night, sniffing the air. He loved the night. He felt good in the darkness hunting his pray. He remembered where he had last sighted the big blond man and began moving cunningly, little by little, silently toward his intended target.

Minutes felt like hours to those in the house. They waited for some sign of relief, but nothing. Finally, the sirens were on their road; George could tell by the encroaching sounds. He hoped Cole was uninjured and able to not only find the man he hunted but George realized that he had not spoken to them of Simone. This concerned him at what that might mean.

The pain suddenly clamped down on his side cutting his breathing into short gasps. He slumped, sliding down the cabinet door he was resting against. Smokey whined nervously and licked his face and hands. They watched and waited. Cars skidded to a halt, heavy firetrucks engines that were noisily straining to pull themselves up the hill quieted as the engines came to idle. The drivers silenced the sirens and George could see the reflection of the red, blue and yellow lights flashing all around the house bouncing off the broken glass and stainless steel appliances behind him. He heard people yelling emergency items banging, being drug out of fire trucks and ambulances. Floodlights began spotting the dark rooms, then the loud speakers came on blearing into the night and filling the house with piercing, brassy voices. Explaining, which George always found humorous, "This is the Police . . ." well who else arrives with such commotion and force. George turned to Helen, weakly requesting her to answer the Police loud speaker, "Honey, shout out to them, let them know we are okay and that the intruders have been neutralized.

"This is Helen Booker, my husband has been shot and needs help. All our intruders are down and please come in, we are behind the kitchen island, help us, please!"

The police approached the house with caution, weapons up and eyes scanning the area, observing all the carnage left over from the gunfight that had occurred only minutes before. An Officer shouted out, "Put all weapons down and push them away from you."

The closer the Officers came the more of the slaughter they smelled and saw; the blood and bodies danced eerily into their vision as the lights bounced over the killing area. Once the officers had affirmed that the intruders were down and had removed the weapons; another form of chaos rapidly ensued. First responders swarmed the entire building, shouting "ROOM SECURE." EMTs were all over the three found squatting behind the kitchen island. Police were asking questions at the same time that EMT personnel were attempting to establish vitals and extract answers from the three concerning their medical conditions. Everyone was in shock, this was Pimsler, Colorado, not Chicago or New York; not one of the Officers nor any of the EMT responders had ever seen a crime scene like the one they were witnessing now. As they entered the house by the same route the intruders did, they slipped and stumbled over the destruction confused as to how this could have occurred in their beautiful little city.

"Mr. Booker!" George recognized the voice, Danny Cline, Robert Cline's son who he knew he could trust.

"Put your weapons down girls, slide them away from you and don't mention Cole just yet, okay?" They both look bewildered at that request but he knew they would obey. "Over here Danny!" George called with a weakening voice. Suddenly the whole world lit up. People were everywhere. Highway patrol vehicles were in the yard. County Fire rescue, Pimsler city Patrol Cars and the county ambulance service. George thought the firefight was confusing but this was a mad house with questions flying from everyone. They were asking what happened. Were you shot . . . did you fall? Did you strike your head; did the fall knock you out? George looked over at the girls and they, too were being bombarded with questions by both police and EMT's, all the while being wrapped in blankets and being examined for shock, injuries as they dug for information. George looked at the girls who were showing signs of shock and fatigue. *This is going to be a long night*, George thought. He felt funny, dizzy; sick to his stomach and very light headed, he was losing his adrenalin. His vision blurred, then narrowed and darkened. He could hear Danny Cline talking but it was as if he was far, far away and in a tunnel . . . a dark tunnel. He felt as if he was falling but not fast, from George's perspective, everyone was entering a world of shadows.

The last thing he heard was Danny Cline, "George stay with me, George! George can you hear me?" Danny heard George call for Helen,

"Sweet Pea?" Then George asked, "Where's Cole, is he okay?"

Cole had moved around to the front of the property. When the emergency vehicles arrived, he used the noise and commotion of it all to move quicker through the underbrush. As he suspected, Martin was moving away from the possibility of capture as well. Cole heard him first, then saw a flash of white before everything went dark . . . too far from the lights up the hill at George's house. Cole anticipated Blondie's escape route. Cole matched his pace without being heard or seen by the big man. Cole had traveled this route earlier, thinking that Martin and Deputy Ortega also had walked the distance from where Captain Henry was lying dead. Cole heard a car door shut and a car engine start. He began running. Lights appeared and he saw a patrol car backing down the roadway away from the Bookers residence. The car was trying to turn around in an area of the road that was too narrow . . . straight down on one side and straight up on the other. Cole picked up a rock. He ran faster focusing in on the driver's window. He had to get there before Martin got the car completely reversed and heading the opposite direction. Cole stretched his stride length. Martin was making one more adjustment in the U-turn and was looking to his right, down the road, as Cole approached from the left.

Martin's driver-side window exploded with the rock coming through the window striking him on the shoulder followed by Cole coming into the vehicle all the way to his waist shoving Martin across the seat and forcing his head into the computer console. Cole backed out of the window holding Martin by the head. His right hand was full of Martin's hair and his left was across Martin's face with his fingers under the bigger man's nose pressing the cartilage up toward Martin's eyes. Martin's eyes filled with tears, he reached up grabbing Cole's hand as Cole jerked him all the way out of the patrol car. The two men exited the window with the car slowly rolling downhill. As the two men cleared the window, Cole rolled his body to the left landing on top of Martin. During the fall, Cole repositioned his right arm so that when he landed his fore arm was across Martin's throat. Cole landed with his knees up under his torso directly on top of Martin's chest. Cole heard the air depart Martin's chest with a rush and a groan through his nose and mouth. However, with his arm across the big man's throat; no air could return. Martin gasped and clawed like a drowning man. He kicked and thrashed at Cole. His eyes were wide with desperation. Cole drew his head down onto Martin's chest straddling Martin's torso, like an MMA fighter, then, true to form, Cole began to pound on the big man's soft sides. No air could possibly reenter the big man's lungs. Cole heard the patrol car crash into the trees off the roadway not far down from where he was beating his would be killer into submission. As Cole's blows began the intended damage, Martin pulled his arms down to protect his sides. Cole went instantly from his sides to his head, then down to his sides again as Martin tried to protect his head, raining down elbow strikes and fists, in seconds, the big man lost his ability to defend himself altogether. He was not out but as close as one could be without being unconscious. Cole flipped the bigger man over on to his stomach and repeated his belt trick, trussing Martin's hands behind him; lifting him to his feet holding on to the belt. Martin cursed Cole through the pain of having his arms jacked up behind him lifting the entire weight of the big man by his shoulders and awkwardly bent elbow sockets.

"Glad to see you got your breath back. I would have hated to have had to drag you behind the patrol car, Marty."

Martin, coughing and splattering blood as he swore at Cole, promising he would see him dead. Cole reached up and struck Martin hard across his right ear causing it to ring and swell even more. "Marty we are going to be civil to each other, aren't we?"

"What do you want?" Martin said spitting the words out through absolute hatred.

"Well, first of all, what happened back where you ran Preacher Pete off the road? Did an ambulance show up?"

"No, the man woke up and beat me in the back and head with a rock. I woke up to Ortega taking the handcuffs off me."

Cole began to laugh, "So the little man slammed a rock into your head," Cole felt pride well up in him for Pete. "And then what happened?" Cole still laughing.

"I told you he knocked me out. I don't know what happened next."

"So the deputy is your pal, I am assuming. You and he went up to the Bookers home to back up the other murdering thieves trying to get Simone and to kill the others. Is that right?"

Martin didn't answer. Cole had his hand on the belt that held Martin's hands. Cole wiggled Martin's arms and hands, "Is that right?" Cole waited a breath. No answer from the big man. Cole, pulled back hard on Martin's arms and kicked his right leg out from under him. Martin hit the rocky road flat of his back banging his head and crushing his hands under the weight of his body.

Cole squatted down pushing his knee into Martin's sternum, "Like to cooperate or do you want me to show you more tricks?"

Martin was coughing hard, trying to regain his breath yet again.

Cole continued, "I don't know Martin but I'm-a-thinkin' about cuttin' a finger off every time you make it hard on me. That would be better than slammin' you around. Don't you think? So I am going to roll you over and start asking you questions and if I don't get the answer quick enough . . . I cut a finger off." Cole flipped Martin over onto his stomach. Martin heard the distinctive click of a locking blade opening and locking in place. He tried to get his feet under him to run but Cole jumped on his back. He was setting on Martin's shoulders facing

Martin's feet. Cole gathered the belt and pulled it up hard, then touched Martin's little finger on his left hand where he had a beautiful diamond pinky ring.

"I decided to go ahead and cut this one off first before I ask questions just to let you know I mean business. Okay?" Cole knew the threat of gross pain was at times as terrifying as the act itself. He didn't figure on the response he got from Martin. Cole held the blade to the finger and pressed the blade into the flesh bringing blood.

"What do you want to know, MAN? Ask me! I'm not in love with any of these guys! Come on, ask your questions!" Cole heard the fear in Martin's voice. Curious, Cole thought; did Martin's fear come from his own torturing of people? Cole did not know how Martin loved to make people scream in pain but when faced with the possibility of his own torture experience he could not stand the thought of it, for Martin knew the ultimate result, disfigurement and eventually death.

"The girl is missing, where is she and who took her?" Cole waited.

"David Clark, I guess."

"Why is he after her like this?" Cole was confused about this whole thing.

"She knows too much, and David is afraid she is going to tell. He's going to fly out to California to his studios and put her in some porn films or maybe another kind of film." Martin did not tell the whole truth.

"There's got to be more to it." Cole said to himself as well as to Martin. Cole was silent a moment contemplating this new information.

"Fly out from Pimsler Airport?"

"Yeah."

"Where in California are his studios? And what other kind of films are you talking about?"

"Santa Barbra. Off the Pacific Coast Highway. I have the address in my wallet. It's on my business card. I don't know just other films." Martin was being vague for good reason, known only to him at the moment.

"You have an illegal business and you have a card that tells everybody where it is?"

"It's not all illegal!" Martin protested.

"You people are stupid. How many local cops are involved with your operation?"

"One on the sheriff's department, I guess you got him and maybe three or four on the PD. Captain Don took care of all the security . . . so I'm not sure how many." Cole was digging in Martin's back pocket for a business card.

"How many are as actively involved in the business as you are?"

"Two PD guys. What are you going to do with me?" Cole could hear the twinge of fear in Martin's voice. "I haven't decided yet." Cole's was distracted digging in Martin's back pocket pulling out his wallet. He clicked on his flashlight and became lost in shock, as he looked through pictures he found in the wallet; grotesque photos of a nude Martin with what looked to be naked, dead women.

"Are these women dead, Martin?" Martin stiffened. Cole felt nauseated just being this close to a man this mentally ill. Criminally ill people always keep mementoes of their victims; Martin was no different. Cole was beginning to get the bigger picture of Martin's business. Cole didn't know what to do with this monster. If left for the police, he could conveniently escape while awaiting trial or he might never even make it to the jailhouse. He was not willing to lose his eye witness. He was sure he could make Martin sing like an opera star, to the right people.

"Get up!" Cole was fuming.

What separates the good from the bad; evil from the righteous, Cole wondered as he drug Martin off the ground. *Is it knowledge of right and wrong? Is it the law that one chooses to obey or not? No,* Cole thought *it is the constant driving powers of love thy neighbor more than self. It is above all this worldly filth and weakness toward evil. It has to do with God. It is not in man to do good.* Cole was sure of it, *it is God in man that drives him to protect the innocent, feed the hungry, heal the sick and love the unlovable. For man does not do this inherently. There has to be a God above all . . . this can't be all there is to life?* Cole felt empty but was determined to first get to the underlying cause of this craziness, protect his sister and then to the greater questions concerning life, his own life!

47

Wealth and power can corrupt but evil is designed to take life, all life.

David's G5 took off from Pimsler Executive Airport destined for Santa Barbara, California, with Carl, Sunny, the four girls and Simone; who were fated for unspeakable horrors for others' wicked ecstasy, depending on which side of the camera you were on. David patted himself on his back for his stealthy snatch and escape with Simone while all the others were keeping the Bookers busy. He hoped Little Dave killed them all, even Joan. He had no other use for her . . . kill her boys. It charged him up just saying the words in his mind. And he didn't even give them their fees! David laughed to himself and thought, *Well, that is the way it goes boys, win some and loose some.* But now what to do about Randal; who was none too happy about leaving in the middle of the night with children on board. David knew Randal would tolerate a lot of nasty business, but was wondering how far he would go before he had enough.

This, in Randal's mind, was way over the top. When he asked David about it all he received a glaring look and David raising his voice shouting, "Drive the plane!" No other response. Randal had never trusted David and knew in his heart of hearts that David was not, in any way, a man he needed to associate with; but the money was to good and he had made the excuse of saying to himself,' I'll get out someday.' But some day never came. David had always concerned him but, now, he could tell something had changed in David; he seemed a darker and more sinister man.

Randal flew the plane, like the good little pilot he was . . . no further questions asked, no further answers needed, as he contemplated escape.

David knew Randal knew too much about his business. Something was going to have to be done about Randal, although, David did not know just what and was not sure when. After all, he needed him for a little while longer.

David sat in the back of the plane allowing Carl and Sunny to handle the girls. "Keep them quiet!" Was the only order he gave the two. David was in deep thought concerning his dilemma. He knew he was a smart guy, after all, how could he have kept an organization this size, this lucrative, this long and have kept off the local police and federal boy's radar; if he weren't good at what he did! But now he needed to consider alternatives. David mentally went through his present circumstances. *First, where was Don and why was he not answering his phone? Surly the intruder didn't get the drop on Don? Who was this intruder? Had Martin gotten away; he wasn't answering his phone? Did Martin end Pete's life? Who was this intruder! And why was he intruding? How much did the Police know? The good guy police,* not his rent-a-cops, he despised cops but realized they were a necessary evil. So the first conclusion; *forget the others.*

He needed to protect himself, *if they were not man enough to keep up, then they are on their own. They can pull themselves out of the swamp. By the time this plays out,* David thought, *I will be long gone. Secondly,* he contemplated, *I need to get to my safe and clean it out. Get the cash and prepare to leave the country. Third, I know I have a buyer for the four girls. I'll even considered taking a discount to move them faster. I could get $200,000 for all four, at discounted prices; they were prime property. With what I have in the safe and the money I can get for the girls; this would help get me set up somewhere else. Now, what to do about Simone?* He looked at her long and hard. She was gorgeous and he was captured by his lust because of her looks . . . that was all that mattered anyway. There was no love in him, not as a righteous man loved. He knew in the right market she by herself would bring $250k, even as tarnished goods. She was stunning, a young and beautifully developed women, despite the loss of her virginity. He again mused, *I will bring her back to the back with me and take advantage of the long flight.* However, He scowled, *if she started a fight it would create a problem with Randal, what an idiot. Randal did not know what he was missing.* David dismissed the idea for the moment.

So review the plan: Call the buyer, arrange a meeting and a transfer of the girls; COLLECT THE MONEY . . . TODAY! Get to the office, empty the safe. Walk away and take Simone with me. Carl and Sunny? If they are caught . . . they cannot be trusted. Once the transfer is completed get them back to the office . . . I have a gun in the safe. I'll do it myself! I don't even have to clean up . . . I'll be out of the country before anyone finds them. Then off to the airport again and where to go? Somewhere where there is no US extradition. Where? I will call my attorney; he'll know. Then get Randal of my back after he flies me to wherever. Can't leave him walking around, he's mad at me already. He would walk straight to the police. Sorry Randy old Pal, you've been a great pilot and I know you have enjoyed the fringe benefits. But as they say, 'it's just business.'

David sat back relaxed and confident that he had a well-oiled plan and he could execute it with precision. He was happy in the optimism of his pending good fortune. A rich man with rich ideas and unafraid to do what was needed to accomplish them. He thought, *Sounds like some of our politicians.* He laughed out loud knowing how many of those politicians he had done business with.

48

Light and life. Are they the same thing?

Emergency crews were transporting George and had allowed Helen to accompany them in the ambulance. She was worried . . . he had passed out and had not revived. The paramedics said his blood pressure was low and had him on oxygen with an I.V. drip in his arm but everything else seemed to be stable, whatever that means. The crew had already contacted the ER doctor and were receiving further instruction; the ER was preparing for a gunshot victim based on George's age, weight, ethnicity and vitals. Helen was reassured that George was in great shape for his age and not to worry. They we're going to do all they could. He will be fine, they kept saying to her. She worried . . . then she prayed and had told Joan to pray before she left in the ambulance with George and the EMTs. Joan had already been praying about everyone involved in this fiasco. How could all this have happened and where was her brother! She was horrified to realize that things like this really happen to people in the United States of America. Joan prayed more specifically. Her phone rang, she moved away from the Law Enforcement Officers to take the call. They were too busy taking photos, measurements of where all the dead lie, gathering evidence and interrogating the deputy that Cole had trussed up like a chicken dinner, to notice she had stepped away from them. The interrogators could not get information fast enough from Ortega; he had to write all his answers. One side of his face looked like a basketball and the other side was black from being slammed into the wall. Cole had broken his jaw and dislocated his writing arm's elbow. Therefore, he couldn't speak and was writing with his left hand which was cuffed to his broken right arm. The police were waiting for another EMT to transport Ortega to the hospital. He was still in hand cuffs although the responding Officers had moved them to his front so he could write.

"Brady Cole, are you okay? Where are you?" She said half in tears.

"I am just fine Sis. What's going on there?" It aggravated her sometimes with how cool and calm he always seemed to be. *Sometimes,* she thought, *he needed to be human and scream or cry or something.* But that was not Brady Cole; her Brother and her hero.

"Well, the emergency crews have transported George to the

hospital. BC, he passed out and they could not revive him! I'm scared for them."

"Sis he lost a lot of blood. He's a fighter though and he is in good hands; let them do their magic and we will see, that's all we can do. Do not second guess this, it won't do you any good" Cole said trying to comfort his Sister with truth. "What else has happened?"

"George told us, of course, before he passed out, not to mention your name or your involvement yet. At least not until we have a chance to talk to you."

"A good Marine to the end, George is a wise man, Sis. I am going to have to thank him for his insight. I think this David guy has Simone and is heading to California. He is a bad man, Sis." Cole did not want to upset his sister any further . . . he didn't tell her of David's porn studios and the possible involvement in Martin's murdering women . . . someone had to take the photos Cole had taken from Martin. "I think if we're going to get her back, in one piece, BS, I need to head that direction as soon as I can. Is there any way you can get a picture of this man to me?"

"Oh, BC . . . I knew he was wicked! Yes I can, I think he is in the church directory. I can take a picture with my phone and text it to you. How are you going to do all that? David is so dangerous. Don't go by yourself." She was frightened for him.

"The church directory! He goes to church with you?" Cole was shocked.

"Well . . . yes," Cole could tell that statement embarrassed her. "He is a Deacon . . . crazy I know. Things happen in an imperfect world big brother."

"So you guys don't screen applicants before they join the church or something?"

"If you're really interested I will explain how it all works when I see you again. But I want you to listen and not make fun of everything. This is the most important thing in the world and you need to hear it, okay?" She felt she was being a little pushy but she thought she had to be with such a knot head.

"Okay, I will. I promise. I am interested, Sis, very interested. And don't worry; I won't be going alone. I need to make some calls. I'll call you back in a bit. Okay?"

Before Cole could hang up Joan came back with another concern, "Do you think you can get her back before he does something horrible to her?"

"That's the plan. Let me get this going and I'll call back in a bit."

Joan didn't want to let her brother off the phone, "All right but you call me back ASAP. Okay? Cole, I love you, take care of yourself, please." Joan knew how dangerous David was but as family goes, sometimes, they forget or even underestimate their own warriors. Cole thought a prophet has no honor in his own home; after all these years. "Okay, I'll call you back, Sis." Cole said a little exasperated.

Cole pushed end and dialed his teammates.

Joan was approached again by one of the officers, returning to ask more questions, when she and he suddenly heard thrashing noises in the bushes. The officer, placing his hand on his service weapon, walked toward the noise, readying himself.

All during the fire fight as he wondered through the woods . . . Pastor Pete went in and out of consciousness. He passed out twice but revived and walked toward the shouts and gunfire. Now he had a clear path because of the noise, all the lights and people. He knew he needed help after wondering in the woods falling, scrapping and cutting himself in the underbrush . . . he was worse off than when he had started.

Pete stepped out from the bushes not knowing where he was, delirious from blood loss, exhausted, hypothermic and dehydrated. He stumbled reaching out his hand toward the two and collapsed. In a course whisper, "help . . . please, Help me." The last words Pete spoke before his eye closed.

49

*The Lord said, I will blot out man whom I have created from the face of
the land . . . For I am sorry that I have made them.*

God

Cole snatched up Martin and headed for the patrol car. It was still idling with its headlights shining into the woods. The patrol car had idled down to a curve in the road a hundred feet from where the two had struggled for supremacy and struck a tree not twelve inches off the dirt road. The buddy bumper had absorbed the impact of the crash keeping the car from sustaining any real damage. Cole walked around to the front passenger's door pushing Martin in front of him. Cole opened the door and pushed Martin down on his knees bending him face first onto the seat putting his left knee between Martin's legs, pressing his knee forward against Martin's backside, pinning Martin to the car. Cole then looked through the deputy's brief case and pulled out plastic-cuffs. He replaced the belt with the cuffs, moved the briefcase to the backseat placing Martin in the front and seat belted him in. Then just as an added precaution, Cole took two more plastic-cuffs strapped his feet together making it doubly difficult for Martin to move in the already tight space. Cole jumped in the driver's seat and turned the unit around, figuring that it would be easier for them to sneak by the ruckus at the Bookers home than to drive by the roadblock down the dirt road where Captain Henry lay dead; if there was anyone working that crime scene? Cole did not want to chance it. He also needed to pick up his go bag he had hid off the roadway before he entered the Booker's home. He had to be precise and quick about recovering the bag. He was in a stolen patrol car and had basically kidnapped a citizen; a citizen that looked like he just went through a meat grinder, the left side his head behind his ear was hugely swollen, one eye closed from an elbow strike, one tooth missing, an ear that was quickly turning cauliflowered and clothes that were bloody and ripped to shreds. Not to mention what a lawman would think if he saw Martin zip-tied up like a bag of beans. If caught it would mean time wasted and losing the girl for good. Cole stopped at the spot where he had left his bag. He looked at Martin, tore part of Martin's shirt that was in rags already and stuffed it in his mouth, just in case, dirt, blood and all. From where Cole was retrieving the bag he could see the Booker's property and hear voices. He listened and overheard Joan and a man talking. Cole could tell he was an Officer of the law. He could tell by the calmness of the conversation that things had smoothed out and she was being taken care of. He jumped back into the car keeping the door open, putting it in gear and idling the vehicle down the road as quietly as possible.

Cole knew that the police would figure out that there had been another shooter as soon as the departments M. E. began looking at the angles of entry and exit wounds, as well as, the expended brass. George would have to come clean about him. Cole decided to make a beeline to the airport and wait for Goose. He turned to Martin, "You look horrible, man! But I think this will make you feel better. We're going to California." Cole picked up his cell and dialed Hatch.

Cole explained the situation to Hatch who advised he would get the Team together, load up necessary equipment catch commercial flights to Santa Barbara and call when they were together at the airport. Cole hit end looking at Martin, "Son, you now have a heap of trouble coming your way. We are going to have a serious conversation about your partner's California organization. I want to know all about it, including who his partners are. Is he selling girls internationally? What kind of assets does he have access to? Has he recruited local police as his security? How does he transport the girls he sells; where does he make his porn films, who are his directors and actors, everything, Martin." Cole looked back out the windshield and followed up with, "I am not going to go easy on you any longer. I will get all the information I need . . . it will be up to you how I get it. But make no mistake . . ." Cole looked back at Martin who was looking at Cole with part of the rag hanging out of his mouth, "I will get all the information you have. That's a promise."

Martin, needed to swallow badly but could not because of the rag, he just looked away. For Martin saw that Cole's face had change from human to beast and it startled him.

Cole was not just going to get the girl back but after seeing Martin's photos; Cole had decided to shut David Clark's entire operation down putting them out of business permanently. If he had to chase the man and his group around the world he would jail them, cripple them or kill them but he was going to stop them. Moreover, he knew his team would back him to the end.

The sky was turning pink and orange as the world turned east looking for the Sun. It was close to five in the morning and cold in Colorado. It had been a long night and Cole was ready for someone else to man up so he could get a little rest. He drove the now stolen patrol car through the airport entrance. Hiding it between two hangers, Cole unloaded his bag, gathered more plastic cuffs and anything else he might need that the deputy was not going to be needing any longer. It was as quiet as a grave at the Pimsler Executive Airport. The only noise that could be heard other than the bird's chirping was Martin's moans as Cole drug him out of the car shoving him against the patrol car and balancing him on his zip tied feet. No mercy asked, none given, of course he couldn't ask with the rag in his mouth. Cole heard the distinctive roar of the twin Beech coming in for a landing. Hopefully they could get off the ground and away from the airport without being seen. Cole's last responsibility was to wipe the car as clean as he could of all his fingerprints. Lock the unit up and stand by for Goose to taxi the plane close enough to board with Martin, without being seen.

50

We leave this world when our jobs are done.

GEORGE Brian Booker Sr., was reading his own obituary in his mind's eye as he came out of the drug-induced coma. He heard an angel's voice softly speaking to him, "Booger can you hear me, Hon?"

Booger's eyes fluttered as he attempted to focus on the face that had been by his side for almost 50 years, "Give me a kiss before my wife gets here, beautiful . . . if she sees you she'll spank both of us . . ." Booger waited a beat before his face betrayed his humor, "Hi Sweet Pea." His voice was still weak and hoarse from the oxygen and drugs used during the surgery. He puckered his lips for a kiss as Helen took her turn running her hands affectionately through his hair and placing her soft palm against his cheek, leaning in close to his face, she replied, "The doctor said not to get you excited . . ." She straightened up backing away her voice flat, "So that kiss will have to wait."

"Aw, Sweat Pea."

There was silence between the two as Helen puttered around the Hospital recovery room. George lay with his eyes closed as he pushed his mind and body closer to full consciousness. He began to remember the trauma of the fire fight at his home. He began to recall all those that had been involved. His mind began to ask questions. He felt warmth close to his face, then the soft lips of his lovely wife. "I couldn't play the game any longer." She said as tears rolled down he cheeks, kissing him again and again. Her eyes, filled with tears. "I love you, my hero. Let's not do anything like this again Booger. I don't know what I would do if I lost you."

"You're not that lucky Sweat Pea. I'm here for the duration. How are the girls?" His voice grew stronger just by her presence, gaining a serious tone.

Helen was not ready to explain everything to her husband who had an over grown sense of responsibility to everyone in his life. But she also knew he would not stand for anything but the whole truth once his mind began to ask questions. "Booger are you sure you are ready to begin this conversation? You just got out of surgery. The doctors are saying that you need to rest and recover before you begin to concern yourself with anything."

"Where are Joan and Simone, Sweet Pea? I need to know if everyone is all right."

"Joan is fine she is in the hall waiting to come in and see you."

"Well, bring her in." Helen walked to the door and called out to Joan who entered and walked to the side of George's hospital bed.

"How are you, Joanie?" George said it as if she was his daughter.

"How am I . . . how are you? I'm not the one who has been all shot up."

George chuckled and smiled at her, then reached for Helen's hand. "Well, better me than you girl. I got more body mass to protect my vitals with than either one of you. Tell me, how is Simone? Is she okay? She didn't get hurt in the ruckus at the house, did she?"

Helen let go of George's hand and walked to the other side of the bed, sitting down on the edge taking his right hand. "Pull up that chair Joan." Helen ordered.

"What's going on girls? What's happened to Simone?" George said moving his eyes between the two women seated on either side of him. The two traded glances before Helen unloaded the rest of the story. George laid still looking into Helen's beautiful face knowing that once he pressed her she would tell the whole story. Helen knew her husband well and knew his strength of character. He could handle the truth and would not stand for anything but the truth once he asked for it. Helen spoke of Simone's kidnapping and Pete Donny showing up all beat up and shot. All the dead in the house . . . the shock of seeing all the evil that people do. "Is Smokey okay?" George's eyes went sad a little when he asked about his buddy.

"Yes, honey, SMOKEY is fine. He's at home waiting for you." Helen said with a smile knowing George's love for that big dog.

"Where's Cole?" George asked.

"Well, when he went out of the house to stop any more attacks on us, he never came back." Helen replied. George looked at Joan, "Did the police pick him up?"

"No, we would know if they would have picked him up. I think he is looking for whoever took Simone. Once he got outside the house all the firing stopped, you know. I think he found the last ones and then went to find Simone."

"Do you think David got her? You know, I saw David look in the front window just before the shooting started."

Helen quietly responded, "Yes, we think David broke in and snatched her out of the house during all the confusion. But we don't know if it was actually David or one of his men."

George continued his thoughts. "Well, I know Cole could not let the police find him there. I am sure he thought it best that he go after David or whoever. You know his number one priority, now, is recovering the girl and finding David and his henchmen." George said with disgust in his voice. The door to the private recovery room opened and the surgeon strolled in looking at the three. "Well, George, I can see you're in good hands. How are you feeling?"

Typical of the Booger's resilient nature, George responded with more strength in his voice than his body had, "Shoot me full of some go juice, Doc. I got things to do."

"Slow down, big guy. You have been through a lot. We gave you enough blood to jump-start a Clydesdale. Let me take a look here." As he took George's wrist in his hand feeling for a pulse. The doctor then pulled George's eyelids back one at a time, taking a look in his eyes after which he began to listen to his heart and chest area with his stethoscope. He walked to the side of the bed that Helen was on pulling up George's gown looking at his wound and pushing all around it, as doctors tend to do. "How do you feel, George, honestly?"

"I have felt better but . . . I think I am okay. What kind of damage did the bullet do?"

"God was on your side there. It passed through without hitting any vital areas. Your biggest problem was blood loss and now possible infection. We have cleaned the wound, put in a drain port, shot you full of antibiotics and as you can see, we are letting it drain. Hoping that will keep any infection from growing. I think you'll be fine if you give yourself the time to recover." The doctor said that while looking hard into George's eyes, knowing his patient.

"I hear you, Doc." George said. Helen spoke up as well, "We hear him too, Booger. Just so you will know. And we are going to do everything he says, understand?"

"Yeesss, Sweet Pea, I understand you're in charge now. Can't fight the establishment lying flat on my back." George said eyeing his best friend and wife.

The doctor turned to leave, but as he got to the door, he turned back, "There are two state troopers out here that want to speak with you. Are you up for it?"

"Sure, Doc, send them in. And, Doc, thanks for all you did for me," George said appreciatively.

"Just doing my job, George. But I do not want to see you in here, ever again, with bullet holes in your body . . . okay?"

"It's a deal. Thanks again, Doc." He turned and held the door open for the Lawmen, "Not too long boys, he's still pretty weak." The two acknowledge the doctor's orders, then entered the room looking at the trio.

51

Victory loves preparation.

Goose taxied the E 18 Beech to where Cole directed him. Goose brought the plane to a stop, setting the brakes, leaving the twin engines running, exiting from the door on the portside of the aircraft. Stepping onto the tarmac Goose hollered out, "Who's this?" Taking a hard look at the big bloodied, blond guy all trussed up.

"My witness." Cole hollered back. "We need to interview him when we have time. Here look at these pictures I took off him." Cole handed the photos to Goose.

"What the—are these women dead?" Goose stood dumbfounded as he tried to take make sense of the grotesque photos.

"Yeah, they are. Say Martin, explain your snap shots to Goose." Martin turned away leaning against the patrol car with the rag still dangling from his mouth.

"You are a sick puppy, son." Goose spit in Martin's direction, then handed the photos back to Cole, "What are we going to do with him? I vote we get up to 20,000 feet and throw him out?" Martin turned wide-eyed looking at the two men debating his fate.

"I need him for a while. He has information that we need but after that I'll turn him over to you, if you want? You can dispose of him." Both men knew the next trustee for Martin would be the Santa Barbara District Attorney's office, although they were not only going to get the information they needed . . . they were going to scare Martin to death doing it. Goose walked over to Martin and pushed him down on the asphalt. Seeing that his feet were zipped tied together it didn't take much effort on Goose's part. The big man slid down the side of the patrol car doing the best he could not to injure himself. Martin muffled a curse at Goose, muffling out strange pain sounds as he hit the ground. Cole took out four more zip-ties connecting two together and placing them around Martin's thighs just above his knees and two more in the same manner around his arms just above his elbows. They picked him up and hauled him to the plane sliding him in through the door like a sack of potatoes. It took both Goose and Cole to shove their prisoner into the Beech E 18. Goose log rolled him into the cargo area in the back of the plane strapping him in with the cargo net. "You be good, boy. Or I will come back here and throw you out of MY plane myself. Understand or do you need a demonstration?" Goose pulled the zip tie tighter on Martins wrist looking the psycho in the eyes. Martin was afraid to even try to say anything . . . it was his first time to be at the mercy of another person, he didn't like it and didn't want to aggravate the situation. Besides he instinctively knew this man strapping him in had no compunction about doing what he threatened.

Cole sat in one of the six captain type lounge chairs that extended back and made into a bed of sorts. He shut his eyes and felt Goose pull the plane into the air. The morning was turning exceptionally bright, as far as Colorado mornings go; the clear and cool air seemed to suspend the light, giving the ground a golden glow. Cole was glad the sun was behind them as they climbed into the western skies pointing the nose west.

He was exhausted and stressed from the chasing, the gunplay, the killing; capturing a truly demented soul and now the thought of another pursuit of evil. The kind of evil only people can perpetrate on people. But is evil fueled just by people? Cole wondered in the darkness of his mind as he allowed his thoughts to vanish into the recesses of his sub conscious. He wanted to think more about the deeper reaching possibilities of eternity but his mind was as tired as his body. He allowed the plane's droning engines to lull him into the restless no man's land between sleep and consciousness. He heard Goose singing Silver Wings followed by On the Road Again. He wished Goose either had better vocals or that he would shut-up. Goose got to the end of On the Road Again and fell silent. Cole began slipping into comfortable darkness when the words of the song 'The Lonesome Whippoorwill' by Hank Williams began ringing in his ears. Loud and proud like Goose does everything. Discipline will always rule the day . . . Cole enabled that area of his brain and slipped into the comfort of darkness despite Goose and his rancid singing.

The plane flew on while images of the dead came back to life, playing with Cole's emotions, dancing in front of his eyes like a nineteenth century slide show; images flickering in darkness as he glimpsed them as if through candle light. He watched Captain Don die again, witnessing the hole in his chest spread out as a red rose opens its petals. He watched as dark fire lay across Captain Don like a blanket spreading out on the ground consuming his body. Cole moved and moaned in his sleep, rolling over to his side trying to find a comfortable spot for his mind. He felt the heat when his team took down the two Mexican Policemen. He heard the shotgun blast out the rubber bullets but it was not bullets, it was a liquorish fire. A sticky black flame that engulfed the two men, hot even from great distances. He flew through his dream like an apparition; appearing here, then there. He felt fear, deep fear. He struggled to escape from an unfathomable abyss that he could not see but felt, it clawed at him, pulling him closer to certain death. There was no light but he could see, no wind when he flew but he felt hot air. No odors but the rancid smell of burning flesh, no sounds but the distant screams of the dying. Horror surrounded him. Martin came out of the shadows wearing blood soaked clothing holding the dead women in his left hand and knives in his right. He had no face, no eyes, and no nose; just a crooked mouth laughing at him . . . he heard the dead women calling him to save the children. He looked at them as Martin twirled them and played with them, he saw their dead mouths contorted, although speaking. Cole was sweating and fighting the monster in his mind tearing away any semblance of peaceful slumber. Cole wanted to cry but men don't cry. He found himself on the edge of a precipice somehow aware that he was going to be thrown off or lose his balance and fall to his death. When he heard a voice . . . sweat and gentle, "Cole . . . Cole, save me, Cole." Cole turned in his dream looking for the location of the voice. "Cole, help me!" The tiny voice called him.

He became frantic and called out, not knowing if it was his dream or reality. "Where are you!" Cole cried out, "I CAN'T FIND YOU!"

"Cole, save me. I'm here!" A sweat voice crying in pain and anguish for Cole to rescue her.

He was in a panic. Martin twirled the women, throwing their dead decaying bodies in his path. The abyss clawed at his feet and legs drawing blood and digging into the muscle of his calves. The dark fire was all around, hindering him from seeing, burning his eyes and hands as he groped for direction. The darkness was like thick mud, clinging to any part of him that touched it. He tore his way through it. He fought his exhaustion created by the pain from the abyss and fire. The fear of not being there to rescue, the tiny voice crushed in on him, heightening his fear, but he pushed on. He fought the monsters that he could not see. He fell onto the sticky, black fire. He cried out in the pain only defeat can bring. Defeat from the knowledge that your failure caused the torturous death of the innocent. He began to weep in profound sorrow. He cried out, "Dear God, help me! Help me save them!" He buried his face in his hands trying to wake fighting his slumber. It held him in darkness and would not let him go. He rolled in the chair and begged God in his mind to release him from this agony. As he lay weeping trying to push himself out of the mire . . . he felt tiny hands lifting his head. The hands lovingly holding his face, gently raising him from his peril of certain death. He opened his eyes looking at his savior. Tiny Callie, affectionately lifted him speaking softly, "Jesus loves you Cole. He will save you as you have saved others just like me." Her appearance was bright; shining like a golden light was glowing from behind her face. Cole felt comfort, peace, even reconciliation with God.

He looked around and saw others he had rescued standing and smiling at him. Even those that didn't survive the attempted rescues were there enjoying the company of the saved. They were clean and in white clothes, standing in bright, warm light. There was no fear, no blood, and no anguish seen on their faces. All were content and joyful. From the far end of the scene a bright light began to glow brighter and brighter; a wonderful voice spoke from the Light, "Come to me all who are weary and heavy laden, and I will give you rest. Take My yoke upon you and learn from Me, for I am gentle and humble in heart, and you will find rest for your souls. For My yoke is easy and My burden is light." He felt Callie's arms wrap around his neck and squeeze tight; as his eyes opened her voice faded into a soft echo, "We love you Cole."

Cole felt strangely consoled. He sensed a release from the stress of the dream or was it a vision, he didn't know. All he recognized was that there was more to this spiritual stuff or whatever you called it, than he knew and he was more determined than ever to find out. He reached up and rubbed his face feeling his wet cheeks realizing he had been crying throughout his dream. He wiped his face on his shirtsleeve, set his chair up right and touched Goose on the shoulder. "Where are we?"

"We're in the plane. Where do you want to be?" Goose spoke over his shoulder, understanding perfectly what Cole was asking but could not help himself.

"Okay, how far from Santa Barbara?"

"Oh, forty-five minutes or so. You were rather fitful back there. Bad dreams?" They all had dreams, some worse than others, none of which they were willing to talk about. Goose understood a warriors struggle.

Cole turned to his prisoner, easing himself to the back of the plane avoiding a response to Goose. His mind swam with more questions than answers from his dream. However, some answers he decided he was going to uncover before they touched down in Santa Barbara.

Cole grabbed the dangling rag and jerked.

52

"Now know the full power of evil . . . it makes ugliness seem beautiful and goodness seem ugly and weak."

August Stindberg

David had made his call to his buyer while in the air. The buyer was called the Gringo; a filthy, sweaty, obese American who found it easier to bribe the Mexican Police with little white girls. Allowing him to do his criminal activity down south of the border rather than to live in America and fight the system; after all the system was always looking for his type.

The G5 touched down and taxied to a hanger rented by David's organization. The plane disappeared into the hanger. David ordered that one of his cars stored in the hanger be brought close to the plane. Telling Carl to close the hanger doors before Carl and Sunny made the transfer of his girls from the plane to the limo. When all was secure he would send Carl to the buyer's place of business and consummate the sale of the girls. He then would proceed back to the studios and collect his stash. He looked at Sunny, concluding, she had worked too long for him. He smiled to himself.

"What's so amusing?" Sonny asked as she observed his mannerisms.

"Just thinking of all the happy times coming, that's all. Get these girls out and into the limo." David ordered. He didn't like talking to dead people and that is what Sonny was to him . . . a corpse! She obeyed and hustled them into the limo where they waited for the subsequent possessor of their life.

****

It had been several hours and George was feeling a little stronger. Helen and Joan left the hospital to go home to rest and clean up. The state troopers had asked all the questions they needed to at the moment with the stipulation that they would return as they needed. George knew they would return. You can't have a shootout at your house with five dead biker types, one dead cop, a deputy sheriff half beat to death at the crime scene; who tried to kill civilians, a kidnapped girl and not have weeks of questioning. So, he knew they would return. He also knew he needed to speak with Cole at some point and soon.

The nurse entered his room with his lunch. "I've been meaning to ask if there is a man in the hospital named Peter Donny?" George waited for an answer.

"As a matter of fact there is. He is just down the hall. Is he your friend?"

"He's my preacher. He was on the way to my house when he was accosted by the same men that attacked my family and me. How's he doing? Is he hurt badly?"

"Well, he is in much worse shape than you are. He was beaten severally and shot in the back. But he is stable and awake." She stated as only a trauma nurse can.

"I was thinking of going to see him . . . in a little while, of course." Booker was looking at the disapproving stare from her.

"It might do him good, when you feel better yourself. I'm sure it would make him feel better. He is in room 512W. Down the hall and turn to the left at the nurse's station. His room is the first on the right. He will not be leaving anytime soon and you will not be getting up without my permission and assistance . . . understand?"

"Thank you. I'll go see him when we are both better." George waited for the nurse to leave. Then wolfed down his dinner. Slid out of the bed, wincing at the pain, tied his gown tighter and started dragging his IV drip pole down the hall with him. He had to see Pete . . .

****

Cole was on his cell diverting Hatch and the team to San Diego based on intelligence he had gathered from Martin, without much persuasion at all. Hatch advised the pilots of the charter plane and they adjusted course.

Time was on the team's side.

Cole had probable buyer information and possible location of the sale. They had vehicles standing by ready to transport the team into Mexico.

****

David was making good time with the hoard he had and knew he would make even better time coming back, without the extra cargo, of course. He found extraordinary joy in the thought of killing Carl and Sonny, it was like an inside joke that nobody else knew about or a special treat for being good. Whatever it was, he enjoyed the thought as much as he would enjoy the destruction of the two, who unfortunately for them had been good employees for several years. Their reward for trusting me, he mused. He laughed out loud drawing questioning looks from all in the car. He just flashed them his winning smile, then turned, staring out the window.

****

Cole and his team, along with Martin, planned to set up a hide, an obscure observation point so they could witness the possible transactions between David and the buyer; 6 miles south of Tijuana one half mile off the coast. The land came off a small beach, up approximately two hundred feet to the roadway and several hundred yards inland to the highway. Then crossed the highway to another set of bluffs that towered over the entire area. From the second bluff area, they had a commanding view of all the traffic and any activity where Martin thought the transfer might take place. Martin had informed Cole that David Clark used this desolate area many times when he brought merchandise into the country. During their trip down Cole had called the priest requesting information on any trusted operators in the Tijuana area. Priest replied without hesitation, "Chu need to call Susana Flynn. Che es Norte Americana but speaks fluent Español. Che's been working de border looking for runaways and stolen children por cinco años. Che lives right on de border. Che de one; has DEA background. Well trained in cobert operation just like chu Cole. But gaab it all up to rescue de children. Chu will like her; che numero uno. Bery good."

"Thanks, Beto. I have another request."

"Chute, Cole, anyting, mi amigo."

"When can we get together and talk about Jesus Christ. I have some questions." Cole was hesitant asking him about Christ in front of his team but he knew if he mentioned it to the priest; the priest would hold him to it.

"Mi esposa and I will come to San Diego before chu leave and I will tell chu all about Hem. Chu needs to ask Susana too. Che is a lover of mi Jesus Christos. Che will tell you all about Hem. Chu start there and I will finish, okay. It es a deal! And Cole?"

"Yeah, Beto."

"It es about time!" The Priest laughed an excited laugh full of joy. "I will be praying for chu safety. Vaya con Dios, Cole."

Again Cole felt that strange joy, a deep sigh of relief like a great burden had been taken off his back. He felt light and happy. His emotions ran high, so high he wanted to cry with joy. He knew that he had made the right decision, maybe the first right decision in his life. He was glad to have made it and even more so to know people that cared for him enough to be willing to answer the questions he had. He actually could not wait. He was full of a strange, deep in your belly joy and yet fearful at the same time. He was fearful that this transfer could end in more bloodshed, leaving him with profound guilt so great Christ himself could not help him. He wanted to pray but didn't know how. He didn't know what to pray for or who to? He was sure if he did pray God would not want to hear his prayers. So, he would have to wait and get right with God first before he prayed. He settled back in the vehicle waiting for Goose to signal that the black stretch Lincoln Limousine was coming into their area of operation. Cole said a prayer under his breath anyway, hoping to be heard, that this was the right spot. He knew they had only one shot at this . . . surely God did too?

Susana's phone began to ring . . .

53

But there is one technique that reigns supreme as king of all propaganda weapons—lying.

Kupelian

David and his group were still several hours away from meeting the Gringo. They were not anywhere close to San Diego and still had to travel through the border crossing, slowing their progress even further. David knew it was going to be dark when the transfer took place. He hated Mexico despite the fact it provided him with quick money and drugs. But he really hated Mexico at night and in the middle of nowhere to boot. David himself never ever went across the border, Martin and Don both knew this, always allowing Don or Martin to do all the transfers or drug pickups. He stayed on the US side waiting. He was a little alarmed this trip because he had never let Carl or Sonny take the lead nor carry any money for him. It had always been Don Henry or Martin. Neither of them were available this trip. Which reminded him, he needed to call them, picking up his phone, he dialed both men . . . neither answer. Which was unusual, they both always answered his calls . . . no need to leave a message. It was disconcerting to think that they could have been killed or worse arrested. Thinking back to the events on the road to George Bookers house, remembering the man they had encountered, David thought, maybe this stranger was more than he thought he was and actually bested the two. But Little Dave and his happy band of killers would have handled him if he had shown up at the Bookers home. *Oh well, as long as I am free, who cares! They can all die . . . more for me!*

He turned to the others in the limo and began a quick strategy session on the transfer of girls and money, then became very precise on the return route to the US. He was always specific with location of their meet, with the transaction events, such as the time spent traveling to or meeting with a buyer and anal with his details when it came to the money, his money!

He gave them detailed instructions on where they would need to rent a van or an SUV for transportation into Mexico that could not be traced back to him or his illegal operation. Then how much to pay each boarder guard and the names of the guards that worked for the Gringo, not forgetting to mention who sent them and what to say to alert the guards to the opportunity and most important . . . how to pay the guards so that things went smoothly. Directions on where they were meeting the Gringo. Then how they would get the money back across the border without being detected. That would be the Gringo's expertise and his people to detail that information to Carl. He hoped, this would be a walk in the park. He had done this hundreds of times however, he had one caveat; neither Don nor Martin were going, it was Carl and Sonny going in by themselves. David knew this would be the greatest flaw in the plan.

He glared at them and with his last instruction, he added brutishly, "You two idiots screw this up, and I will kill both of you. Do you understand?"

They both nodded and wonder why they were doing this. Fear was creeping in on them from both sides of this deal. At first it was just concerning this Gringo guy, now it was their own boss. It was quickly becoming a no win situation for them. Carl turned and looked at Sunny, then looked down at his hands.

54

It was for freedom that Christ set us free;
therefore keep standing firm.

Paul

As George rounded the nurse' station he heard one of the nurses call his name and begin to scolded him for being up and walking about. He sped up, as much as his pain and the IV pole allowed. He glanced over his shoulder and saw one of the nurses get up from her computer to come after him. He tried to quicken his pace, knowing his pursuer would soon be on top of him. The nurse was laughing at him . . . he reminded her of a three-year-old runaway as he turned into room 512W. She followed him in and observed him set down in the guest chair and grab the armrests looking down at his feet. She could tell he was going to stay despite her objections.

She looked him in the eye, "Mr. Booker, you should not have walked down here and besides Mr. Donny is resting!"

Over her shoulder she heard her other unruly patient chime in, "He's fine nurse. We will only visit a minute." Pete was extremely weak and his voice relayed his condition.

"Well . . . only a minute." She shook her finger at Booker, "Then right back to bed with you, young man, you hear me?" She was as big as Booker and had hands of a steel worker.

"Yes, ma'am." Booker response resembled a school boy trying to duck out of class.

"When you're ready to go back to your room you buzz the desk and I will bring a wheel chair and take you back. No argument! Understood?" She said with more force in her voice this time.

Again, "Yes, ma'am."

She looked Pete up and down as he lay in the bed, then shut the door behind her.

"Don't give her any trouble George . . . she'll drop kick you back to your room." Pete said feebly and they both snickered and moaned as the pain flared.

"No kidding she's tougher than both of us." George retorted. He limped to a chair by Pete's bed and eased himself down into it. He felt the cold vinyl on his backside realizing why the nurse was laughing at him.

"How are you feeling, brother?" George asked.

"Well . . . for being beat in the head with a rock and kicked so hard I have broken bones and shot in the back, I'm doing okay, I guess. The doc says I am going to recover, I just need time." Pete's face was swollen black and blue, with some areas already turning green and purple. His lips were puffy and blood caked. The white of his one open eye was filled with blood, which made it hard for him to focus and harder for George to look at him. What with the stitches in his head, flakes of dried blood on his pillow and sheets; he had dirt and blood matted in what hair he had left after his attacker pulled handfuls out and the nurses shaved the rest off so the doctors could stitch him up. He looked more like Frankenstein than a human. The nurses tried to clean him up the best they could but poor Pete was a mess. The only clue George had that this was Pete, was the name tag on the door. The shell that held his friend was unrecognizable.

"You had said some things that concerned me yesterday. If you feel up to it I would like to talk to you about it?" George said hoping Pete would want to talk about it for at least a minute or two.

"I know. I have said some things lately that have concerned me as well. Like doubting God's existence and power to save me or even love me. I am afraid, George. Afraid that God has turned His back on me." Pete said turning his head toward the window.

George was quiet for a long moment as they both contemplated Pete's declarations. "Do you believe, Pete?"

Pete knew what George was asking him, "Yes, I believe in God and his Son Jesus Christ," Pete said with tears in his eyes. "But I feel like Thomas . . . I need to see more or know more somehow. I just feel lost. I am not what I used to be . . . more questions than answers. I feel like I am in a dark hole and cannot climb out."

"Can we talk about this, Pete?" George asked with true empathy in his vice.

"I would like to . . . I . . . I'm just so ashamed of what I have done, I don't know where to begin. Besides all this, I can't find my Mary. Neither Mary or Simone has come to see me. I'm afraid something bad has happened to them, George."

"I'll call Helen and see if she can locate them. Is that okay with you?"

"Yes, that will be great. Thanks, you have always been a better friend to me than I have been to you. I want to apologize for that."

"No worries Pete." George picked up the bedside phone and called his home number. Helen picked up on the third ring. Listened to what

George's request was, agreed to look for Mary and he put the phone back on the receiver. However, George was not ready to disclose any details about Simone just yet. "We will find out something soon. I want to continue our talk if you feel up to it?"

"I would like that, thank you." Pete was ready to get some things off his chest and George could tell.

"I want to begin with where you are right now. We all have seasons of doubt. We all question the truth of the scriptures or our own belief at times. Thomas doubted the Resurrection but it did not cost him his salvation. But, never the less, doubt cannot be the reason for us separating ourselves from God the Father or His Son Jesus Christ. It should be the thing that drives us to dig deeper."

"George, you don't know what I have done over the past few months and years. I have separated from the truth and sinned terribly, leading people away from God through my own arrogant stupidity. I see that now."

"I am going to let God deal with you through His Holy Spirit on that point . . . all I want to do is to remind you of some things . . . okay?" George waited for a response.

Pete weakly agreed, "Okay, remind me."

"Peter the Apostle wrote in 2 Peter 1:12; 'I will always be ready to remind you of these things, even though you already know them . . .' You know the things I am going to say. You, more than likely, have said them to others in their times of crisis. But I am going to say them to you. I want you to be patient in your hearing of these things as we together approach God's throne. Can you do this with me?"

Pete was looking at George as a son would a father, "Yes, I can. I know I need help."

"You have found yourself in a pharisaical position. What I mean by that is . . . what John wrote in chapter 12 of his gospel, 'Many believed but because of the Pharisees they did not confess Him (Christ) so that they would not be banned from the temple. For they loved praise from men more than praise from God.' From those Pharisaical actions, Satan sneaks in and feeds you lies, Pete. What is interesting is what followed this quote from John 12:42 . . . John writes, 'Then Jesus cried out, '"The one who believes in Me, believes not in me but in Him who sent me. And the one who sees Me sees Him who sent Me. I have come as a light into the world, so that everyone who believes in Me would not remain in darkness. If anyone hears my words and doesn't keep them, I do not judge him; for I did not come to the world to judge the world but to save the world.'"

George continued, "Pete through all our struggles in this life we tend to look at God as the god that deals out punishment only and we forget His main purpose is not to condemn but to save us from ourselves. We have the free choice to turn our back on him Pete but He will not turn His on us. For His purpose was never to condemn only to save. We confuse ourselves with this thought - 'There is a hell and if we are not careful He will send us there' . . . not true! Listen to verse 48; "'The one who rejects Me and doesn't accept My sayings has this as his judge: The word I have spoken will judge him on the last day.'" Never forget we damn ourselves to Hell, God does not. There is a certain fear that we need to recognize though . . . God has all power and will allow those men, who reject His Son and blaspheme the Holy Spirit, to choose condemnation to hell . . . even believers. But the key word here is the word 'reject.' He presents it and we choose to accept or reject His word of truth and life. The fight you feel now is God's Holy Spirit fighting Satan's demons over your soul. If there was not this great struggle inside you, then your choice would have already been made by you in the rejecting of God's truth and in that, the condemnation of your soul to hell. Pete the scriptures say that, 'all good things come from the Father of heavenly lights.' That one good thing is again seen in verses 49 and 50 . . . "'For I have not spoken on My own, but the Father Himself who sent Me has given Me a command as to what I should say and what I should speak. I know that His command is eternal life.'"

"Pete, what Jesus spent His time on earth to tell people is one thing . . . I am here to take you to heaven. Nothing else! It is up to us to hear and believe His words of eternal life. So point one is Jesus had one mandate from His Father . . . SAVE THE WORLD, period!"

"Now what happens to those believers who fall from grace? This is a difficult place to be found. For some say even though you fall into unbelief which is blasphemy of the Holy Spirit, you will never lose your eternal salvation because you are an adopted child of God's or those same ones say if you do fall from grace even though you had confessed Christ as King and Savior, you never really believed or you would have never fallen from grace. Therefore, hell is where you deserve to go."

Pete was lying still and listening to George. "What do you say George?" Pete asked.

"I say read the scriptures honestly. See what Jesus says about those who confess Christ as King of their lives and then fall into Satan's grasp. The first thing is a little word that we believers tend to ignore . . . 'If.' This word is used in scripture to denote conditional concepts. There will be wise men that will disagree with me in this area of discussion. However I believe if people are honest with the scriptures they will come to the same conclusion. Remember Ananias and Sapphira in Acts? As Paul told the Galatians Christians in chapter five verse four that they had fallen from grace . . . only a Christian can fall from grace."

"Yes, I do."

"Well, if we back up to Acts 4:32 to the end of chapter 4 we see Luke setting the story line for what happened to Ananias and his wife Sapphira. The whole group of believers at Jerusalem was of one mind and heart. Which led them to do things we have forgotten today. They, as a body of believers, agreed together to share all things as each determined to do for the good of the church. The sharing is exemplified in verse 36 with Joseph, better known as Barnabas. He sold a field and pledged all the money to the Lord bringing the proceeds of the sale to the apostles, laying it at their feet for them to give to the poor as the whole church had determined. There was no misunderstanding with what Barnabas had done . . . sold the land and gave all the proceeds of the land sell to the church, which was Barnabas' committed decision he made to God. Pete, he did not have to sell the land and when he did sell the land he did not have to give the whole price to the church. He could have dedicated part of the proceeds to the church and kept part of it if he so chose. The point is not the selling of the land nor the keeping of some or all of the money made off the sell; the point is that he was being honest with what he promised to God. Peter is going to make this point in verse 4 of chapter 5. My argument is simple . . . what was the choice made by Ananias and his wife? It again was not the selling of the property nor the keeping of it but what they said they had dedicated to God. They made a promise to the Apostles, the church and the Holy Spirit to sell the land and give all to the church. But when the time came they both agreed to lie about the amount made. They broke covenant with God through blaspheming the Spirit of God through their lie. They both died that day. I believe they separated themselves from God by their choice. I know this sounds cruel but remember it was not God's choice it was the man and women's choice. Let's think of Hebrews chapter 10 beginning in verse 26. The writer of Hebrews makes a clear distinction here between the believer that is accepting the grace of Christ and the believer who is not. He makes the distinction in believers . . . not in a nonbeliever and a believer.

How he does this is in verse 26 by saying 'FOR IF WE' . . . we know the writer is a believer because he is writing about Christ and he includes himself in this most personal of discussions . . . the damnation of a Christian's soul. Also remember he is beginning this discussion with the little word 'IF' denoting a condition. Now Pete, some say that the writer is speculating on this topic. That it cannot really happen to Christians because this would contradict other scripture concerning the promises and power of God. Two things come to my mind on this . . . first this is dealing with Christians. Only a believer is in a position to stop believing in something, whether that something is in God or gravity. The second; the Hebrew writer is not dealing with God's omnipotence he is dealing with man's freedom of choice to stop believing in the Holy God thus blaspheming the Holy Spirit.

"Pete notice what the writer says . . . 'For if we deliberately sin after receiving the knowledge of truth, there no longer remains a sacrifice for sins.' The condition is the possibility to sin to the point of no return. In the book of 1 John; John speaks of two types of sin . . . one sin not leading to death and the other is leading to death, this is in 1 John 5: 16 & 17. Of which John says do not pray for the sin leading to death . . . Why? Because there is a sin that a Christian cannot come back from! In Hebrews he writes in the sixth chapter in verse 4 through verse 12 about an apostate Christian in even stronger language . . . 'For it is impossible to renew to repentance those who were once enlightened . . .' Pete this is a truly terrible place for Christians to find themselves. Remember, Paul said to the Galatians, 'You have been severed from Christ, you who seek to be justified by the law; you have fallen from grace.' This is not left for interpretation, this is a statement of fact. Paul says, 'You have fallen.' Who falls? Only those who were standing in God's truth, saved people, Christians. However, you have to understand how a Christian knows he or she is in that place or not, and this is by what goes on inside them. In their heart and mind."

"What do you mean George? What goes on inside, I don't follow?" Pete looked so exhausted George thought about letting him rest and continuing later.

"Do you want to rest, Pete. We can continue this later if you're too tired right now."

"No, please go on. I want to hear what you have to say." Pete tried to scoot up in the bed but couldn't.

"Remember what Paul wrote about in Romans 7, his description of his struggle with his own sin?"

Pete nodded and weakly responded with, "Yes, I do."

George smiled and continued, "Good, in verse 14, Paul begins, 'For we know the law is spiritual but I am made out of flesh, sold to the power of sin. For I do not understand what I am doing, because I do not practice what I want to, but I do what I hate. And if I do what I do not want to do, I agree with the law that it is good. So now, I no longer am the one doing it but it is sin living in me. For I know nothing good lives in me that is, in my flesh. For the desire to do what is good is with me but there is no ability to do it. For I do not do the good that I want to do.' Do you see the struggle Paul is having?"

Pete nodded in agreement.

"This struggle is deep inside of Paul, in his heart and mind. Paul continues the second part of the same verse, verse 19, 'but I practice the evil I do not want to do.' The great apostle Paul is fighting within himself, just like we do, Pete. He continues in verse 20, 'Now if I do what I do not want, I am no longer the one doing it, but it is the sin that lives in me. So I discovered this principle. When I want to do what is good, evil is with me. For in my inner self I joyfully agree with God's law. But I see a different law in the parts of my body, waging war against the law of my mind and taking me prisoner to the law of sin in the parts of my body. What a wretched man I am. Who will rescue me from this body of death? I thank God through Jesus Christ our Lord! So then with my mind I am a slave to the Law of God, but with my flesh to the law of sin.'" George stopped there for a minute as Pete contemplated what had been said.

"Pete listen to the next verse and give these verses time to sink in because I am talking about all men and women, everybody that has ever lived. The overwhelming question has been, 'Is this all there is to this life?' Like the man said 'Life's tough, then you die, and that is it.' No, it's not, because Paul says in chapter 8 verse one . . . 'Therefore there is now no condemnation for those in Christ Jesus.' So, Paul, in one place says there is no condemnation and in Galatians 5:4, he says you have fallen from grace? So which one is true? Both, the principle is that a Christian can fall from grace and loose his salvation by his own choice, Hebrews chapter 6 and chapter 10, as well as what Christ says to the churches in Revelation 2 and 3, "I will come and remove your candle stick . . . 'IF' YOU DO NOT REPENT." But our God is great and powerful enough to accept us back into His Church if we repent from the only sin that can condemn us eternally . . . blaspheming the Holy Spirit, unbelief. So we see that we are safe in Christ but at the same time our safety is conditioned on asking for repentance as we live in the grace of Christ. His love is unconditional but his relation is based on our belief and desire to grow into becoming like Christ over the course of our lifetime. This takes recognition of our struggle, like Paul explained in Romans 7 and the growth of our relationship, from our side as seen in 1 John 1:5-10; by asking for forgiveness as we recognize the sins we commit. Now Pete, this is not an in and out relationship. I mean, I sin and I am not saved anymore, then I ask forgiveness and I am saved again, John clearly states that this cleansing is a onetime, forever act or a continual act once cleansed we are clean. But as Paul stated in Hebrews chapter 6:4-6, a Christian has to work at losing their salvation. Read the steps that one goes through to come to that point of rejecting Christ. It is a difficult and determined downward spiral to get to the point of trampling Christ under one's foot. Christ will not give up your soul easily. Even if you are working hard at rejecting Him.

"The first thing to ask yourself, Pete, if there is a struggle inside of you? I can see there is because you have shown it. The second question is; is it too late for you to repent and turn back to Jesus? The first question answers the second . . . no it is not too late. Third; what do we do now? We recognize the truth of the scripture that Christ is on your side, no matter what, as long as you have that willing heart of repentance. Pete, Christ loves you and will never condemn you as long as your faithfulness is to Christ. Our sins cannot stop us from His loving, saving grace. 1 John1:9; says 'If we confess our sins; Christ is faithful and righteous to forgive us our sins and to cleanse us from all unrighteousness.' So as we confess those sins we know we have committed, He will forgive all those we have forgot or didn't even know we committed. Our relationship with Jesus is built on conditions, condition one, our acceptance of His offer; condition two; the recognition of our sins and our need for him to forgive us as we fellowship with Him in His glorious light through our obedience to His commandments and agreement on our part by confession of our sins. We must recognize we all sin and we sin continually. His part is to forgive us as we recognize our sin and request His powerful intervention in our lives to save us. By our trust and faith in Jesus to fulfill His promises to us by His power alone."

George could tell Pete was exhausted, so as he rang the nurse's station he touched Pete's arm and said, "Remember his love is unconditional although we must acknowledge our part and that is to obey His word as best we can. Christ Himself admonished His churches in Revelation to endure to the end and you will receive a crown of life."

Pete lay still looking at the ceiling. He turned his head slowly locking eyes with George, "Pray for me, George. Would you, please?"

55

How do you win a fight? More bullets and more bombs!

Cole was on secure satellite phone listening to the ringing of the number Beto had given him for Susana. He waited . . . it rang with no voice mail; it just kept ringing. Finally, a female voice came on the line, "Hi can I help you?" Cole knew the recipient had encrypted the call on her end as well or had possibly established a trace on him.

"The Priest gave me your number and said you might be able to help with a problem I have."

"The Priest? How is Father Miguel Sánchez doing these days?" The female asked without a hint of larceny in her voice. "Well, I am not sure how Father Sanchez is doing but Beto is doing great." Cole knew there was only a handful of people that knew the priest by his nickname.

The phone was silent for a moment, "What is your name, again, please?"

"Brady Cole Williams. You want my social too?" He waited for a response; none came. "I was told to ask for a Susana Flynn. I need help with a recovery. Are you Susana?"

"What church in which town does the priest work?"

"He neither works as a Priest in the formal definition nor does he Pastor a church any longer." Cole realized he had to go through the vetting process in order to ease the degree of paranoia of those that work in secrete.

"Well, I'm well aware that an unwed Mexican male travels a rocky road, knowing how much Mexican men love their women." She said in a matter-of-fact way.

"Well, Beto married a woman he rescued. I believe he actually killed a man saving her life. I'm in a bit of a rush here. How about we just phone conference Beto in and you can vet me that way. I'll give you his phone number. That sound good?" Cole needed conformation of assistance or he needed to move on to someone else.

"Well, Mr. Williams, what can I do for you?" Her tone changed slightly from interrogator to approachable but they were not friends yet. "Beto told me you're a man that didn't waste time. What do you have?"

"I have been in and out of Mexico many times and have never once heard of you. What's your back ground . . . if I might ask?" It was his turn.

"I was with the DEA for eleven years; my last station was deep cover in the State of Sinaloa around Culiacan. I got sick and tired of watching all the young girls being sacrificed to the gods of lust, drugs, and later killed on the altar of secrecy. I quite the Agency and opened up a private rescue business here on the border. Been hard at it for five years now."

Beto's words came back to his conscience mind "Chu will like her, Cole.' "You sound like my kind of gal, Mz. Susana. I do not know your location but I am six clicks south of the over pass to nowhere off highway 1Delta, just outside of Tijuana, half a click in from the beach. I am waiting on a very nasty individual who has several young girls with him and my understanding is he will sell them to a man called The Gringo."

"The Gringo." She repeated with disgust in her voice. "I know that name well. What do you need from me?" Cole could tell she was getting friendlier, with the mention of the Gringo.

"Need you to take the girls that I am not here to recover. Give me alternative transportation along with cover fire if needed. I will need for you to take into custody the Gringo as well or have him taken. Seeing that I and my team are here as tourist it might prove difficult for me to tote Mr. Gringo back across the line, you understand. And besides, I know Beto would love to make the Gringo's acquaintance, if at all possible."

"Is your team armed? The Gringo is just as nasty as the men you are expecting, I'm sure." She responded coolly, exposing her professional side.

"Only handguns, those we could bring across the line undetected. We do have night vision and infrared spotting scopes if this thing goes longer than we think. I understand that they transfer the cargo in a quarry of some type located on the west side of 1D. It is about seventy-five to one hundred feet deep. Perfect for concealment and has only one way in and one way out. We have that under surveillance. Can you enlighten me on the Gringo?"

"He traffics in the white sex-slave trade. He also pushes large amounts of cocaine but his stock in trade are the girls. He has quite a network that he uses in his trafficking business. He goes nowhere without a 4 car convoy. His car roams between the second or third in line. There are usually eight to twelve in his protection group. They carry automatic weapons such as folding stock AK 47, CAR 15 assault rifles with handguns, of course. They mean business if confronted." Her voice had the tone of maliciousness to it.

"Sounds like he could start his own little war, are you available for back up in this?"

"I am. I've activated my people. We are on the move as we speak. I want this guy worse than you, I promise. If you can deliver him you'll become my new BFF, Mr. Williams."

"Well, all righty, then. I'll see what I can do. There are five of us. I have one on high ground spotting with night vision and the others scattered out strategically. I just need some heavy fire power backing us up. What is your ETA, Susana?" She liked the way he said her name.

"I am forty minutes out from your location. But my team leader is in Tijuana with three shooters. They can be there in fifteen. Good enough for you?" She was proud of her team and Cole could tell.

"Good enough for me. When you get closer to my location notify me of the type and color of your vehicles. See you in forty-five."

"Roger that."

"Oh, by the way . . . Susana?" Cole caught her just before she clicked off.

"Yes, Mr. Williams." She said his name as if it was a cover name; not his real name.

"We may need your assistance in moving seamlessly back across the border. If you have any suggestions I would love to hear them."

"If everything goes well I will move you across myself."

"And if it all falls apart like Humpty Dumpty?"

"No worries. We have contingency plans for basket cases."

"I do not expect that but good to know. Thanks." Cole hit end on his sat phone wondering what Beto meant about him liking this woman. He supposed he would find out soon enough.

The men were strategically placed around the entrance of the large whole in the ground. They, like ghosts, could not be seen, waiting for the arrival of the evil that kept them in business.

Cole keyed his bone mic and spoke to his team, "Heads up boys. I have Beto's counterpart coming in to give us hard cover incase the fireworks become too loud for us. They will arrive in two groups . . . ETA for group one is fifteen minutes . . . second group on scene will be thirty minutes after the first's arrival. The Gringo travels in a four car convoy . . . AK's and Car 15s with sidearms. She sounds like she knows this guy well. There could be as many as twelve shooters with the Gringo. Goose, how's the view on the hill?" Cole waited for an answer.

"I can see your pearly whites. How's that for ya?"

"Perfect. Test night vision as soon as it's dark enough, ten-four?"

"Roger that."

"Does everyone feel they have enough cover and concealment? Any questions or last minute suggestions before we go silent?"

"Hey, BC . . . you said this is a woman backing us up?" Blake was asking.

"Affirmative."

"What does she look like?"

There was a long pause . . . "Any other questions, hopefully from someone in control of his senses and that thinks like a pro?" BC ignored the chatter that Blake started. Seconds later all went quiet.

Twenty minutes had passed when Cole's phone rang. A thick Irish accented male advised, "We are 2 minutes out from your location. Where do you want us?"

"Exit at Punta Bandera. Go to the underpass, follow the road to the left. Take the left 'Y' follow it to Comino Vecinal, which will be the next left. Take that road to the first half circle turn, look to your right and you will see me parked in a small open area. Need type and color of your vehicle, please?" Cole waited.

"A blue Nissan 4 door sedan. Pretty beat up on the passenger's side. It has some rust colored body putty on the front fender and left rear quarter panel. Mexico plates, yellow and black."

"Well, you guys sure fit in here; I've only seen three thousand of those since I arrived in Tijuana four hours ago. Any other distinguishing marks, scars or tattoos?"

"Four big redheaded Irish boys - help any?" The operative said with a laugh.

"So, it's just the car that has a disguise. Okay, I know what to look for, thanks. I'm standing by."

Cole was relieved for the backup but also for the darkening skies. He hoped it would be completely dark before the bad guys arrived. He waited for the new operators to show.

It didn't take long before car lights moved across the parking area. The car stopped with its headlights illuminating Cole's vehicle; they waited but there were only three red-heads in the vehicle.

Cole took the initiative and stepped from the shadows slightly behind and to the left of the Nissan. The man on the phone was not lying. All three were large redheaded Irishmen. And they literally stood out like volcanic islands in a sea of brown and black. The rear passenger turned and saw Cole approach their vehicle.

He immediately alerted, "On the left!" Causing a flurry of activity inside the vehicle. The driver's door swung open and a large male slid out half crouching behind the car while the other two had raised weapons angled in Cole's direction for quick response if needed. Seconds later, a second redhead stepped from the Nissan with a short barrel automatic assault rifle drawn.

Cole called out, "Cole Williams, easy men, easy. I'm here to meet with Susanna Flynn." Cole had his palms out so they could see he held no weapon

Cole shook hands with Sean the obvious spokesman of the group, who introduced him to his brothers Jon and Albert.

After the pleasantries, Cole asked, "I thought there were four of you guys?"

Sean turned and called to the fourth brother, "Gilbert, come on down, son." Then turned back to Cole smiling, said, "Sorry, but one cannot be too careful, in Mexico." In his thick Irish accent.

Cole smiled and began quizzing them on weapons and strategy, as he watched the one called Gilbert saunter into the increasingly attentive circle of men. Gilbert was toting a large bore rifle with night vision, slung over his shoulder.

Cole shook Gilbert's hand and the two men acknowledge one other like warriors often do, as Cole continued his explanation of the overall situation. Cole detailed what information he had, which was not much, for an operation that had so many ways it could go wrong. For example, Cole had no ETA on the bad guys. He was not 100 percent sure this was even the spot. But if it was the spot, he figured they had limited time to set up an ambush and as far as Cole knew, limited resources. Cole's goal was to keep the two suspect groups, David Clark's group and the Gringo's, from interacting. Hopefully, stopping the smaller of the two groups on the main highway and the larger, more heavily armed, down in the bottom of the quarry. However it worked out, the overriding goal, was to keep the girls safe from any of the potential gun play.

Sean suggested, "If the Gringo shows first we let him proceed into the quarry. Then we let our shooter take out the engines of all four of his cars. One shot each threw the block or the driver's heads, whichever works the best. If the sellers show we take them before they turn into the quarry. Swarm the car secure the girls, then turn our attention back to the Gringo's group. We have the high ground and can gently persuade them to die or give up?"

"What if the sellers show first?" Cole responded.

"We have some IEDs that are designed to stop a vehicle. We have to be precise with the timing, set the IEDs along the road leading into the quarry. We let the sellers pass the IEDs and go to the bottom of the quarry. Then, as all four of the Gringo's cars are safely below elevation, we trip the trigger and stop Gringo's lead car and his trail car. We then in lighten him and his men to their dire circumstances, which is give it up or die." Sean stood confidently with a crooked little smile on his freckled face; his blue eyes shining in the dimming light.

"I like it! How are your IEDs triggered?" Cole wanted more Intel.

"Three ways. We can trigger them manually from up to two hundred meters or we have set an infrared trigger on the devices themselves, which trips the trigger when a vehicle breaks the beam. We have a timed activated trigger as well. So we can set them at the location and turn them on after we have left the location."

"Beautiful. Let's get it set up now. I don't know what kind of time line we are dealing with, so we got to move speedy-fast." The small group of operators looked at Cole and chuckled at the speedy-fast comment.

Cole ignored the looks, "I'll advise my guys. Once you have set the IEDs, call me and I will expose my guys so that you can set up with them." Cole knelt down and drew out the quarry, the highway with the road going down to the bottom of the quarry with the hills on the east side of the highway. "What does your sniper shoot and where does he want to set up?" Cole asked. The four Irishmen discussed the topography of the site and determined the best position for their shooter.

Sean explained, "My brother shoots a 7.62 X 51 / .308 Winchester, with armor piercing rounds. He has night capabilities with a W/A NX 3.5-15X50 Nightforce military spec scope. He is excellent at night up to 200 meters, good out to 300 or so. We think the best place for him will be to set up close to the mouth of the road. He will position himself for either scenario, take the Gringo going in or coming out."

"I can tell this ain't your first rodeo. I look forward to seeing him at work." Cole chuckled.

Sean responded, "Brother, we're from Ireland. We've been in all sorts of rodeos before." Cole laughed but noticed he was laughing alone. These men were serious and dangerous.

"I'm glad we're on the same side, Sean. Let's get set up." Cole turned to his headset and began informing his team of what was going on.

It was just minutes before he was informed that the Irish were in position. Cole knew now it was a waiting game. He hoped that Martin was telling him the truth. He was relatively sure of it but Martin was a criminal and Cole knew most stretched the truth to some extent but criminals, lied all the time, for no good reason. So it was a gamble at best.

Cole's cell rang, "So what do you think of my brothers?" Her voice was softer now that she knew Cole had met her team.

"Your brothers in arms or your brothers, like brothers and sister?"

"Brothers, as in brothers and sisters." Her voice was lite as if it had a smile in it.

"You mean to tell me all of those men are your brothers?" Cole sounded shocked.

"I mean to tell you all four of those darlings are my blood and bone brothers. I brought them over here ten years ago to get them out of Ireland. They all have military experience and served with honor. I'll tell you more if I get to know you better and if we like you."

"Okeydoke, then. Well, I like them so far . . . as long as your sniper brother can hit his target and not one of us."

"He'll hit his target." She said it with steel in her voice. "I'm at the exit. Sean gave me your 20." Cole's phone went dead.

It was a beautiful quarter moon night with a cool ocean breeze, no smog just clear skies with stars popping out here and there in the darkening canopy. Cole sat on the hood of his car waiting. Thinking about how this situation was going to play out. He knew no matter how well one planned, it would all change in an instant when the first shot was fired. He bowed his head . . . he assumed God loved all people —so a little prayer from one who was struggling to believe in Him, might be heard if by chance all the stars and galaxies in the heavens lined up. He began to ask God for protection just as car lights washed across the parking area.

The second group arrived. Susana, as Cole had been calling her, stepped from her vehicle along with two others. "Cole?" She said with just a hint of Irish. Her hand was extended as she approached him. Cole was glad he was down wind . . . she smelled great. He took her hand feeling her strength and softness at the same time. He looked down at her and held her hand a little longer than was necessary but she didn't seem to mind. She introduced him to the other two. Another female named Carmen and small older man named Hector, some of her in country contacts. They shook hands with Susana leading the conversation, "Well, are my boys set up?"

"Yes, they seem to be a very professional. Beto told me you guys were good." Cole said looking at Susana in the fading light. He could tell she was in great shape not like a model but like an athlete. Like a soldier. She wore Levis' with a nice fitting blue gray T- shirt, lace up boots and a ball cap. Her hair was pulled back through the hole in the back of the cap. Cole could tell she was a fine looking woman. Not that that mattered to him, of course. She was five foot seven, maybe 125 to 130 pounds. In the fading light her hair was dark and he could see her eyes but could not make out the color. Cole stepped back several steps since he had not taken a bath in three days and had been wearing the same clothes from his sweat stained brim to his crusty socks, he had a three-day-old beard and knew his hair was matted with greasy residue, he was glad he wore a ball cap. His breath stank and he felt the fuzz growing on his teeth. He knew he was a pretty sight. He offered her a stick of gum as he shoved several pieces in his mouth.

She had the other two wait in her vehicle, explaining to Cole that the two Mexican citizens were there to take control of the girls once the teams retrieved them. They were the best she had seen dealing with the initial shock associated with recovery of kidnapped victims and the process of reintroduction to family and kin. She stepped close to Cole, "I can tell you've been on the job a day or two. Where did the chase begin?"

"Pimsler, Colorado. And, yes, I left one situation around Culiacan and fell right into another. Have not even had time to shower or shave as you have so kindly pointed out. So, I suggest, you might want to stand up wind." Cole said it with a chuckle, not denying the gravity of his statement.

"What? Remember the redheads? I've had plenty of experience with stinky boys." She said with laughter in her voice.

Cole's earpiece popped with Goose's voice. "Got a black SUV entering the exit ramp. Stand by." Goose said to everybody that could hear. Cole called Sean's cell. "Black SUV heading your way. Our seller might have switched vehicles. Stand by."

"Do you want to ride with me or do you need your vehicle?" Cole questioned. Susana moved quickly toward her car speaking over her shoulder, "Pick me up at my car." Cole moved into the driver's seat and cranked the engine, pulling the car around to where Susana was standing by the now open trunk pulling out her gear. His car lights lit her up and for the first time he could see her face clearly; beautiful auburn hair, porcelain skin and in much better shape than he first supposed. She moved like an athlete, smooth and with practiced purpose. Her shoulders were broad accenting an already small waist. He could tell her legs were firm and strong under the Levis' she wore.

She turned and moved across the front of the car looking at him through the windshield with big green Irish eyes. Cole just stared at her with his mouth opened as she moved with coordinated precision to the passenger's side of the vehicle. *Chu will like her Cole*, Beto's voice resounded in his head.

Susana jumped into the car while putting on her vest as she spoke to Cole, "My name is Susan . . . Sue or Suzie . . . not Susana. That's Beto's name for me not mine. Okay?"

"Yes, ma'am." Cole said as he pushed his vehicle down the dirt road toward the quarry, still starring at his passenger. "My name is Brady or Cole or Brady Cole or BC or Williams or you can call me 'hey, boy,' but ..." both of them in unison stated the next commonly used phrase known to all military and Para-military types, "just don't call me late for chow." They laughed together. Cole looked at her and said, "You too huh?"

She had a lovely smile, "Yeah. Me too. Didn't you see the brothers I grew up with? Thirty seconds late to supper and you had to wait for the next meal." She laughed out loud and Cole thought, Beto was right, I think I like this gal. But as was the nature of the business . . . relationships built in this business were seldom successful.

Cole stopped his car under the overpass that led back to the quarry. He waited for someone to direct the teams. Everything was silent. He sat still looking out the windshield expectantly waiting for some kind of information. He turned his head to the right and Sue was looking at him.

She looked a bit longer as if trying to think of something to say or understand him better. She could only come up with, "What do you think?"

The radio crackled again with Hatch's voice, "We have visual of one black SUV entering the quarry. It is proceeding down to the bottom. We will allow the vehicle to set up at the bottom. We will observe and wait for instructions."

"I think its show time," Cole said to Susan. Then answered Hatch, "Roger that. Who's with Sean?"

Hatch again, "He's with me BC."

"Hand him your headset." While Hatch passed the set off, Cole spoke to Goose, "Goose do you see anyone on the highway."

"Not a soul, boss."

"Roger that."

Sean came on with his Irish lilt. "Sean here."

"Sean, this is BC. We're going to improvise."

"Roger that." Sean said without hesitation.

"Can we take the single vehicle now? Is it possible for your shooter to disable the vehicle? Then we will converge on it take the girls out of harm's way and set back up for the Gringo?"

"If we have the time and they have no weapons we can do it easily." Sean's voice betrayed his excitement.

"We need to move now. Get an approach plan and get your shooter ready to put several rounds in the block of that car. Let me know when you're ready. Goose!"

"Goose here." Goose sounded extremely professional.

"Can you see the occupants of the SUV?" Cole quizzed Goose. Goose responded, "Stand by one."

"I count four, what appears to be young girls in the far back and two adults in front."

"Roger that. This has to be our group. Everybody listen up. We are going to take the vehicle down now. We need to begin an approach of the SUV and get as close as possible on foot without detection. Set up strategically in case we need to take the two adults out. Once we are set, Sean's shooter will disable the SUV. Then both teams advance in force. Need at least two flash bang grenades. The shock will give us the opportunity to grab the adults and recover the children. Questions?" Cole was not waiting for questions or objections. "Sean, I need your shooter to wait to disable the SUV after we get close and are set. Seconds count. If the SUV begins to move take out the driver. We do not allow it to exit the quarry. Everybody copy?" All copied the transmission and agreed. "Goose keep an eagle eye on the highway for the Gringo, copy?"

"Roger that. No vehicles in sight at this time." Goose stated.

"What do we do?" Sue asked, disappointed she was not included in the fray.

"We have good men on the ground. We let them do their thing. If the Gringo shows we create a diversion. The most important thing is that we recover the girls. Agreed?"

"Agreed." They waited. Listening to the headset BC had removed and was holding between them so they both could listen. Cole thought, man, she smells good!

Minutes later Hatch squawked, "We're set. Ready shooter . . . fire when ready." The night was still and dark; BC and Sue had their windows down they both found themselves involuntarily holding their breath waiting for the shots. It seemed like forever then, "Fire in the hole, fire, fire, fire . . ." BOOM! BOOM, BOOM! The shots shattered the stillness of the night. They did not hear the rounds hit the SUV which Cole thought he should have, but then he realized, sitting under the overpass the echo was still reverberating.

The duo heard two successive pops of the flash bang grenades and silence again . . . no further gunfire. Good news to people who understand combat.

Cole's headset came to life, "We have two in custody and four young women."

Cole responded immediately, "Hook the two up and put them back into the SUV and strap them in tight! Take any communication devises. We want the Gringo to see people in that vehicle. Move the girls out of the quarry to a safe location. Get set up to take the Gringo. Advise when you are set. Everybody copy?" All affirmed Cole's transmission. Sue sat quietly watching her new found friend command the two teams and listened to the respect her team was giving him in their obedience to his orders. Her arms were crossed on her chest as she sat sideways in the seat with her back against the door. She was eyeing him hard, trying to conceal a smile at the same time.

"It's unusual that my brothers take so quickly to another's commands."

"So, you impressed?" Cole said with a smirk on his face.

"No. Not yet." She said flatly turning her head, she looked out the windshield never letting the competition see that you are impressed by their handling of a situation. Cole was looking at her . . . my, my, you are one good looking woman. His thoughts were interrupted.

"I have four fast movers southbound on highway 1D as in Delta; maybe two clicks out."

"BC, we're set, girls are safe." Hatch sounded out of breath. "Roger that. Goose has four fast movers coming your way . . . stand by." Cole responded.

"Roger, standing by."

"Shooter ready?"

"Shooter is ready and standing by."

"IED's activated?"

"Switch on. We have set the IEDs on the road down into the quarry about thirty-five to forty feet below the ground surface," Hatch stated.

"Good decision, If we stop them there, they have no room to move or to mount a counter attack. Gentlemen we must take the fight out of them before the fight starts! I do not want any dead bodies if we can help it. Open up high and with lots of firepower. Let them know we are serious. If our sniper can blow a round or two through the cars informing them they cannot escape, we will have turned them and they will give it up. Agreed?"

Sean came on, "Agreed BC." Sue looked at Cole, "Well, I'm impressed now."

"Fast movers approaching exit ramp." Goose was going to give blow by blow, "On ramp. These guys are not slowing. You should have visual in five, four three . . . now."

Hatch responded, "Have fast movers in sight approaching quarry road." Hatch paused a beat. "On quarry road." The IEDs were directional fire controlled and set on the outside of the roadway next to a straight drop to the bottom of the quarry.

The idea was to blow the IED forcing the lead vehicle into the dirt wall on the driver's side of the vehicle; trapping the lead car and trail car against the dirt embankment leaving the rear of the vehicle in the road blocking egress which would trap the other two between the two disabled vehicles. Before Hatch could transmit further instructions, all parties involved heard the distinctive explosion of the infrared triggered IED. The lead car reacted as planned, skidding into the dirt wall bringing down a mound of dirt on top of it and sloughing off a section of roadway. The second car crashed into the back causing a chain reaction with the third and fourth. The fourth car tried an ineffective evasive maneuver resulting in the driver's loss of control. The nose of the car glanced off the rear bumper of car three sliding toward the edge of the seventy foot drop off. The driver had no control which was an advantage to him in this case, as often is the case, a driver will over correct causing a worse accident. Although this was no accident per say, the car came to rest mostly on the road with the right front tire and bumper dangling off the edge of the roadway. No need for another explosion. Hatches voice came over the radio, 'Fire, fire, fire!" The whole world lit up with gunfire. Four of the seven men moved to the side of the quarry where they could direct riveting fire down on the vehicles driver's side while three of the seven fired on the passenger's side of the vehicles; leaving no room for the occupants to exit either side or fire from the inside of the vehicles. Seconds later the firing ceased. The silence was deafening. Hatch was giving the occupants time to consider options. Car three apparently had the Gringo in it . . . the backup lights came on and the heavy vehicle slammed into car four pushing it off the roadway plummeting seventy feet to the bottom of the quarry on its roof. Car three was speeding backward up the road.

Hatch yelled, "Sean, fire the IED . . . STOP THAT VEHICLE!" Another ear-splitting boom went off as car three swerved into the dirt wall. The car had been too close to the IED upon detonation, lifting the rear of the vehicle off the roadway pushing it onto the side of the embankment. The car landed with the rear bumper holding the rear wheels off the ground and the front bumper jammed deep into the road surface placing it permanently in a tail up nose down position. Hatch again, "Fire, fire, fire!" Another withering series of rounds began punching holes in every part of the vehicles that was not occupied by human flesh. When firing ceased this time car doors were being opened and Spanish voices were heard, empty hands appeared above heads and frantic shouts echoed, "No mas . . . no mas!" The occupants began lying down on the roadway in the traditional style - arms out to the side, legs spread and faces in the dirt. The group on the edge of the quarry overlooking the road approached the nine remaining banditos. Five perished in the affray. Four in car four and the driver in the lead car had been crushed by the dirt wall that came in through the front windshield and the driver's side window.

Cole and Sue arrived at the scene with the two in country contacts pulling in shortly behind. One of Sue's brother's was interviewing the girls. He was, Sue said, the gentlest of the four. He was young, tall and handsome; he was also their team sniper. Although the girls were devastated by this ordeal . . . they were all standing skin close to him holding a hand or an arm or a piece of a shirt . . . shaking uncontrollably, crying but answering all his questions without hesitation.

When the two in country contacts arrived, the girls had to be coaxed into believing it was okay to go with them. They finally persuaded the girls that Carmen and Hector were there to help get them back to the US and to their parents. Sue's youngest brother stretched out his arms and began to herd them toward the waiting vehicle. As he moved the girls moved with him, Cole laughed as he observed the tall man move as if he had ten legs and one head. The girls refused to enter the vehicle until their dashing bodyguard sat with them in the vehicle and explained that he would be along shortly. Goose came flying down from his perch in the van Cole had rented earlier in the hopes they would have several presents for Beto.

Cole again took command, "Gentlemen we need to move off station ASAP. Truss up the prisoners get them in the van. Snake get to the bottom and bring up the two in the SUV. Sue do you have a safe house that we can get our mob to? We need to dump some vehicles and transfer the others to Beto."

Sue took offense. "This mad man is mine for now! I'm not giving him to Beto until I'm through with him!" Cole was stunned as he saw her Irish come out.

"No problem, girl . . ." Cole held his hands up as if he was surrendering. He heard laughter behind him and turned to see Sean laughing at him.

Sean said, "Don't fight a redheaded Irish women Cole . . . you won't win."

Cole turned back to Sue smiling, "What happened to the BFF statement for getting him to you? Gee. Let's clear this war zone and get to your safe house. Okay? We can fight about who gets who later." Cole was proud of her standing up for what she knew to be one of the best finds she could possibly come across. She was passionate about stopping all the Gringos in the world and saving as many lives as possible. And he knew he was going to be her BFF for a long time to come. Things like this were never forgotten in the world of shadows. Blake the Snake and Scottie were handing off Carl and Sunny to two Irishmen who drug them up by any means they could and hustled them to the waiting vehicles.

"Cole!" Scottie shouted out getting his team leaders attention.

"Yes, sir." Cole responded out of respect for his people.

"Sean's boys found this in the Gringo's car." Scottie dropped it on the ground at Cole's feet. It had weight to it. The dust kicked up from the sides as the bag hit the ground with force. Cole squatted down beside the bag and felt around the zipper. He then took a gravity operated Osborne designed Bench-made green handled knife with a black razor sharp four-inch blade out of his pants pocket and flicked the blade open. He cut a four-inch slit in the bag two inches from the zipper and clicked on a small flashlight. Cole carefully slid the flashlight into the slit and stretched the bag up and out just enough so he could look into the bag. After careful examination he was sure it was not booby trapped; he looked up at the men around him, "You're not going to believe what's in here!" The group gathered as Cole unzipped the bag revealing the contents . . .

56

Forsaking the right way, they have gone astray.

Peter

David sat patiently waiting for word of the transfer. He knew how long these things took. Carl was still within the time limits he had set for the duo to deliver the girls and collect the money. He pulled Simone over and sat her on his lap. She began to fight him, "Don't touch me!" She yelled it in his ear. She found herself on the floor of the Limo with her left ear ringing and a burning sensation on her cheek. David had her by her hair, pulling her back up on his lap. "Simone, if this is going to work, honey, you are going to have do what I say. I can be very nice or extremely harsh. Which do you want? The nice me or the harsh me? Chose."

She was almost in tears, "The nice you." She had her head down holding her cheek and wouldn't look into his eyes. It was his eyes that she hated. She could see his evil and hatred for all the people he looked at. Why hadn't she seen this before? She knew Joan saw it that was why Joan didn't have anything to do with him. His eyes had frightened her too.

"Good choice, you set right up here and we will occupy the time the best we can while we wait for Carl and Sunny. Okay? No more problems, right?"

Her heart was beating faster now, her fear level was up and she was trying to survive this nightmare. "No more problems." She said it in a weak little girl voice.

57

Brethren, my heart's desire and my prayer to God for them is for their salvation.
Paul

Cole opened the mouth of the bag wider so all could see. He stood up and shined his flashlight into the bag illuminating its contents. The bag was what the Gringo had agreed to pay for the girls. Sean whistled, "Well, what now BC."

Cole looked at Sean, "Let's load up boys. We are going to use this blood money to trap a monster." He moved to his vehicle and got in preparing to follow Sue in hers when his passenger door flew open and Sue slid into the seat.

Cole was looking at Sue as he keyed his mic, "All riders accounted for? Sound off boys." Each sounded off accounting for the Irishmen, the girls, Carmen and Hector along with the prisoners.

"You riding with me?" Cole said eyeing the beauty setting beside him. "Yep, I'm riding with my new BFF." She said as she flicked her hair away from her face. "Which way girl? You're the boss now."

"South on 1 Delta to Cibolas del Mar, then we will turn east onto Mexico 3. We have a Ville with a dirt strip up in the hills. We'll regroup there." It was close to 2330 hours. It was dark and there was no traffic to be seen anywhere. People didn't call the policia in Mexico; they just hunkered down and hoped the fight wouldn't come to their front door. They knew the police were as likely to steel from them or steel one of them as the bandits would. Besides, everybody within earshot would think it was another cartel killing off its rivals and nobody wanted a piece of that, not even the big bad Mexican Police.

"Ten-four," Cole responded to his new BFF. The train blew out of the area heading south on highway 1D as in delta. Cole keyed his mic again. "Do we have a girl among us named Simone?" Cole waited for his answer.

An Irish accented voice came back over his earpiece, "Negative on Simone." Cole answered, "Roger, thank you."

"Who's Simone?" Sue asked.

"The girl I was sent down here to recover. I really need to interview the two that were in the SUV as soon as I can. I need to know the next move the American side of this crime scene is going to make and what he's going to do with the Simone kid, if he still has her."

Cole had already begun formulating a plan in his mind to catch his prey.

"We can stop just about anywhere along this road and no one will see. You can interview them and we don't mind helping you get your information. My brothers are great at scaring the pants off bad guys." Sue look mischievous in the dim dashboard light.

"Okay. You say where. We need to get a fix on their boss. Then figure out how to get the girl back." Cole looked at Sue for a long time as he watched her contemplate a place to pull over. He was trying to get the courage up to ask her about Jesus when, "Beto told me you had some questions about Jesus Christ?" Cole looked dumbfounded. "Well . . . uh . . . yea. I had some . . . uh . . . questions but I can't think of them right now." *What? What's the matter with you, this is a perfect chance to get information and you can't think?*

Sue turned in her seat and looked at Cole through the dim dash lights. "You know every one of those big Redheads I have are Christians. Do you know what each one of their biggest concern was before they came to believe in Christ?"

"I have no idea," Cole said flatly.

"Can God forgive me for what I have done? The first thing I had to teach them was that Christ is the original warrior God." She was waiting for the response she knew he was going to give her.

"I thought Jesus was this meek and mild pencil neck that hung with the women and taught Sunday school class to the kids. I can't seem to picture him as a warrior in any way." Cole was thinking this girl is nuts.

"There's a place about six or eight miles down the road where we can stop and ask the scumbags your questions."

"Okay." Cole figured she dropped the Jesus talk because she can't prove Him to be a warrior.

"I don't have my Bible but let me tell you a story, then I want to quote a Biblical description of Christ to you . . . is that okay?"

"Quote away, sister." He really liked listening to her.

"Okay." She chuckled at his response. "First before I start quoting I have a question I want you to think about. If God is the creator of all creation . . . where do warriors come from . . . the good guy warriors? Just think about that while I tell you a story." That immediately peeked Cole's interest . . . Where do they come from? "Early on during the conversion with my oldest brother I realized that if Christ was not shown to be a powerful man in His life on earth, Sean would not have had any faith in Christ to lead him to salvation. So the first thing I did was to show him the inner strength of my Jesus. A big thing with all my brothers was to know if their buddies had their six, ya know?"

Cole nodded, "Yeah. I know. We always tell each other 'I got your back.' That is a huge thing with us as well."

"Christ taught his disciples this . . . 'No one has greater love than this, that someone would lay down his life for his friends.' The first thing Christ did and the first thing we know about Him is that He laid down His life for you, Cole. He had your six before you were even born." Sue stopped talking and watched him.

Cole turned and looked at her, "Sounds like my kind of team leader. But how do I know He is my friend?"

"Great question. Are you part of this world?"

"What? Part of this world?" She lost him with that question.

"Yeah, are you part of this world?" She pressed the question.

"Well, I guess so."

"You're not from another planet, right, you're part of the good old earth. Our earth, right?"

Cole laughed. "Yes I am part of this earth. I come from Texas. The center of the world, you know."

Sue laughed at that, "Well, we'll talk about what's the center of the world at another time. But I am glad you're part of this world because in John 3:16 Jesus says, and I quote, 'For God so loved the world, He gave His One and Only Son, so that everyone who believes in Him will not perish but have eternal life.' Cole, God did not say except for Brady Cole Williams . . . He said everyone who believes will not perish but have eternal life. You see He died to save you before you even knew He was your Friend. I would call that a pretty good friend, wouldn't you?"

Cole stared ahead not answering just thinking about this Jesus. Why would He do that for me, of all people? Sue interrupted his thought, "Here's the spot. Just up ahead on the left." Cole saw the turn in, signaling the others with his left blinker to follow him.

58

Having a heart trained in greed, accursed children; forsaking the right way, they have gone astray.

Peter

David was outside the Limo pacing and holding his cell phone in his hand impatiently waiting for a call. Periodically he would glare at Simone through the open window. Then follow his threatening looks with, "You better hope he calls me." Or "If he doesn't call I am going to have to sell you to make up for my loss!"

Simone could tell he was exasperated and it frightened her to her core. He turned and kicked a rock as he stomped back to the car. David was angry, beyond angry. He was furious thinking Carl could have double crossed him. He jumped behind the steering wheel banging the car into drive as David headed back north toward Santa Barbara. He was going to kill Carl ever so slowly if it was the last thing he did.

59

Many will follow their sensuality and because of them the way of truth will be maligned.

Peter

The group learned that David Clark had production offices in Santa Barbara. He owned several houses in the area where the film crews would actually make the porn movies. Carl also told them where David was waiting for Carl and Sunny to bring the money to him. They had no idea he had left the area thinking the two employees had absconded with his cash. Not one ounce of torture had taken place during the interview. The three were so freaked they gave David up before the questions had begun. No loyalty like the loyalty found among thieves. Cole also learned that Simone was with David as his hostage or Carl said as his new girlfriend. The recovery group stepped off to the side out of earshot of the prisoners to discuss a state side capture plan. They could call the police and have David picked up on suspicion knowing once the Police got the girl, Simone would tell all, if she survived. Or they could go get him and recover the girl themselves delivering him to the nearest PD. Carl and Sunny both said David had no compunction about killing the girl if he needed to. They also said that if things didn't move fast enough his plan was to leave the country especially after the Colorado shootout. The clock was ticking. The group decided to approach this from two directions. Head directly to the US and the waiting plane at Montgomery Field in San Diego; pick up the plane with Goose flying Cole and his team to Santa Barbara, hopefully getting there ahead of David and Simone. Sue's Group on the ground following up on the road attempting location of David and the girl according to the description of David's vehicle given to them by Carl and the known route Carl had driven coming down. It was a long shot but they were going to try. They loaded up and headed north on 1D back to Tijuana and the US border. Cole found himself alone with Sue again as they sped north. Sue picked up her cell and began dialing an old friend who still worked for the DEA. She waited for someone to pick up, "Hi Tag, it's Sue. How's it going?" She waited as the person on the other end spoke. "I'm sorry I am calling so late. But I have a situation and was wondering if I could get a little help." Again she waited . . . "Well, I have been out doing the things I do and have got four to bring back. I was wondering if I might get you to help me with a smooth transition across the big muddy?" Again a pause. "Great. Also I will be traveling with about nineteen in all. I know it's a herd, I will need housekeeping to take care of seven, is that possible . . . I will explain it all on the other side." She waited and ended the call with, "You're a dream Tag. Santa just moved you to his nice list. Tell Ruth Ann I can't wait for our next girl's night out. Love ya." She punched end and laid the phone in her lap.

"Love ya?" Cole said quizzically.

"Yes. I do love him and his wife. They are my best friends. Besides he helps us across the border all the time. He has very secure contacts on the Mexican side." She said proudly.

"I thought I was your BFF? I'm hurt." Cole gripped the wheel with both hands.

"You're my newest BFF and only if this Gringo thing works out."

"Oh, so now we have conditions. I thought if I delivered him I was instantly your BFF. I didn't know that he had to provide information too." Cole laughed. She enjoyed his laugh. He laughed like a man who hadn't laughed in a long time or who was uncomfortable with happiness.

"Now where were we before we were interrupted by the Gringo and our job?" Sue laughed. "Oh, yeah, my quote!" She said it like she was excited about reciting Bible verses.

60

But these, like unreasoning animals, born as creatures of instinct to be captured and killed.

Peter

As David drove north himself he called Randal. "Hey, get the plane down to San Diego airport. I've had a change in plans."

"Yes, sir," was Randal's only response.

David thought, *Now that is the way all my employees should respond.* "I'll be waiting. I'll explain everything when you get here." David ended his call without waiting or caring what Randal had to say. He looked over at Simone who was curled up starring out the window. He thought he could see her trembling. He turned the control for the air conditioner down to sixty-eight degrees, cooling the interior down considerably.

61

But when the kindness of God our Savior and His love for all mankind appeared . . . He saved us.

Paul to Titus

"John, one of Jesus' disciples . . . have you heard of him?" She asked wanting to know the level of biblical knowledge Cole had.

"He wrote one of the gospels. He was Christ's best friend, I think."

"Yes." She said impressed. "Anyway, he also wrote the book of Revelation and that is where my quote originates. Revelation 1:12 . . . I am going to give you a description of your Sunday school teacher . . . John wrote, 'I turned to see whose voice it was that spoke to me. When I turned I saw seven golden lamp stands and among the lamp stands was One like the Son of Man, dressed in a long robe and a gold sash wrapped around His chest. His head and hair were white like wool— white as snow—and His eyes like a fiery flame. His feet were like fine bronze as it is fired in a furnace, and His voice like the sound of cascading waters. He had seven stars in His right hand; a sharp double edge sword came from his mouth, and His face was shining like the sun at midday.' That is your Sunday school teacher Cole. What do you think of him?"

Cole just drove. He had never heard a description of Christ this way. He was trying to wrap his mind around the description. "Powerful," was all he said.

"If you think that was powerful, then you will love this . . . this is the one I love and the Christ that holds me in his grasp when I need Him the most. 'Then I saw heaven opened and there was a white horse. Its rider is called Faithful and True, and He judges and makes war in righteousness. His eyes were like a fiery flame, and many crowns were on His head. He had a name written that no one knows except Himself. He wore a robe stained with blood and his name is the Word of God. The armies that were in heaven followed him on white horses, wearing pure white linen. A sharp sword came from His mouth, so that He might strike the nations with it. He will shepherd them with an iron scepter. He will also trample the wine press of the fierce anger of God, the Almighty. And He has a name written on His robe and on His thigh:

King of kings and Lord of lords.' The ultimate Warrior King, don't you think?" She was looking at him throughout the entire quote. Trying to read his expression, trying to know if who Christ really is made a difference in his thought process. But Cole was looking straight ahead. He didn't look at her, he didn't comment as with the first description, he just looked out the windshield at the road and the dotted line flicking past the car. The car was dark inside and the silence hung heavy, she thought Cole looked angry.

Cole broke the silence, "Why is He portrayed so feeble in the sermons I've heard . . . why is He so . . ." Cole could not think of another word to describe Christ, "so . . . weak!" He spoke as if he was angry at her for telling him about her Christ.

"Because people don't know Him Cole or they forget the two sides of love . . . the soft and the strong. The strong making the soft possible. Often not even those who preach about Him know Him as well as they should. They would rather have the Gandhi god; the passive more than the fierce fighter of evil. They want the Savior God they feel they can control rather than the Hero God who is a strong commander. People believe that all we need is love, like the song the Beatles sang and everything will be roses. But the truth is evil is always present . . . evil people driven by evil gods that rain evil down on the weak minded and scared masses. Just like the Gringo and the guy we're after now. If we are not standing for the strong side of love . . . who will? It is no different in the spirit world, demons and devils following Satan's rule. They wreak havoc, tempting people to do evil, destroying lives. People don't want to see the ugly part of life but when they do who do they call? Those who can deal with the ugly, those who really have a greater love for their fellow man than those who scream 'I'm a pacifist' and the reason is because it takes great love for a man to give his life for his fellow man. Pacifists have never understood that. They refuse to understand. And if it weren't for people like us who keep evil in check, then evil would rule the day and all life. But once the evil is back in check they want you to disappear. Their weakness will not allow them to look at your strength."

She was quiet for a moment, "And beside we equate Christ with those that teach us about Him too. If they are weak or if their social standing in the community is one that holds little respect, then people begin to see Christ in the same light." He was quiet again, brooding about this overlooked information. Silence engulfed the interior of the car once more, except for the thump, thump, thump of tires on asphalt.

She felt she needed to expand this thought of Jesus as a powerful man, "You know this strength was seen in His life on earth as well? John wrote about him causing a cohort of armed Roman Soldiers and temple guards to step back and fall down with just His spoken word. It is an amazing story. Another time a demon possessed man attacked

Him and his disciples as they were getting out of a boat. This man had been chained up but broke the chains and lived in graveyards. He had an entire region afraid of him. When he saw Christ he charged the group, the Bible does not say this but I believed all those tough disciples ran back to the boat but not Jesus. He stood His ground alone unafraid. As the demon possessed man in all his demonic fury flung himself at the Christ, Jesus stood fast asking him his name . . . 'What's your name' He said. When the man got close enough to tear any other man to shreds he fell on his knees in front of Jesus and said, 'My name is Legion for we are many.' Right there and then Jesus sent the devils away into a herd of pigs that rushed into the sea and drowned saving the demon possessed man's life and soul. He is strong enough to lead you and those redheaded brothers of mine, you know." His head swung sharply looking at her but said nothing. They had reached Tijuana by now. Traffic was light but the closer into town they came the heavier the traffic became. Tijuana is a 24/7 city of ugliness.

Anything a person wanted he could have in Tijuana. The cartels had killed over 37,000 people in the last five years and many more would die before the good people stood up and changed the direction of life in Tijuana; a terrible place to find yourself, if you are a young girl, in the hands of sex traffickers.

She ventured a question, "What are you thinking Cole? Are you angry with me?" Sue was a lot of things as all people are but fearful and timid were not on the list.

"No. Confused, I guess."

"How so?" She asked.

"I have this desire to get to know Him but don't know how. And now with this description I want to know this Man even more. It's funny if my guys heard me say this they would think my cheese slipped off my cracker. I don't even know what I am saying. All I do know is that what I have been doing and the way I have been living . . . well this just can't be all there is to this life. There just has to be something else. I want to know what that something else is." He turned and looked into those emerald eyes curtained by auburn hair.

She smiled and said, "There is more."

Cole's headset that was lying on the seat between them began to come alive with voices. Cole picked it up and listened. The Gringo wanted to make a deal! Sue picked up the headset speaking into the microphone, "We are not stopping until we get him to the US line. Tell him he will have to hold until then. Tell him I want to deal too. Copy?" Goose confirmed and the caravan continued to roll through one, if not the most, dangerous city in the world.

Cole was not through with his discussion, he wished they were some place different. Some place without the interruptions. His desire to talk was not for him to know her particularly but to know what she knew about this man Jesus.

"So how do people get to know Him? How is this friendship forged?" He spoke quietly into the windshield.

"This question has many answers to it. It is that the God of heaven draws all men to His Son first. Listen, few realize that God the Father calls men to Christ. Men begin to have an interest or questions, as you began to have, then that interest begins to light a fire and people begin to investigate . . . ask more questions, that is God's drawing. God always makes Himself known to all who seek Him. The Gospel of John is called the Gospel of Belief. We will spend some time in that book as soon as we can but for now Romans 10:14 says something you need to hear, 'But how can they call on Him in whom they have not believed in; how can they believe without hearing about Him and how can they hear without a preacher?' First step is for you to be introduced to Christ your Savior. Second step is to realize that the only place you can find truth about Him is in the scriptures. Again in John 20:31, John writes, 'But these are written so that you may believe that Jesus is the Christ the Son of the God, and by believing you may have life in His name.'

So you see Cole, God has called you first by putting the questions in your mind. In Ecclesiastes 3:11, Solomon writes that God set eternity in the hearts of men. I believe He did that for the purpose to make men search for God. This is what you have been doing . . . searching. Then He introduced you to the priest and to me. Now look at us learning about Christ. John writes in 1 John 5:13, 'I have written these things to you who believe in the name of the Son of God, so that you may know that you have eternal life.' The book holds the secrets to life everlasting because it teaches you about the Savior. You see, Cole, there is something more beyond this life . . . much more."

"Okay, so how do I believe? I mean where do I start? I don't know if God can even accept me? Sue you of all people know what this life I have led does to a person or what a person has to do sometimes who leads a life like I have led? I am afraid He will tell me where I can go and it ain't heaven."

"First, remember . . . is He calling you? I vote yes, He is. Second, has He brought people into your life that has answers to your life's dilemma? I vote yes, again. Remember you can't get all your answers in a quick fifteen minute fix. After all it took thirty-five or forty years to get where you are. There is some unraveling that has to be done. Do you remember the demonic I spoke of?" She waited for him to answer.

"Yes, I do. But how do you know that really happened in the first place?"

"I will answer that question in a little while. I want to ask you, do you believe Jesus Christ is the Son of God?"

Cole hesitated a moment thinking of his answer, "Yes I do."

"Step one God calls you; He has chosen or elected you; Step two God sends a preacher; Step three you begin to believe. Those are the first steps toward salvation." She smiled her enchanting smile at him as if she had won the lottery.

"How do you know you're saved?" He thought that was a simple question.

"Some very smart people think all you have to do is say a simple prayer asking Jesus into your heart and voilà you're saved. The examples of salvation in scripture are different than that. That is all we have to go by is what the scriptures say. Without scriptural examples we have nothing. Romans 10:9 says, 'If you confess with your mouth Jesus is Lord and believe in your heart that God raised Him from the dead, you will be saved.' Most modern religionist stop there and says if you do this it is all you need. Then go and find a church to your liking and worship with the Saints. But before Paul, who wrote the book of Romans, ever got to chapter 10 he wrote in chapter 6 a description of the saving act and where it comes from and how one is put in touch with it. I want to say one does not negate the other . . . chapter 10 is not more important than chapter 6 and vise a versa. Both are equally important. You cannot come to knowledge of salvation without confession and you will not confess without belief in Christ. According to Paul one must also understand and obey what Paul writes in chapter six verse 2—11 which says, and I will paraphrase some of it, 'How can we who died to sin still live in it? Or are you unaware that all of us who were baptized into Christ Jesus were baptized into His death? Therefore we were buried with Him by baptism into death in order that, just as Christ was raised from the dead by the glory of the Father, so we too may walk in newness of life." It is through baptism that we come in contact with Christ's death, killing sin and gaining the ability to walk the new life. We die in the act of baptism spiritually. There is nowhere else a person can come in contact with Christ's blood except in the watery grave of baptism. There is nowhere else a person can die and be raised again to walk a new life except through the watery grave of baptism. Peter says in Acts 2:38 'Repent each one of you and be baptized for the remission of your sins and you will receive the gift of the Holy Spirit.' Again in Acts 22:16 where Paul's conversion is recorded, Ananias says to Paul 'And now why delay? Get up and be baptized washing away your sins by calling on His name.' Even in 1Peter3:21; Peter says baptism does now save you.' Cole this is how you begin the relationship of friendship with Christ . . . you believe, repent, obey and are baptized, all by and through His grace and love for you. This is also how you know you have been saved. All of this comes from faith given to us by the grace of God. It comes from no other place. We are saved by God's grace alone. It is by His grace that we can know what He established in His word to bring us into that saving relationship, which is that true and complete friendship with His Son Jesus."

They both sat quiet as Cole maneuvered the car through town closer to the US and Mexican border. He had heard every word. He was glad she road with him. After all she made the car smell so much better and he knew she had the words of Christ he needed so much.

62

Do not let your heart be troubled, believe in God; believe also in Me.

Jesus

The transfer and the border crossing went smoother than Cole had expected. He was glad of that but knew he was on a limited time schedule, so the pleasantries were going to have to be cut short if he was to catch David Clark. He and his team needed to get moving. Sue assured him the girls were taken care of and the priest was going to be contacted about the Gringo.

The group was at the DEA safe house preparing to separate. He watched his team interact with Sue's brothers and was pleased with how well they meshed. Cole walked out of the house after he said his goodbyes and 'thank you' to Sue's group.

"Hey, you just going to mount up and say hi ho Silver, away?" Sue said following him outside.

Cole laughed again and thought I haven't laughed this much in years, strange, "No, I was going to say goodbye to you. But you had that crowd of guys around you and I wanted a little privacy."

Sue's left eye brow rose, "Oh, a private goodbye. Hmm."

Cole stepped toward her invading her space . . . she let him, "I want to say two things."

"Okay, if you think your tough enough, big guy." Her face was smiling with open, transparent honesty.

"I am. So, first I want to say thank you for talking to me about Christ. You seem so sure about Him. I heard every word. I am going to follow up with it all as soon as I get this kid back. Which brings me to my second point . . . when's our next Bible study?" He locked his eyes on to hers. He looked deep into them as if trying to read her thoughts.

She did not break his stare, "Anytime you want, Mr. Williams. You call me anytime you want. Now you need to understand I do not ever say that to any man, especially in this business. But I am going to say that only once to you. I want you to call me, understand? You go get that girl and then you call me. If you need help with retrieving her we are here for you. But regardless of any of that you better call me." She had reached out and slipped her fingers between the buttons of his shirt and pulled on it, letting the material slide across her fingers, then stepped back from him, not breaking their gaze, "It's up to you, Mr. Man. Okay?"

Cole didn't understand the rapid heart rate he was experiencing nor could he understand the trembling in his chest . . . it was far from cold . . . he stared not wanting to go anywhere . . . regretting the need to go chase David Clark.

He deliberately stretched out his hand toward her, her smile was captivating his very soul . . . she swayed slowly side to side as she took his thick strong hand in hers . . . she blushed and blinked as she felt his strength and the warmth of his hand.

Goose pushed hard on the van's horn letting a long loud blast out, "Let's move it!" He yelled from the window.

Sue jumped a little and they both laughed. Cole turned to leave but Sue held tightly to his hand. Cole turned back and looked at his new BFF, "Don't worry. You and I have a date. I will see you soon!" She melted and softly shook her hair all around, "I'll be waiting." Her voice lost the control of the professional and sounded a little more girly girl than she really wanted but she didn't care. She liked this guy and she could tell he liked her.

It was out of character for him, especially with all the men standing around but he lost his inhibition. Stepping back toward her he reached around her shoulders and felt the warmth, gentleness and the woman he had come to admire in such a short time, "I will be back Sue." He stepped away looking into her eyes once more feeling emotions he had forgot he had. He held her shoulders a moment longer, then turned disappearing around the van to his car.

Hatch was behind the wheel and led the team north. It was quiet until Hatch broke the silence, "It's about time, son. We all thought you were going to be an old maid."

Cole was staring out his open window watching the sun show its beautiful bright face over the peaks and Cole thought His face is as bright as the sun shining at noonday, wow!

And the chase goes on . . . to defeat the evil that steals, lies and kills before it kills again and to lay hold of the Christ who is capturing the hearts of men.

For though we live in the body, we do not wage war in an unspiritual way, since the weapons of our warfare are not worldly, but are powerful through God for the demolition of strongholds. We demolish arguments and every high minded thing that is raised up against the knowledge of God, taking every thought captive to obey Christ.

1 Corinthians 10:3–5

THE END

ABOUT THE AUTHOR

JMW is currently a successful entrepreneur. Former Police officer and former Marine. He is a graduate of Seminary School and an ordained minister. He lives all across the country.

Find more books by JMW at **amazon.com/author/j.m.w**

Made in the USA
Coppell, TX
22 May 2020

26166692R00146